BLOOD OF A KING

BEYOND THE ETHER
BOOK 2

MYRANDA RAE

ONE

"ARE YOU SURE THAT–"

"I'm fine." I grit through my teeth.

I'm not fine. I am the farthest thing from fine. I've never actually been less fine in my life. Every breath feels like shattered glass dragging through my ribs.

But if he asks me again, I'm going to scream.

Every ten seconds—every ten seconds—it's the same thing.

"Are you alright, Kiah?"

"You're breathing really heavily, Kiah."

"I could carry you."

"Do you need help?"

He didn't want me to come. I pushed it. I argued. I insisted. Now, I would rather die than admit to him that this is physically too much for me to handle.

I truly thought that my ribs had healed enough.

"Kiah—"

"Oh my god, Canaan! Stop it!" I snap, flinging my water bottle into the dirt. "I'm sorry, alright? I thought I could do this. I don't want to slow you down. But I can't go back by myself."

"Come here." He grabs me; this time, he isn't asking.

"Wait—Canaan—" he covers my mouth with his hand. He physically shuts me up.

His wings snap open violently, and he lifts us up, the wind taking us higher by the second.

"I'm going to move my hand," he whispers near my ear, voice like gravel. "When I do, keep your mouth shut."

I nod, or try to, and he slowly peels his hand away.

"I'm looking for something."

"I mean, yeah. That's the whole point. We're looking for–"

"Not a portal or Shadowrithes. I'm looking for a mare."

"A horse?"

"Yes." He glides through the air. "If you won't let me carry you, we'll ride."

In the distance, four dark shadows race across the ground. He dips down, bringing us toward them.

Those aren't just horses.

"Wow. Look at them."

"They are beautiful, but dangerous. They will heed my commands, but they might not be particularly pleased. Stay close." He tightens his grip on my waist.

Great.

He speaks something into the air, a command that makes all of them stop running immediately. I didn't understand the words, but my body reacts to them, like it understands somehow.

"I'm going to lift you onto her back," he says, his tone shifting slightly, softer under the steel. "And then I'll sit behind you. Don't argue."

There's no point. Not when I'm shaking, not when everything hurts, and not when the only thing keeping me together right now is him.

He climbs on behind me and wraps his arm loosely around my waist. Leaning back, I rest my head on his shoulder.

How long is this blood-bound bullshit going to last? I can feel it flowing through both of us, absolutely ravaging all rational thoughts or maturity. It's tangled into my bones, down to the marrow; it's in my organs. I can't escape it.

He's hot, then cold—then I am. I'm annoyed at him, but then I look at him too long, and I find myself leaning in to try to kiss him. He glares like he can't stand the sight of me, and then in the next breath, he's carrying me around, concerned about every little thing.

I hate it, but it simultaneously makes me feel warm and fluttery inside. I want to push him away, but when he's close, I feel safe and protected. When we're this close, all I can think about is how he smells and how good his hands feel when they're on my skin.

It's a roller coaster, a violent spinning, swirling, jerking, whiplash-inducing, carnival ride that's poorly put together and teetering on the edge of a breakdown. I'm nauseous, and I want to get off. I want to throw up. I want to scream at the top of my lungs.

But then there are moments—moments where he touches me like I'm precious, moments where I see something raw in his eyes—and in those moments, I don't want to get off at all.

"Stop." He growls.

"Stop what? I'm not doing anything."

"You're thinking–loudly." His voice is strained.

I start to ask him what he means.

Please, if there is anything merciful and good in the world–he can't read my mind, can he?

"Canaan!" Calais calls from above us. "The cove!"

He waves his hand at her, not dismissing her but sending her ahead. "We'll meet her there."

"The cove?" I take the opportunity to change the subject. We can't talk about that, especially not in this position.

"We'll camp for the night. When the sun sets, we'll want to have shelter."

The horse carries us through the tall, grassy fields onto a road surrounded by trees. The forest has not been particularly kind to me recently. Fear creeps into the corners of my mind.

"Are there monsters out here?" I'm only half kidding. I don't want to sound fearful, but this fucking place is a nightmare. "Anything desperate to kill me or eat my bones?" A shudder rolls down my spine.

He grunts and tightens his grip. "No."

Desperate to keep him out of my head, I hum quietly. If I'm thinking about song lyrics, I'm not thinking about his body pressed to mine.

I'm practically on his lap. His thighs are behind mine, pressing tight to the horse to keep us steady. No saddle. No reins. He's just gripping it with his legs...

So much for not thinking about him. The harder I try, the more he seems to wedge himself into my brain.

"Kiah." He growls. "Stop it."

"What?" I gasp.

"Wiggling like that. You're..." The tension in his voice is cut off as he tightens his grip and sends the horse galloping forward.

This is worse.

I understand the sentiment. The faster the horse runs, the faster we get to the cove, but this...

His hips rock behind mine. To keep steady, I have to move my hips too—stay loose and fluid so that I can keep balance.

We're both doing it, at the same time, rocking with the motion of the horse's body.

I feel him.

All of him.

Covering my mouth with my hand, I swallow the gasp that wants to escape.

Holy shit.

It takes everything in me, every ounce of self-control, not to turn around to look at his face. I want to. I need to see it.

But I don't.

Pressed right into the seat of my pants, he's so hard. It's hard to tell in this position with the clothes and motion, but it feels big. Enormous.

A whimper crawls up my throat, tickling my neck.

My body moves, just a subtle shift, but he gasps, and I moan. It all happens too fast. I don't know why I did it. I blame it on my blood–it has a mind of its own. It forced my hand. The blood pressed my ass back into his raging erection–not me.

The horse yields to him, coming to a quick stop. He jumps down so quickly, I feel like I'm falling. My feet hit the ground, and he storms past me.

"Calais!" He yells, his anger booming through the trees. "Come, take her to the water. I'll be back."

He's in the air, carried away by the wind before she even responds.

"There is a small cave here that will be a suitable shelter for tonight." She steps onto the path. Her hollow eyes meeting mine. "Where did he go?"

"Oh, I don't know." I shrug, following her to the small wooded area.

The little cove opens up like a secret tucked behind a wall of trees—magical in a way that feels unreal, like it was stitched together from a dream. The water is cool and impossibly blue, the kind of blue that makes it look enchanted.

At one point in my life, an enchanted lagoon would have been exciting. Now, I'm worried about what might be lurking in the depths of the crystal clear water.

The cave isn't dark or ominous like I expected. Instead, it's warm with the faint scent of moss and dirt. A soft wind moves through it, carrying the distant sound of trickling water. As far as caves go, it's nice as far as caves go. Tucked away and quiet. Safe.

Lowering myself to the floor, I rest against the wall and watch Calais.

She wades into the water like a ghost, her movements slow and dreamlike. She looks like a shell—hollowed out, emptied. The pain in her face is a physical feature.

I don't know what to say. What could I possibly say? There are no words big enough, no gesture gentle enough to touch the wound she carries. It's not just emotional—it's physical.

When I found out that they were getting married, I was surprised. They didn't seem like what I thought a couple looked like. I thought love looked a certain way. But I was so wrong.

Now, it's carved into her. The grief and loss are like a shadow that follows her around. It's in her sunken eyes, the haggard sound in her voice, the way her skin doesn't glow anymore.

She's still beautiful—otherworldly, ethereal—but the beauty has changed. It's colder now, like starlight or snow. There's no warmth in her anymore.

She reaches down into the water and plucks out a fish with her bare hands.

Every day spent with them makes me feel smaller and inferior. They can do everything. If their legs get tired, they fly. If there is an enemy, they fight it with a strength that I can never obtain. I could live in the gym, build strength and muscle, and it would still pale compared to them.

She comes out of the water with three fish that she caught in a matter of minutes.

I want to offer to help her, but I'm too embarrassed. As she starts to bring sticks and dried leaves to make a fire, I wrap my arms around my legs and watch. She doesn't need my help. By the time I pull myself up from the ground, she'll be finished.

I don't even know how to gut a fish. I'm fucking useless.

As I stare at her, the gentleness of her movements, Canaan lands on the ground between us. His wings are spread wide, blocking the dimming sunlight from the cave completely.

He turns, looking directly at me. There is no moment of searching, no question—he knows exactly where I am. This weird string ties us together.

The look on his face is hard, indifferent. But again, his actions don't match. He walks toward me, holding his hand out. A piece of fruit.

"Thanks." I take it, rubbing the soft, warm skin with my fingers.

"Eat, then rest. We will stand watch through the night."

"I would like to take a shift."

His mouth forms a straight line.

"Wait," I hold my hands up. "I know I'm not strong enough to actually fight, but I can sit here at the mouth of the cave and watch. My eyes aren't injured. Let me help. That way, you can get a few more hours of sleep. I want to help." My voice cracks, which only adds to my shame.

"Kiah–"

"Please! Please, let me help. If I see something, I'll wake you up immediately. I won't try to do anything myself. I won't go investigate. I won't assume it was my imagination. I won't hesitate. If there is so much as a twig snapping in the distance, I'll get you. Please, don't make me feel even more useless and pathetic than I already do. You need to sleep and rest, too. Let me do this."

I'm not sure if it's our conversation or her stress, but Calais disappears into the treeline, leaving the fish on a rock on the edge of the small fire.

"When your body is fully healed, you can—"

"Canaan, you're suffocating me!" I pull myself up from the ground, much more slowly than I wish I could. It doesn't give off the same effect as jumping up and storming away.

Brushing past him, I avoid the water and step into the trees.

I'm not stupid enough to venture too far off. I just want to be far enough to breathe without him watching me.

Calais is sitting on a large rock just a few steps into the water. I freeze, I don't want to disturb her.

"He can't let anything happen to you." Her voice is quiet.

"I know–"

"No," she shakes her head, turning to face me. "You don't. He can't." She emphasises it more. "Your blood is mixed together now. Your lives are linked. He cannot allow harm to come to you; it's in his veins. Your pain is his. He is overbearing." She chuckles, the first time I've heard it in so long. "But it's not out of cruelty. It's out of his control, it's biological."

"How long will it last?"

She shrugs and looks out at the water again. "You might feel like you're useless, but you did something no one else could have. My blood wouldn't have saved him that close to death. You were willing to sacrifice yourself for his life. If I had lost both of them..." Her voice fades. "You are not useless or pathetic."

The water is cold against my feet as I step into it, climbing up onto the rock beside her. Wrapping my arm around her shoulder, I wait for her to push me off. But she doesn't.

Instead, we sit in silence, looking out at the reflection of the sun setting on the water.

TWO

"I'LL TAKE THE WATCH NOW." He kneels down beside me. "Get some rest."

I look at him, rolling my lips into my mouth to keep from arguing. I don't know how long my shift was, but it was less than two hours. Much less. Probably closer to one hour.

Remembering my conversation with Calais, I scoot back, going deeper into the cave so he has more room to sit. "Did you sleep?"

"Yes, thank you for standing watch."

I scoff and laugh. "You're a terrible liar."

"I'm not lying." He looks surprised, but his outrage is fake, I can tell.

"You didn't sleep at all, did you?" I lean back against the wall of the cave, trying to find a position that's even slightly comfortable.

"No." He reaches for me. "Come here. Put your head on my lap."

I'm not going to argue. This cave is uncomfortable, and I am tired. This might be adding to our problems, but I don't care right now.

Dropping my head into his lap, I close my eyes immediately. His body moves around me, shifting slightly, until he places something warm over my chest.

Peeking my eyes open, I watch as he spreads his shirt over me like a blanket.

"Thank you."

"Sleep."

"Fine." I pout.

Despite myself, it only takes a moment to start feeling myself drifting. His fingers are in my hair, scratching lightly at my scalp. I think, in this barely conscious state, that he might be braiding it.

The thought makes me feel warm inside.

Warm. Soft. Safe.

Then, suddenly, not.

It's so abrupt that it takes me a moment to even register the change.

The grounding touch of his hands is gone, and I'm alone in the dark. Cold.

"Oh, for fuck's sake!" I shout into the void. Every expletive I have ever heard flies out of my mouth.

He's dragging me to hell. He's going to hear my displeasure about it.

This place is just darkness, a black hole. There is nothing, no sound, no light, just black as far as I can see. I'm just suspended in it. There is no coming, no going. I just hang here, helpless, waiting.

I know he must be nearby, but I feel utterly alone.

Then, when I let my body be still, I hear it.

There is a sound in the distance, trickling water. Just drops somewhere far away. It's the only sign that there is any life in this place.

"Kiah, darling!" He emerges from the dark like a fucking monster. "I am shocked to see you!"

"Yeah, unfortunately, I can't say the same for you, you fucking piece of—"

"Ah, ah." He wags his finger in my face. "What kind of hello is that for your lover?"

"You're not my fucking lover! You tricked me. I never would have slept with you if—"

"Have you and Canaan..." he arches his brow instead of finishing his sentence.

"What?" I gasp. "No! Of course not!"

I wish I could say he looked like shit. But he doesn't. He looks powerful, well-rested, healthy. Deep down, in a naive, girlish, hopeful part of my brain, I wanted him to be wracked with guilt. To spend every night awake, haunted by the image of my dying face–of the betrayal–of the people he killed. But of course he's not. He's proud of himself.

"Has he not told you?" He starts to laugh in that high-handed way that always bothers me. He knows something I don't know.

"Told me what?"

"Oh, this is amazing." He looks so thoroughly pleased that it makes me sick to my stomach. There are very few things that I wouldn't do right now for enough strength and power to kick his ass.

"What do you want, Elion?"

"I just had to see this for myself!" He shakes his head. "I didn't think you would make it over in time to save him. I definitely didn't think he would give you his blood." There is amusement written all over his face. "I cannot believe you're still alive."

"Well, it's not for your lack of trying. Where is Cheyenne?" I fold my arms over my chest, trying to shield as much of myself from him as possible.

"She's perfectly safe and quite satiated." He licks his lips.

Fuck. My insides clench, not in a seduced, longing way, but in a nauseous way.

"You know," he inches in closer. "If you gave yourself to him, it would help. It would remedy all. Tell me, do you ache? Do you feel it all the time, thumping like a pulse beneath the fear and confusion? It's there, isn't it? Focus your attention on it. Throbbing. Pulsating. Longing. He would cure that for you."

"Fuck you!" My hands shake, all the rage in my body cruising through me.

"Sorry, love." He lets the tips of his fingers graze my cheek. "You'll have to ask him for that now." The sparkle in his eye is too much to bear.

Lunging forward, I throw my balled-up fist at him as hard as I can.

But my arm barely moves.

I can't make any part of my body move. I'm submerged in a thick, clear liquid. It's like glue surrounding me. It wasn't there before, just one second ago.

"What is this?" I panic, my muscles jerking, but I don't move an inch.

"It's not real." He smiles. "It's a figment of your imagination."

"Elion! Let me out!"

As soon as the words leave my mouth, I fall, dropping straight down like there is nothing below my feet. My mind flashes back to when he dropped me.

My body tenses, and I scream, bracing for the impact.

But instead of hitting the ground, I lurch, bouncing, then dangling like my body is tied to a string.

Looking around frantically, I try to find him, but he's gone.

Full-fledged panic.

"Wake up, Kiah! Wake up!" I scream, desperately searching for something, anything. There isn't a rope; nothing is actually holding me up. There isn't anything to grab onto. "This isn't real." I pinch my eyes closed. "It's just a nightmare."

Hot tears burn down my cheeks.

I can't wake up until he releases me. He just left me here. I know he's cruel and that everything between us was just a means to an end. But this just seems...

I'm trapped.

My mind won't focus. I can't think of a plan—I can't think of anything. Pure, raw panic seizes me, dragging me down into the depths.

Is this a real place? Is it made up in his mind? In mine? Will I just stay here until I die?

"Canaan!"

I don't know why I screamed for him. He's not here. He can't save me. But for some reason, he is the only thing that cuts through the chaos in my mind.

His face is like a cord tethering me to reality.

"Kiah." His voice echoes around this place, surrounding me on all sides. "Pull yourself out, Kiah. Follow my voice. Come back."

Taking a long, slow breath, I focus on him. He's here somewhere. Find him.

"There you go, Kiah. Just like that. Follow my voice."

Rich and warm.

Pinching my eyes closed, I feel my way, following him.

"Open your eyes, you're here. You're safe. I've got you." He cradles me against his warm skin.

"Canaan?" I blink my eyes open.

We're in the cave. I never left.

"Is this real?" I don't want to let myself believe it.

"It's real."

My skin feels slick with sweat against his. I'm too warm, but I can't let go. Clinging to him, I bury my face in his chest, trying to swallow down the sob that's fighting its way out.

His arms wrap around me, holding me close, and I can't contain it anymore.

"I thought I would die there. He was just going to leave me there forever. It was so dark, and I was falling." I gasp between sobs.

"His connection to you is weaker." He runs his hand over my hair. "Our connection is stronger. He can't keep you there. I can come get you."

"You can?" I lean back to look at his face.

"I'll come in after you. I promise. He can't keep you there."

Maybe it's my body coming down from such a high place, so tight with fear. Maybe it's the sincerity in his eyes. Maybe it's the way his hands hold me gentle but firm—he's not letting me go.

Maybe it's a mixture of all of it.

Whatever it is, it barrels through me on a warpath. It won't be constrained or held back.

Holding onto him like he's going to disappear, I try to catch my breath and stop the tears. They won't obey.

His hand runs slowly down my spine, a soft, reassuring touch. But Elion's words play back in my mind. I feel out of control. The moment doesn't call for this kind of anguished neediness.

Things that shouldn't be flashing through my mind float around like bubbles. They aren't memories; they haven't happened. It's worse. It's a fantasy.

I see him above me, his body on mine. He bites me, and I don't fight back. I like it. He kisses me, and I suck on his tongue. My body is on fire.

"Throbbing. Pulsating. Longing. He would cure that for you."

My breath catches at the same time that his body tenses. His muscles flex beneath his skin.

"Canaan."

"Don't—" He hisses, the hand on my head gripping my hair. "—say my name right now, Kiah."

I'm not going to mention what Elion said. I wouldn't even know where to start or how to get the words out.

"Where were you?" His voice is strained, but I appreciate his effort to change the subject.

"I don't know. It was pitch black."

"There was nothing? It was just the two of you? You couldn't see anything else? Smell something? Hear something?"

"There was dripping. It sounded far away, and I couldn't see it, but it was a steady dripping."

"Like rain?"

"No, like a single drop."

He hums, his fingers absentmindedly moving through my hair again, over my scalp and down the length of my braid.

"What did he say?"

"He was taunting me."

About fucking you...

"I tried to hit him, but he had me submerged in a thick liquid. I couldn't move."

"You tried to hit him?" The amused chuckle doesn't help me forget the sexual tension at all.

"Yes." I narrow my eyes. "What's funny?"

"If you had been able to move, you think you would have been able to hurt him?"

"Are you mocking me right now, Canaan?"

"Certainly not." He is.

"I could hit you!" I know I probably can't, but it's the principle of it.

"Oh, I'm sure."

"Don't try to pacify me!"

"I would never. I'm sure you could hit me." His eyes make me feel irritated and fluttery. Damn him.

"I'm not as strong as you, but I bet I could do more damage than you think." Before the idea even fully formulates in my head—to throw a fake punch to test his readiness—he spins us, pressing my back into the ground beneath his body.

A whimpering sound comes out of me. It just happens. I can't control it.

He's between my legs, letting just enough of his weight press down on me. My mind drops into the depths of hell—a hell that they created. I'm just stuck in it, lost and touch-starved.

His eyes are so intensely focused on my mouth, I'm sure he's going to kiss me.

It's just the blood. This isn't real.

But it feels real. Nothing has ever felt so real.

I want it to be real.

My body, my blood, it's reaching out to him. I feel it rushing up, pooling beneath my skin like a hot, sensitive bruise.

"If you're ever able to hit me—" His breath fans over my cheek, his lips so close.

"If I'm ever able to hit you, I just want you to admit that you underestimated me."

"Alright—"

"On your knees."

A groan rumbles in the back of his throat, and his hoarse, ragged breath stutters. "Fine."

We don't move. Not forward or back—we just sit in this position, so close, but too far.

When he abruptly pulls away, I gasp and do the same.

Did I learn nothing from the last fae prince? How many times do I have to put myself in this position?

THREE

SITTING BESIDE THE FIRE, I stare out at the water. I find myself looking at it often. Deep down, I still expect something to come creeping out of it to get me.

But it's not really the water that has my heart pounding like this.

Pulling my knees to my chest, I stare at the slowly dying embers and try to bury the embarrassment.

I took things too far last night. Now I can't look him in the eye. Why did I do that? I was teasing him. It's like I couldn't even control it.

I heard myself. But it's like my mouth was moving without my brain's permission. I was flirting with him—challenging him.

And to make matters insurmountably worse, now I can't get the image of him on his knees out of my head.

It's burned there, taunting me.

God, to see him like that would be...

He is power. I've recognized it from the start, but since he drank my blood? It's more than power. It's something more, something deeper. I want to reach out and touch it, to feel it in my hands, to let that kind of strength and intensity soak into my skin—just for a moment—just to know what it's like.

When he flipped me and pressed his body to mine—I'm afraid of what I would have done if he didn't have the self-control to pull away. I would have given him whatever he asked for.

Even now, removed from the situation, I would give him anything.

My throat is dry as I try to swallow down this ridiculous feeling.

When he comes back from the water, his wet hair tied up on his head, I gulp. An audible fucking gulp. His eyes meet mine—fire and fury. Rage radiates from him. Unfiltered and raw, he pins me down with his stare.

I took things too far.

Turning quickly, he storms past me. "We're leaving as soon as Calais returns."

The more I think about it, the more I think Elion might not have been lying.

"Focus your attention on it. Throbbing. Pulsating. Longing. He would cure that for you."

His words repeat, again and again. Festering.

Throbbing...

My cheeks burn. I can't bring it up. If I speak those words, something bad will happen. Just thinking about it is making me feel flushed and uncomfortable.

"Ready?" Calais drops out of the sky. "Canaan is waiting for you."

"Ready!" I jump up and dust off my pants, pretending that everything is fine.

If I ignore it long enough, this will all go away. The blood bond must be nearly over by now. I'm too afraid to ask him how long it takes to disappear. I keep telling myself it's ending.

"Let's find something today." She looks at me with determination before shooting up into the air, and she's gone, like an apparition— one second she's here, then it's like she vanished.

Walking down the path, I mentally prepare myself to see him, to sit on the horse with his cock pressed into my ass while we roll our hips with each step. That's completely normal and not torture at all.

When I step out of the tree line and onto the road, I freeze.

"Canaan! What the fuck?" I don't mean to yell, but the words fly out before I can stop them.

He's standing beside the horse with his shirt open while he ties up his hair again. He looks like hot, wet, sticky sex incarnate.

"I can't do this!" I throw my hands in the air. "I'm walking."

"Kiah." His voice sounds like sex wrapped around my name. I can almost hear it, how he would sound seated between my legs, growling like that.

"No!" I point my finger at him. "No! Don't try to talk me out of it. I would rather break all of my ribs again than to sit on that fucking horse with you." Only after saying it does it occur to me how bad that sounds out loud. "I mean that respectfully." I back away.

He sighs and runs his hands over his face. His wings twitch with frustration. "What do you want to do, then?"

"I don't know. I just can't sit there with you again. Last time–" A shudder runs the length of my spine. Last time...

"I will restrain myself." He looks so fucking ridiculously, other-worldly, absurdly handsome that I want to pluck my eyes out so I don't have to see him.

Elion's taunting voice comes back into my head.

THROBBING.
Pulsating.
Longing.

CHECK, check, and check. Present and accounted for.

Is there a cliff nearby that I can fling myself from?

"That won't help." I cross my arms over my chest, hoping he doesn't see that my nipples are rock hard.

I feel like a teenage boy going through puberty. There is absolutely no controlling it—it's all impulse and hormones.

Ask him. Just do it. Woman up and ask him if there is something about the blood that makes me want to sit spread-eagled on his face.

Once I say it, I can't take it back. It will be out there, in the air.

Shaking my head, I regain control of my mind and look at him.

Huge mistake.

He's smoldering. "Kiah. Get on the horse."

"Um, ok." Any defiance I thought I felt is squashed.

As I step forward, he grabs me, spinning me around so that my back is pressed to his chest as he lifts off the ground and onto the back of the horse.

"Holy shit." I gasp.

He holds me tight as the horse starts to gallop up the growing slope of the hillside.

When we reach the top, Calais dips down from above the clouds. She is leading the charge.

Minutes tick by, the scenery around us a blur of trees and tall grass. We crash through a river and across a rocky field.

My hip bones hurt as we hit every bump hard. At least I'm too busy looking for signs to hyper-focus on the way our bodies are pressed together.

A valley stretches out in front of us. A vast basin of golden flowers.

Calais stops, hovering in the sky.

Squinting, I watch her. Waiting for something—anything.

It looks like she sees something because she takes off like a bird diving for prey.

We follow behind her from the ground, racing beneath her shadow.

It happens so slowly that I don't notice it at first, but then it hits me. Something feels strange. I recognize it. The air is heavier, and there is something–unnamable, that just feels off.

"Canaan?" I instinctively grab the arm that's wrapped around my body.

"You feel it?" His voice is so calm that it eases the tension in my chest.

The mare comes to an abrupt stop. The air is colder here, damp. My skin prickles, goosebumps rolling down my arms. I remember this feeling. It's so subtle, but it makes me feel insane, like hearing something that isn't there, or seeing something move in the corner of my eye, but every time I look, there isn't anything.

His arm tightens, and my eyes dart through the field, searching for whatever it is that he's seeing.

"Oh, god."

It looks like a wave at first, just a black mass in the field, rolling through the flowers.

"I'm going to spin you around. Hold on to me."

He doesn't give me a chance to answer before he spins me with no effort.

"Wrap your arms around my neck."

I do it without hesitating. Even in moments of chaos, I know he will keep me safe. This is the best place for me.

Canaan lifts up, leaving the horse behind. The Shadowrithe is now a fully formed man, sprinting through the field toward us.

Calais swoops down behind him, flying straight into him without slowing down or hesitating. She tackles him to the ground, and they roll. A mess of darkness and wings.

I can't tell who is who or which one is winning.

Neither one is holding back. This is a fight to the death. Bloody and brutal–they each try their hardest to kill the other.

Closing my eyes, I take a breath.

"She's got it," Canaan reassures me.

"Are you sure?"

She screams and jumps up so that his body is beneath hers. Not a scream of pain, but triumph. The jagged blade of a knife plunges into his chest, and she flays him wide open. Blackness like tar spills into the grass.

She's not done.

Bending down over his body, she starts doing something that I can't see from this distance.

Blood flows from his body, little streams running in all directions in the grass.

"What is she doing?"

"We die by exsanguination or by having our hearts penetrated directly. She is doing both."

"Better safe than sorry, I guess." I swallow the thick, dry ball of panic in my throat.

He hums, his hand stretching flat against the small of my back. It's comforting, but it makes the flames grow again, just a bit.

When she finally stands, his heart is in her hands.

With the graceful ease of a fae princess who did not just rip a monster to shreds, she floats up toward us. Her body is covered in his dark blood. "Let's find the portal. It's still open, or he wouldn't have been guarding it."

"Portal?" I perk up.

"Keep your eyes open for something that looks unnatural. Like–"

"Like a perfect little circle of mushrooms?"

His head tilts to the side. "Yes. Just like that."

Narrowing my eyes, I focus on the ground. Every rock and leaf seems suspicious.

"There." Calais points out in the distance. "That puddle on the ground."

Canaan starts to bring us closer to the ground, but is still far enough to see if any more Shadowrithes come out.

The puddle is small, just an inconspicuous bit of leftover rain– only the rest of the field is completely dry.

As we get closer, the water shimmers with silver.

"That's it." Calais' face is set in stone. She flies over the water and drops the heart into it.

The silver water ripples once, then sits perfectly still again. It's unnatural. A hedge of grass grows around it. A perfectly symmetrical circle, each blade precisely the same length.

"We have no way of knowing how long ago they opened it. It could be closing already." Canaan sets me on my feet.

"When are we going?" I look at the water that might not be water at all. When no one answers, I turn to find them both staring at me like I've grown a second head.

FOUR

CLOSING MY EYES, I lean against the tree and try to forget everything. All of it. I'm too tired to think about this, but I'm too afraid to sleep.

I can feel him watching me, but I won't acknowledge it. Do not engage.

I'm not going to be the first to break our wall of silence. I don't care how immature it is. Right now, I'm going to be childish.

Just thinking about it takes the simmering rage in my blood up to a boil.

I understand that he's the king here, but he doesn't get to rule over me—not when my home is involved. Who does he think he is? I'm human. That realm is my home.

"Kiah," he says, sitting down beside me. I feel the heat from his body.

Instead of answering, I hold my hand up, keeping my eyes closed.

He sighs, "You're being unreasonable."

He's baiting me into an argument, and I won't give in. Not again.

"This is for the best."

It's not. But I won't explain it to him again. If anyone is being unreasonable here, it's him. He basically forbade me from going through the portal.

"Kiah."

"We can't talk without arguing, so I'm not engaging. Leave me alone, Canaan." My voice holds the sharp edge and icy chill I was hoping for.

I feel him walk away. This is never going to resolve itself, but I'm so tired, I don't have the strength to deal with this.

When I'm sure he's gone, I pull myself up to stand. If I sit for even a second longer, I'll fall asleep. And I can't let that happen.

Walking into the tree line, I start to collect dried leaves and twigs to keep the fire going. It's probably not needed, but I need to stay upright.

"What are you doing?"

I scream, dropping everything I've gathered as I whip around.

"Damn it! Don't sneak up on me!" I clutch at my racing heart.

"I apologize. I didn't mean to scare you." He looks sincere, but I'm too irritated to care. He can be as sincere as he likes, but it doesn't change the fact that he's trying to force me to stay here.

Bending down, I start to recollect everything.

"Kiah."

"Canaan, please stop saying my name like that."

"I am sorry that you're angry. I even understand where you're coming from, but—"

"You don't understand where I'm coming from. That's my realm, you jackass. You are trying to forbid me from going home. I belong there. You're the king here, not there. I am not one of your subjects. Stop trying to lord over me. I am going through that portal unless you physically chain me up. The reason I wasn't able to go home before made sense. You didn't want to risk opening another portal. But there is one open now. Not going through it seems insane."

"I can't keep you safe there."

"It's not your job to keep me safe there." Damn him and his incessant need to keep me safe.

His ring-clad hand runs over his face, frustration etched into his beautiful features. The darkness is back. He looks dangerous. Every word out of my mouth inches him closer to the edge.

He doesn't like being questioned.

I don't like being lorded over.

"Kiah, you don't understand." He holds his hand up, asking me to wait. "Half of the Rimfae disappeared when Elion's betrayal was revealed. The ones that stayed behind, we don't know if it's just part of the plan. We can't trust them. They can't know where you are. This is the best plan. They will expect me to bring you with me. But you will be safely hidden away."

I sigh. "I don't want to stay here, Canaan."

"Your realm is open. The Shadowrithes are there. You can't know the state of your world. The safest place for you now is here. I will stay with you, and Calais will go into your realm and find them."

"Or, you can stay here, and I'll go with her. I bet they would never expect that! When was the last time you were among humans en masse? Has she ever seen a cell phone? Does she know how to drive a car? What's the plan? Is she going to go in there and fly around until she finds them? Do you know where they are? Also, no one in the human realm knows about your existence anymore, so flying is not exactly an option. A kid with a cellphone is going to post a video online, and the government is going to shoot you out of the sky and dissect you in a lab on some military base somewhere." I drop back, sitting in the dirt. My legs are too tired to hold me up.

He inhales and stops. Clearly, he hasn't considered this.

Standing slowly, he stares at me for a moment. I can practically see his mind racing. I bet he doesn't even know what a cell phone is.

"Calais." He abruptly walks away.

Smiling to myself, I lean back against the tree, just for a minute. I can't sleep, but I can rest my eyes.

Even as I let myself relax, I know that it's my delirium lying to me. If I lie here like this, I'll fall asleep. My brain wants to fight it, but my body is giving up.

Their voices in the distance soothe me, lulling me into oblivion.

I know it's happening immediately. I did this to myself.

I'm not in the forest, I'm in a wide open valley. It's warm, and the sun is setting in the distance. The ground is strange, a burnt orange colored soil. It stretches around me in every direction.

"Hello?" I call out. Elion must be skulking around here somewhere.

The air is warm and dry. It seeps into my skin. There is no breeze, just soft heat and the slight smell of dusty air.

I'm standing in the center of a small circle. Little tufts of yellow grass grow in a perfect circle around me. A few feet away, there is another one, a much larger one. And behind me, a smaller one.

They're everywhere.

The grass grows like this, like rings stamped into the cracked red dirt.

Squinting, I look out into the distance. The marks fade on the horizon, stretching out past what I can see.

It's beautiful but eerie.

What are they?

Careful not to disturb anything, I step forward. The dusty desert floor is soft below my feet.

They remind me of the circle of mushrooms or the hedge of grass around the portals. Are these portals? The thought sends a chill down my spine. There are hundreds of them.

Searching the ground, I find a small rock and throw it into the center like Calais did. Nothing happens. The rock lands in the circle, but it doesn't disappear.

I guess these aren't portals, then.

I'm alone. If Elion is here, he's hiding somehow. Walking across the plain, I stop and inspect each one I pass. Some are large enough to lie down inside. Some are as small as my hand, but each is a perfect circle. The lines are clean. The inside has nothing, no grass or leaves, not a stray weed. It looks man-made or designed.

Something like this couldn't possibly grow naturally.

Crouching down, I touch the grass. It's softer than I was expecting it to be.

"Kiah?" Canaan's voice in the distance pulls my attention away from the marks.

Turning, I search for him. Far in the distance, on the crest of a small hill, I see him. His wings are spread wide as he stands, watching me.

This feels different. Canaan is here. I'm here. Elion isn't.

"Canaan?" I whisper, "Can you hear me?"

"Yes." His voice floats toward me.

"What is this?"

"I'm not sure." His presence in this vast place is comforting. Whatever this is, wherever we are, it's going to be alright now. He won't let anything bad happen. "It's a dreamweave. I could feel you being pulled away but..."

"Are you here too?"

"That's hard to explain." I can hear the smile in his voice. "I'm here because you brought me here. Not Elion. So I'm still in my body, you're just sharing this with me."

"Why?"

"I'm not sure. Maybe—"

His voice is cut off by the sound of rushing water. It's sudden and strong, a tidal wave that washes away the entire valley. It's unnatural, it doesn't belong here. Everything is gone in a second.

I feel Elion. He's hiding, but I know he's nearby.

My eyes open, and I jerk upright.

"You're alright. You're safe." Canaan is already beside me.

"What happened?"

"I think it was a mistake. He didn't mean to show you that. His magic isn't as powerful in the human realm. He accidentally showed you something through the tie."

Only now do I realize that his arms are wrapped around me. Clearing my throat, I scoot out of his grip.

"Did you recognize that place?" I have to fill the silence with questions.

"No. You?"

"Not at all." I chew the inside of my lip. "That seems like a place here in your world, not mine."

"I've never seen anything like it." He shakes his head.

A breeze blows through the trees, and we fall into uncomfortable silence. The kind that usually ends in sexual tension.

"When are we leaving?" I blurt out before my brain has time to think about how attractive he is.

He sighs and looks up at the tree as the breeze moves through the leaves. "The plan was to go when you woke up."

"Well, I'm up." I couldn't contain my excitement if I tried. I'm going home. I know it's going to be a logistical nightmare. How am I going to explain any of this to my mom? Or the police? Even with that nightmare hanging over my head, I can't wait.

He stands, holding his hand out to help me up. "Let's go then. Calais is going to stay here, guarding the portal until it closes."

"So, it's just going to be us?" Alone? My heart rate skyrockets.

He nods and steps around me. I swear his hands clench by his sides.

It's not that I want him to struggle. I don't. But knowing that the bonds are affecting him, too, makes me feel less guilty about the thoughts that keep forcing themselves into my mind. The crushing weight of the bond isn't only crushing me.

As we walk toward the water, my legs feel tight. My last experience with a portal was not one that I want to relive.

At least there aren't any crows.

"Ready?"

"Yes."

As I speak my answer, I'm confident. I really am ready.

But then he grabs me, pulling me into his arms, and all the confidence withers away.

"What are you doing?"

"This is the safest way to take you through." We don't know what's waiting on the other side.

"Right." I swallow too hard. "Let's go."

He steps into the puddle, and we sink quickly. My eyes pinch closed, and my fists instinctively bury themselves in his shirt.

"It's ok, Kiah." His soothing voice brushes against my ear.

I blink my eyes open.

I'm home.

FIVE

IT FEELS DIFFERENT. The change is immediate. The air is lighter, it's not pressing down on me. It filters into my lungs differently. Each breath feels fuller.

I'm shell-shocked.

It's such a palpable difference that I never recognized. It's the kind of difference you don't even notice until it's slamming into your senses like a freight train.

I blink, trying to steady my breath, "Where are we?"

This doesn't look familiar at all.

The night air whips around us, an arctic chill that seeps into my bones instantly.

He wraps around me, solid and warm. He doesn't ask, he just does it, holding me against him like I belong here.

"Let's find out."

Rolling my lips into my mouth, I try not to pout. This is unbelievable. It's hard not to see it as purposefully done. The universe is against me. It's a cruel joke with me as the punchline.

Is it necessary that it's so unbelievably cold that he has to hold me? I need distance. But at every turn, I'm forced into his arms.

He's so warm. He is wrapped around me so perfectly, like his arms were made to hold me.

God, it feels good.

With my cheek pressed to his chest, I absorb his heat. It's like a furnace. A big, strong, muscular furnace with perfect hair and shiny white teeth that keep drawing my attention.

I don't really remember the moment I pressed my skin against them. I was so close to death, everything is hazy, but his teeth...

His teeth look different from before. They look appealing now— like I might enjoy having them scraped over my skin. If I focus on it for too long, I can almost feel it. A phantom tingle spreading over me like goosebumps.

He holds me like I'm some fragile thing he is trying to keep from breaking. It makes my inside feel gooey.

"I'm going to take us up to get a better look." He barely warns me before shooting up into the air.

Holding onto him, I watch the world shrink beneath us.

As far as I can see, we're surrounded by nature. A wide open valley spread out beneath us, with a river running through it, and snow-capped mountains on both sides. Far in the distance, the dim glow of lights twinkles on the horizon, like looking at a city from an airplane window.

"I'll fly closer, then we'll walk." His grip tightens around my waist, pushing the air out of my lungs.

"Ok." I gasp, my legs tangling with his.

I know I shouldn't, but I can't help myself- I watch his face as he brings us toward the city with ease. He isn't struggling at all. I know the tightness in his jaw isn't from the strain.

My brain fumbles, trying to find any distraction.

"Are you able to fly so easily now because of the blood?"

Idiot! The point was to draw our attention away from the blood, the bond, this connection. Instead, I pointed a big neon arrow at it! The words just flew out of my mouth. Don't ever mention the blood.

"Yes. Your blood—" his voice trails off as he swallows. My eyes are focused on his neck, on the way his Adam's apple moves.

"Why didn't you ask for it before?" I already opened the door; I might as well walk through it. "I know the bond is difficult, but would you have been able to stop Elion if you had?"

"The Rimfae and Shadowrithes don't have the same blood connection we do. It strengthens them, but they don't feel bonded to the humans they take from. I did consider asking you, but the cost is so great, it made me hesitate. That hesitation had dire consequences." He pauses. "I could have stopped him."

The guilt etched into his face spreads like a living being from him into me. It's cavernous, splitting my chest in half. It's relentless, digging itself deeper, rooting itself there so that neither of us will ever forget it.

"Would you have given it to me?" His whisper is almost lost in the wind, but I hear it. "If I had asked for your blood, would you have given it to me?"

"I don't know." I feel compelled to answer truthfully. Right now, I would give him anything he asked for. If he wanted to drain me of every last drop, I would give it freely. I would give him the breath from my lungs.

But Elion was so deeply buried in my mind, he had sunk his claws in. I don't know if I could have trusted Canaan. He poisoned me with lies and fake affection. He made me think he was a white-knight, rescuing me. He even hesitated; he backed away, denied himself. I was so sure it was true.

But now I see real truth in front of me, and I can't believe I fell for that. I feel this in my bones. It's coiled around my heart.

"The weight of this bond is heavy." I can't tell what he's feeling if it's just the exhaustion from having to carry this, or if it's hatred or disgust.

I don't want it to be disgust. I'm not sure how I feel about the bond. It's strong. There is something out of body about it—I'm not in control of it—but I don't hate it. The more it sinks into me, curling into my organs, pressing itself into every crevice and crack, the more I don't mind it.

I want it to go away, to fade, but at the same time, I don't.

The way he looks at me... It's like a shot of adrenaline each time. I've never experienced anything like the feeling of his fingers on my skin.

My body melts into his, completely comfortable.

I gave him the blood without a choice. He wasn't conscious to consent to it. I can't help but spiral about that. He might not have chosen it. Would he have picked death over this bond with me?

I can't ask.

My heart might not be able to handle the answer.

A road below us cuts through the greenery, winding through the dark. He brings us down, dropping in the middle of the empty street.

"I can walk now." I wiggle out of his arms. It's not as cold here, and the space is necessary. My mind is going back and forth so fast, I don't even know where I stand half the time. It's best I keep myself in check here. Catching feelings based on a blood bond would probably not end well. I've already had one failed relationship with a fae prince. I don't want another.

On the side of the road, a large wooden sign is displayed.

As we get closer, a security shack with an arm barrier sits in the middle of the street.

Panic courses through me, and I instinctively hunch down.

"There isn't anyone inside." He continues to walk toward the sign, never shrinking back or hiding. He walks down the middle of the street like he owns it. I don't know where we are–if we're even allowed to be here–but he clearly doesn't care.

"What are we going to do about your wings?"

"I'll hide them."

"Hide them? Canaan." I stop walking. "With what? A sheet? I hate to break it to you, but humans must have gotten smarter since you closed to portals. People are going to notice those." My eyes move over them, large and proud, spread wide open.

He looks at me, and they vanish.

"Wha–" I gasp. "How?"

"I can stow them. I just don't like to."

"That's handy." I watch him as he walks. It's weird to see him without them.

"Stop staring."

"I can't." I laugh. "You look so different."

"I look the same. I just take up less space."

"No, you look different." The wings give him something other-worldly–something ethereal. Now he just looks like a person. Obviously tall and attractive, but human.

His eyes flicker with annoyance.

I think he's acutely aware of how human he looks, and he hates it.

As we reach the sign, we turn in front of it to read it.

"Lolo National Forest. We're in Montana! This is only a few hours from where I'm from!" I bounce on my toes.

"What direction?"

"Um, west?" I should know that, but I'm more of a landmark kind of girl. "We don't have any money or–"

"We'll fly until we can't. If I bring you home, will we be able to—"

"Yes!" I don't even know what he was asking, but the answer is yes. Bring me home.

"I have money and a car." A wave of excitement rolls over me, but almost as soon as he takes me in his arms and we rise into the air, it falters. What am I going to say to her? How am I going to explain this?

"What's wrong?" His fingers dig into my thighs.

"I can't tell my mom about you, can I?"

"No. If humans have forgotten us, keeping it that way is best."

"I don't know how I'm going to explain this. I don't want to hurt my mom any more than she already has been." Just thinking about her fear and pain makes me sick to my stomach.

"You will have to lie."

"I know." And that breaks my heart.

Leaning forward, I rest my head on his shoulder, pressing my face into the crook of his neck. It happens accidentally, completely unintentionally, but my lips end up pressed into his skin. My body freezes, waiting for his reaction.

"It's so quiet here." He whispers. The gentleness and calm in his voice break my fear. Maybe he didn't notice.

"Is it?" I lean back, looking at his face.

"There is no magic. The hum is gone. I forgot about that."

Closing my eyes, I listen. "You're right." The buzz is gone. The air around us is still, not a living thing–just there.

When my eyes flutter open, he's watching me. His gaze is fixed on my face.

"I also forgot how humans blush." He shifts his body so that his nose grazes against my cheek.

I don't know how to respond to that except to blush more.

"Your realm is still the same." He dips down toward the ground.

"I think you're going to be surprised. We've come a long way since you closed the portals."

"You look different, the clothes you wore when we found you, your hair, the way you speak, but otherwise, you're still the same. Humans have a way about them, an innocence. I think it's the lack of magic."

"Innocence?" I can't hold back my laughter. "I wouldn't call us innocent."

He hums, a smile tugging at the corners of his mouth. "Maybe not."

Leaning in again, I wrap my arms around his neck. I can't look at his face anymore.

Looking behind us, I watch the ground as we pass over it. Trees and fields, roads, and little towns disappear behind us.

"We should go down and see where we are." My heart rate increases. I think we're close to my hometown.

"It's going to be alright, Kiah. Take a breath." He brings us down to the ground slowly.

"This is Spalding." My breath catches in my throat. "We're only twenty minutes away."

"Kiah, breathe."

"I can't." I hold on to his shoulders. I'm unraveling.

"You can. In." He inhales, his chest rising beneath my hands. "Out." He exhales.

"What am I going to tell her?"

"Tell her that we were together."

He steadies me, holding me to the ground.

"I'll tell her we were together." I swallow. "She's never going to forgive me."

SIX

STANDING at the end of my street, I stare down at the row of houses, swallowed up by trees. This neighborhood, these houses, the people, they have been my home since before I have memories.

I don't move. My feet are glued to the concrete, nerves are pressing against my spine. I can already see her face. The hurt and confusion. She's going to be furious. I left without a word. I'm sure she thinks I'm dead. And now I'm back with a stranger beside me.

And I have to lie to her. I have to let her believe that I'm so unbelievably selfish that I would run off in the middle of everything that was happening.

He doesn't speak. He doesn't have to. His presence is steady, quiet, a rock to bind to.

There's no judgment in the way he stands here with me, just strength, silent and unshakable. I can feel it pulsing off him like heat.

My breath stutters. My fingers twitch.

And then, without looking at him, I reach out.

He takes my hand.

His grip is warm, anchoring.

Taking a slow breath, I force myself forward. Standing here isn't making this any easier. "Let's go."

I've walked this strip of cracked sidewalk so many times I couldn't possibly count. For the first time, I feel like a stranger here. This place is the same, with the houses, the porches, and the cars parked in the driveways. I'm the different one.

"When we get there, I'm going to knock." I swallow the thick ball of emotion in my throat. "I don't want to scare her. You should stay on the porch. And don't say anything. Just let me handle it."

"Alright."

"I mean it. Even if you hear yelling. Please, stay outside."

"Kiah–"

"Please, Canaan. She won't hurt me or anything, but she's going to be upset. Rightfully so."

"I'll stay outside." His jaw clenches.

"Thank you."

We walk past Cheyenne's house, and the dim light of the lamp on her bedside table is on. Of course it is. They're still keeping the light on for her, a symbol that they're waiting.

"This is Chey's house." My voice trembles. "That room, the one with the pink curtains. That's her bedroom."

"I will get her away from him." The promise in his voice is convincing, but I can't help but have doubts. I know from experience how easy it is to be blinded by Elion's charms. He had me eating out of the palm of his hand.

Even when I found myself questioning things, I went against my gut instincts.

I can't even imagine the things he said to her, the lies, the sweet nothings.

I bought it all. It's easy for me to understand how she would, too.

"This is it." We cross the street hand-in-hand. I didn't expect to feel like this when I finally got to come home.

This feels like I'm walking toward the gallows.

"Wait right here." I point to the old porch swing I've sat on hundreds of thousands of times with my mom, with Cheyenne, alone, lost in thought.

It seems so small now with him sitting on it.

Taking one final deep breath, willing forward the last bit of courage I can muster. I knock on the door.

It's the middle of the night, but the light flickers on inside almost immediately, and rushed footsteps hit the ground behind the door.

She swings it open, standing there in the same flannel pajamas she's worn for years. Her face moves through fifty different expressions in one second flat.

"Kiah?"

She's happy and relieved, excited and confused, and shocked.

I can see the disbelief.

"Mom!" I melt into her, pressing my face into her neck, wrapping my arms too tightly around her body. She's thinner. I can feel her bones.

We move inside, her icy hands clamped tight around mine. I don't think she even noticed Canaan.

"Kiah..." Her voice trails off as she looks at me.

I don't know where to start.

"I'm so sorry, Mom." I break, my heart cracking down the middle. "I–" I sob, grabbing her and pulling her into a hug.

"I'm going to call the police, ok?" She takes a breath, her years of nursing experience shining through with her calm demeanor. "Sit down here. They–"

"Wait, no. Don't call. Not yet. I can't stay."

"What do you mean you can't stay, Kiah? I promise you, sweetheart, we will keep you safe! You don't have to worry about that. Taylor was here. I'm sure he will take more leave and come back. We will protect you."

Oh, God. This is going to be harder than I thought.

"I'm not in danger, Mom. I'm going with someone. I was with

someone." I have to force the words forward. They stick in my throat, choking me. My body fights against me, and my tongue feels too big for my mouth. I can hardly get the words out.

"What do you mean?" Her face scrunches. "What does that mean?"

"I ran off with someone that I met. He's waiting for me. We're going to look for Cheyenne. You don't have to worry about me. I'm safe. He's a good guy, a great guy. We're–"

"Kiah." Her voice is colder than I've ever heard it. "I don't believe you."

"Mom–"

"No." She shakes her head violently. "No. I don't believe you. You were kidnapped. I'm going to call the police, and they will take him to jail. You don't have to lie to me. I promise you, I won't let him take you again. Anything that he threatened you with is just to control you. He can't hurt you."

"Mom, look at me. Do I look hurt?" I take a breath. I have to do this all the way, or she'll never believe me. She won't let me go. "I wasn't kidnapped. I haven't been brainwashed. I just went with him. He isn't threatening me."

I can see the color draining from her face.

"No."

"I'm sorry. I don't expect you to understand. One day, when I can explain it better, I will, but–"

"No!" She stomps her foot on the ground. "Kiah, I won't let you leave this house."

"Mom, I can't stay. I have–"

Her hand makes contact with my face so quickly that I don't have time to brace myself. She has never hit me before.

I take a stunned step back.

"You should call the police and pull the police report." I clutch my stinging cheek. "I'm going to get a few things from my room."

She grabs me, yanking me back. "I will put you on a psych hold,

Kiah. You're not leaving this house. Over my dead body. It's not happening."

"Mom, I know you don't understand, and I'm so sorry I scared you. I hate myself for hurting you. I'm going to get Cheyenne and bring her home. Then, I'll explain everything. Until then, you have to let me go. I'm an adult."

In the back of my mind, panic is starting to rise, moving up my spine. Maybe I should have broken in and stolen my car. I knew this would be devastating, but it's worse than I thought. My heart aches in my chest. I'm causing her so much pain.

For the first time in my life, she actually put her hands on me, dragging me down to the ground.

"You are not leaving. I will incapacitate you if I have to."

"I wasn't kidnapped!" I scream. "I'm not under duress. I am not staying here. I need my car. I lost my phone, but I will call you when I can. I won't disappear completely. I'll let you know that I'm safe."

"No." She doesn't loosen her grip at all. Her nails bite into my arms. "You're brainwashed. You're not in control of your mind. I won't let you walk back into the arms of whoever took you!"

"No one took me!" My voice comes out like shards of glass, ripping at my throat.

The door opens, and we both freeze. Canaan looks enormous standing in the kitchen. Even without his wings, he looks like more than a man. It's different than before. Maybe it's because he's in my house this time. Whatever it is, it feels like it's dragging me toward him.

"Let her go."

"Who the fuck are you?" Mom doesn't let me go.

"I will protect her." He steps forward. I'm not sure if he's trying to look menacing, but he does.

"No, I will protect her." She digs her nails in deeper. "I don't know what you've done to her, but–"

"I would never hurt her. And I won't let anyone else hurt her." His voice doesn't waver.

"Wait for the police." She grabs her phone with one hand, releasing me just enough for me to slip out of her hold. Little cuts, half-moon marks from her fingernails are pressed into my arms.

Canaan looks at them, probably smelling the blood in the air. "Call your authorities. They will not stop us from leaving." He holds his hand out to me.

I couldn't stop myself if I wanted to; it's as if he's controlling my limbs. I feel myself moving toward him, being pulled by a string that keeps us together.

"Kiah! For god's sake!" She grabs me again, her phone hitting the ground. The muffled voice of the emergency operator calls out. "Help!" She yells. "Please, send help to this location."

Canaan steps forward, calm and completely in control. He's not emotional at all. "Let her go. You're hurting her. Look at her arms." His jaw ticks, the only sign that he's holding himself back or feeling an emotion at all.

"I am doing what I have to do as her mother! She isn't leaving here with you. I don't know what you did to my daughter, but she's not in her right mind." She's still screaming.

Without a word, he takes her hand gently. I can feel it. She releases me from her grip and stares up at him. I can see the awe-struck wonder in her eyes. It's the same way I feel when I look at him. His power and authority are palpable, even here in our realm.

"Kiah, go get what you need. I'll wait here with your mother." The softness in his tone makes my knees wobble.

As I run up the stairs to my room, I hear him talking to her quietly. I can't make out what he's saying, but it sounds gentle–kind.

Even without knowing what he's saying, I know he's being comforting but firm.

Throwing a few outfits in a bag with my purse, I look at my bedroom. This feels like the last time I'll ever see it.

When I come downstairs, the scene is very different from the one I left. My mom is sitting on the couch with her head in her hands. Canaan is standing, watching, waiting for me.

"I love you, Mom." I ignore the tears welling up in my eyes.

"I will keep her safe." He places his hand on her shoulder.

Tears roll down her cheeks as she looks up, her eyes darting back and forth between us.

"I love you, Kiah. If you need anything, call. I'll come running."

"I know you will." I wrap my arms around her and squeeze.

SEVEN

HE LOOKS COMICALLY large in the passenger seat of my car. If my heart hadn't just been ripped out of my chest and stomped on, I would laugh about it.

The cab is suffocating as we pull out of my neighborhood.

"We have to go this way because the police will be coming from that direction." I turn onto the main road and drive slightly above the speed limit.

"Kiah."

"No." I bite into my lip. "Not yet. Give me a minute. If we talk about it right now, I'll start crying, and I won't be able to drive. We have to get away from here."

"Alright." He reaches across the center console and places his hand on my leg.

This is possibly the worst thing he could have decided to do.

Swerving off the road, the car screeches to a stop on the gravel shoulder.

"Fuck!" I cover my face with my hands. We don't really have the time for me to have a breakdown right now.

"Kiah."

"No!" I yell, not really at him, but out into the void. "God damn this bond!" I cry harder.

Not only can I hear the gentleness in his voice–the care. I can feel it. In my bones, in my chest. It's a soft, caring concern that wraps around me as palpable and real as his arms holding me. I'm too emotional to feel that right now. I'm too unstable.

"What if she never forgives me?" The thought feels like an elephant sitting on my chest.

"She will." He reaches for me, placing his warm hand on the back of my neck.

"She might not. I broke her heart!"

"She'll forgive you, Kiah. She loves you. She doesn't understand now, but one day she will." He sounds so certain.

"But–"

"Kiah." His voice is louder and more stern. "She loves you. She will forgive you."

"I hate lying to her."

"I know."

He doesn't rush me. I know we don't have time to sit here like this, but I have to take a minute. Taking deep breaths, I lean back in my seat. I pretend I'm resting my head against the headrest, but really, I'm leaning into his hand. It's like a heating pad. His warmth and calm spread through my skin, relaxing the tension in my muscles.

"Ok." I nod, opening my eyes. "I'm ready."

He doesn't move his hand as I pull back onto the road. We drive like that for several miles, until his fingers move down, leaving my neck to gently graze the little cuts on my arm.

"They're alright. They don't hurt." I try to sound convincing.

He gives a slight now before running his thumb over it again.

"The human realm is unrecognizable now." He says suddenly.

Gripping the steering wheel, I snort. I don't mean to, but the laughter bursts through my lips. "I told you!"

It hits me that this is the first time he's been in a car. He didn't say a word! He just got in like it was normal.

"Why didn't you say anything?" I wheeze.

"You were upset. It didn't seem like the right time."

I swerve just a little bit, my cheeks aching and tears forming in my eyes again.

"What do you think of the car? This isn't a particularly nice one, but it gets the job done."

"It is better than a horse-drawn cart, but I prefer to fly."

"We do that now, too!"

After trying to explain the engineering of an airplane, I can't help but feel pleased. He looks impressed.

I show him how the car works, teaching him the rules of the road, what the signs mean as we pass them, and my very limited knowledge of routine car maintenance.

The first hour passes in a blur of such normal conversation that I'm almost able to forget the shit storm that we're in. Almost. Not quite. I'm not just a regular woman anymore. The ordinary path toward an ordinary life crumbled beneath my feet.

It happened so fast I hardly had time to take notice. One second, everything changed.

Now that I'm home, I feel it. Everything is the same here. But I'm different.

I can't think about it now.

"So, we're driving west, toward Washington. Do we have a plan? Are we just going to stop when we get to the ocean?" Any subject is better than the one running on a loop in my head.

"My magic is weaker here. Not gone, but it will be harder to track him."

Weaker? He definitely doesn't look weaker.

"Remember, he'll be weaker too." He reaches over, placing his hand on my thigh again.

"Are we just driving until we see something?"

"There are places here in the human realm that are susceptible to magic. Long ago, humans called these sites of magic or witchcraft, sacred grounds, or cursed woods. They are just places where the veil is thinner. Portals open more easily in these places, and we can draw from the source. He will want to be in a place like that."

" Well, that's wonderful. But I don't know any places like that!" I pull into a gas station and yank the shifter into park. "How are we going to find sites of magic?"

"We can follow the unexplained deaths." He says it so casually that the meaning of the words takes a moment to click.

"What unexplained deaths?" I blink at him.

"If the Shadowrithes are here, they are feeding. I doubt they have suddenly gained the self-control to leave the human intact." His voice is suddenly heavier.

"Oh, my god." I feel sick. "You think they're just roaming around draining people?" A cold sweat breaks across my neck.

He doesn't answer right away. His mouth forms a tight line as he looks out the window at the gas pumps. "I wouldn't be surprised."

Taking a slow breath, I stare at my hands. "So what do we do? How do we find it?"

"They will have started off exactly where we came through the ether. We will go back there and inquire about the local deaths. Especially the ones without explanation. We will look for people who died of sudden blood loss or cases that are dismissed as animal attacks, but show signs of something else. You'd be amazed at how much humans ignore what doesn't fit their understanding."

My head spins. I'm not an investigator. People aren't just going to tell me about suspicious deaths in the area.

"Um, ok. I'm going to fill the tank, and I'll ask to borrow someone's phone. Maybe there are news articles online for Washington, Idaho, and Montana. Local news is more likely to cover something like that."

This is seriously the worst road trip ever.

"Search for patterns. Clusters of deaths. One is an accident. But there is no such thing as a coincidence. More than one attack? That's a Shadowrithe."

Nodding grimly, I slide out of the car and set up the pump to fill the car.

He climbs out of the car, watching me carefully.

"I'm going to buy a drink. Do you want something?" I think a sip of soda might kill him on the spot.

"I'll come with you." He looks around suspiciously.

Inside, the small convenience store is empty except for the clerk. He's an older man who has a no-nonsense face.

Walking down the aisle, I take a bag of mini powdered sugar donuts and two waters.

"That will be four dollars and twenty cents."

I hand him cash and pluck up the courage to ask him for his phone.

"Do you have a cellphone that I can borrow? Mine broke, and I need to look up a map. Please, I'll be quick."

He looks between Canaan and me, his eyes narrowing.

"Alright." He slides it across the counter.

"Thank you so much."

"Um," we huddle together next to the first row of shelves. "I guess I'll search for clusters of deaths nearby?"

Canaan is looking at the phone like I'm holding an alien. Under different circumstances, I would laugh about it. Right now, there isn't time for that.

"Oh, wow. Look." I turn it toward him. "There is a town in Washington about fifty miles northwest of here where three people have either gone missing or been found dead in the woods five days ago. Authorities are blaming wildlife, but two of the victims were found completely exsanguinated." I read the article.

"That seems like a smart place to start."

"Do you think they're already gone?"

"It's likely, but we won't know if we don't look."

Deleting the search from his phone history, I look up the closest diner and bring the phone back to him. "Thank you. We really appreciate it."

EIGHT

"WELL," I mumble incoherently. "Here we are. Lovely Birdsview, Washington." I open my eyes as wide as I can. They sting with the kind of desperate-to-close burn that only sleep can cure.

I'm so tired, I'm struggling to stay away. Twice, he had to nudge me so that I wouldn't drive into the shoulder rails.

"Kiah." He shakes me. "We need to stop. You're going to kill us."

It's not funny, I know that. But the look on his face makes me cackle. He's huge. A big, flying, fairy king, and he's gripping the handle above the door for dear life. We both died, like really, actually died. But sitting in my car is scary for him.

"I'm sorry." I hold back my giggles. "I'll stop at the next hotel."

The car crawls into the parking lot of the Skagit River Inn. I'm so tired my foot is barely on the gas, we coast in, bumping the wheel stop before stopping.

"Come on, Kiah." He pulls me out of the seat. "Just another minute."

He brings me into the small reception room where a very bored-looking teenager is sitting behind the counter. A TV on the counter is playing a hunting show that he seems very invested in.

"Can we get a room for the night?" Canaan's voice is so formal and serious.

"Um. yeah. Sure." He seems startled. Even without the wings, he is shocking to see.

I think I fell asleep standing on my feet. The next thing I know, he's setting me on a bed and slipping my shoes off.

"Sleep."

"You sleep too." I can't even open my eyes.

"I will."

I fall like a rock, hard and fast. It happened all at once. I'm completely unconscious.

I feel him here, warm and steady. Heat radiates from him; it's comforting.

The bed shifts, his body filling the space–taking all of it.

Fingertips crawl across my skin. His hands work their way beneath it, breaking into pieces in my blood and flowing through my body. He touches every part of me.

He's searching and touching everything. Not violently, but with care. He looks at all the hidden places, watching my memories, looking at the parts of me that I only show myself.

I can feel his appreciation. He likes those parts.

The parts I don't think anyone else could ever understand. He wants them. The quiet, the screaming. The anger and fear. All of my insecurities.

A whisper, not his or mine, floats around us, wrapping us in something silky and soft. A liquid bubble of warmth that holds us together.

I feel him in every part of me, my skin, my teeth, and the marrow of my bones.

His hands, big and strong, with rings on his fingers–I see them, I feel them. The veins look perfect to trace with my tongue. The veins that carry the blood that runs through my body.

He takes my nightmares and locks them away with his. They're similar. Pieces of the same horrible picture.

But it's far away now.

It can't hurt me now.

They travel further, moving over my chest, touching my collarbone, then down, running over and between, squeezing, cupping, caressing. His touch is reverent. It's for me, not him. He's not greedy or self-serving. His exploration is to memorize it, not take from it. He leaves it exactly as it is.

Then further. To my stomach, spreading flat over the growing thumping pressure in my belly.

Heat blooms there, but it doesn't stay there; it spreads.

The tip of his pointer finger touches one freckle, then another. He's counting them, committing them to memory.

A tear slips down my cheek.

My hip bones are next.

My lungs burn for air, but I can't breathe. I'm paralyzed, waiting.

I'll beg if I have to. Please, don't stop here.

And he doesn't.

Now his lips come to my mind. Soft and wet. His sharp teeth are just behind them.

I want to feel them. On my lips. On my skin. On everything. I want his mouth to know me the same way his eyes do. And I want to reciprocate. By the time I'm done with him, I will know every part of him by sight, smell, and taste.

"I would find you anywhere. I would know you instantly in a crowd of thousands. Your skin calls me. Your heartbeat is etched into my bones."

I don't know who says it. Is it me or him? Is it both of us in unison?

We're ripped away. The warmth from his skin is gone. I'm cold and alone.

But I can still feel him. He's searching for me. Wading through the sea. I'm in shark-infested waters, small and helpless. Instead of fear, I feel calm. He'll get to me before they hurt me. I just know it.

They circle around me, closing in. But he comes and scares them away. "I told you I'd come for you. I wouldn't let you stay lost."

I think I'm smiling, but I can feel us drifting. Gravity is gone. I rise into the air, surrounded by droplets of water.

He is the only thing tethering me to the ground. I'm floating away, fading into something endless and pitch black. We reach in the dark, crossing the universe to reach each other.

"Canaan." We spin through space. It's vast and beautiful, but I'm not afraid of it. Not with him beside me. "Kiss me."

"If I start, I'll never stop." His fingers brush my lips.

"Please." I whimper against his thumb.

"We have to resist it."

"Why?" A tear drips down my cheek. This one hurts, like an acid burn on my skin.

"We aren't from the same world. If we give in to it, we will be tortured forever. We can't have each other and have our homes, too."

"That's not fair."

"Life rarely is."

My fingers search his face. I touch the place where his eyes should be, but there are no eyes there.

I don't have eyes either. I didn't know they were missing.

"How do I see you?" I gently search my face.

"With your heart." He's smiling. I see it, crystal clear. He's so beautiful.

"And that's how you see me?"

"Do you feel it?" He takes my hand and places it gently on his bare chest. "Can you feel my heart?"

"Yes." The soft thump against my palm feels like a memory. I know the beat like the melody to a song.

"Now, feel yours." He places my other hand on my own chest.

"It's the same."

"Because we're two parts of a whole, you and I. We are bound in this life and the next. I will always long for you."

A sharp sting bursts through my chest. It's so sharp it makes me double over. "That sounds like torture." I can't catch my breath.

"Yes." He smiles. "But to have this connection. To know someone so thoroughly, to see them, flaws and all–it is beautiful. The final act of great love is grief. It is the price we pay for feeling so deeply."

"But I don't want grief."

"No one does." He wraps his arms around me, taking some of the pain from my chest. "It will be worse if we give in."

"Is this real?" It occurs to me suddenly that we might not be floating among the stars together.

"Yes, and no."

"Which part is real?" I run my fingers over his face. Stopping to press the point of one of his sharp teeth into the tip of my thumb.

"The words, the feelings." He hums. "They are real."

My greedy hands move lower, doing in a dream what my waking body wishes it could. I scratch gently down his chest, enjoying the hiss that echoes around us.

"Kiah, don't make it worse." His voice trembles. I can't stop myself. It's a force more powerful than myself–more powerful than both of us, pulling me to him.

"I want it so badly, though." I feel the tears again.

"So do I, but giving in now will only make it harder later."

"I think that's a problem for us later." I suck in a shaky breath. "Let's deal with it then."

"Consequences be damned?" He smiles, the soft one that makes me weak in the knees.

My fingers move lower, stopping at the waistband of his pants. Just four buttons. That's all that stands between us.

I slip one of them between my fingers.

He doesn't stop me.

I move down, popping the second one open.

"Kiah." He gasps.

I don't pause between the third and fourth buttons; I rip them open.

"Can I touch you, Canaan?"

NINE

CONSCIOUSNESS DOESN'T JUST COME BACK to me; it slaps me upside the head. It's a violent crash of reality. My eyes fly open, and I feel the weight of everything. My chest is tight, and my body feels heavy, like it remembers floating just a moment ago, and gravity is too heavy now.

I can feel him. He's so warm.

The dream is burning in my brain. It's clawing at my skull, demanding to be remembered. I couldn't possibly forget it. I'll never forget it.

I want to turn around and look at him, but I can't. If I let myself peek, I'll fall into a trap. I'll study his perfect sleeping face–memorizing it.

So I stare at the wall instead.

Moonlight creeps in through the uneven curtains. The air is thick and humid. Something slightly sweet and floral blooms in the air. The air conditioner hums, making a hard cranking sound in the silence.

He lets out a huff of air behind me, and my spine stiffens.

I know he's awake. I can feel his eyes on me.

The last thing I said in the dream was, 'can I touch you?' I can taste the words on my tongue.

He breathes again, and I have to look. I shouldn't, but I have to.

"Oh, my god!" I choke and spin back around.

I shouldn't have looked. Why did I look?

He's sitting on the bed, leaning against the headboard with his wings spread wide open.

His shirtless chest is dripping sweat, and the blanket is tenting in a very distinct way. His dark, hungry eyes met mine in that split second, and his jaw clenched.

"You can't dream like that." He grits through his teeth. I don't even have to look at him to know that he's struggling. I can feel it.

"I'm sorry, but I don't have a lot of control over my dreams." I cross my arms, mostly as a way to shield how hard my nipples suddenly are.

"Well, you were very loud."

I gasp and spin around. "No, I wasn't!" As quickly as I looked, I turn again. I can't keep doing that.

His fists are gripping the blanket, ripping it to shreds, like he has to hold on to something to keep himself from touching.

It feels wrong to be here, seeing this. Voyeuristic.

This is private.

But the look on his face. And the rigid tension in his muscles.

Seeing the tent in the blankets reminds me of how it felt to feel it pressed against me.

"Kiah!" He groans.

"I'm sorry!"

Puppies and kittens. Cute cuddly things. Nothing sexy about that. I try to imagine them in my mind, the least sexual things I can think of. Ice cream. There isn't anything sexy about ice cream.

Unless I let it drip down his hard chest and lick it off.

"Kiah!" He snarls again, jumping out of bed. "It will pass. If we just ignore it, it will pass."

I accidentally look at it again. That's not the kind of erection that 'will pass.'

Bits and pieces of the dream come back to me, floating around my head like a cesspool of filthy, horny swamp water.

He's right here. Just a breath away. He's so beautiful and strong–and not just physically. He's beautiful in his bones. Regal in a way that is entirely inhuman. He's not a man. He's something else–something other–too good for a title like that. It just doesn't encompass everything that he is.

Peeking over my shoulder, I watch him pace around the room.

It's like a fever just beneath my skin. An itch I can't scratch.

The longer I watch him, the worse the ache gets.

"Canaan?" I whisper, my body moving on its own with no permission from my brain. "What if we just–"

"We can't, Kiah."

Why? We can. We're adults.

And I want to.

His voice echoes in my head, bouncing off my skull. It's raw and painful. I'm starving. I want it so badly I'm almost to the point of begging.

The ghost of his fingertips traces my skin. I jerk around, but it's not him. He's not touching me. It's the memory from the dream.

I watch his hands flex and clench into fists, still trying not to touch–me, himself–I'm not sure. There are so many ways he could do it. The possibilities are endless. He could touch everything. I would let him.

The monster is growing. It's sharpening its teeth and digging its claws in.

"Why?" I don't recognize my voice. It's so desperate it sounds like an addict searching for a fix.

"We cannot cross that boundary. It's too dangerous, and it will only lead to pain later. It's better to suffer a bearable pain now than to deal with insurmountable suffering later."

"This is bearable?"

He groans, the only answer I get to that question.

If I were to walk into the room right now with no knowledge of what I'm walking into, I would think he was in the most immense pain.

"We're stronger than the bond."

He sounds like he's trying to be reassuring, but he's not so sure himself. The confidence that's usually present in his voice isn't there.

"Right." I nod like I agree. But I don't agree. I don't want to be stronger than the bond. I want to give in immediately.

The only thing holding me back is the bitter taste of rejection.

I can't throw myself at him if he's going to shut me down.

I hate that Elion is the last person to kiss me—to touch me. The thought of his hands on my body makes me feel sick to my stomach.

He took from me under false pretenses. He violated me.

Standing up, I abruptly make my way to the dingy bathroom. The tiles are salmon pink, and the grout is a dirty gray color. It's still cleaner than I feel right now.

Leaning against the sink, I stare at myself in the mirror. I'm tarnished. I can see it on my skin like a physical mark.

It's a scar on my heart that shows through my eyes.

It doesn't matter how many times I scrub my skin; his touch is burned into me. I'll never wash it away.

Everything hits me at once. A punishing, angry tidal wave that swallows me up and thrashes my body into the sand.

I turn the sink on at full pressure, hoping to drown out the sound of my crying. He's right outside the door. We're in a shoe box with paper walls. Now is not the time for a meltdown.

But I can't stop it.

Spinning around, I cover my face with my hands. I don't want to look at myself anymore.

Crying as quietly as I can, I let everything out of me. It feels like I've cried at least one hundred times. It seems like it's all I do, but each sobbing session has been about something specific. Tonight, it's about the way he tricked me. The way I believed him. The way I worry if I'll ever let another man touch me again and be able to believe that he is who he says he is. And the way that I'm already willing, even broken and scared, to let Canaan try.

Everything is crashing down on top of me. I'm caught in an avalanche that's sweeping me away. I can't find my footing.

The bond in our blood is making it all worse.

I need time and space—neither of which are things I can have.

Canaan is trying to do the right thing here. For both of us.

But his blood is wreaking havoc inside of me. It's getting into everything, my organs seeping into my brain. It's compelling me to him, driving me right into his arms. I can't resist it.

There's a small part, a scared, insecure part that makes me wonder if the real reason he doesn't want me is because Elion already had me. He ruined me. Canaan doesn't want Elion's garbage. I'm the fool who opened her legs to a few kind words and a smile...

A loud knock on the door, the kind of knock that nearly splinters the wood, makes me jump.

"Open the door." His voice is low and stern.

"Um, just a second." I panic, looking around the bathroom for a place to hide.

"Kiah, open it, or I'll break it down."

My hand shakes as I reach for the doorknob. I barely twist the knob, releasing the lock, when he yanks the door open and grabs me. His arms engulf me, pulling me into his hot chest.

"It's not that. I promise you, Kiah, it's not that." His fingers weave through my hair. "You are..."

I want him to finish that sentence. I'm what?

But he doesn't. And I don't ask him to.

His arms fit around me so well.

I can feel how much he wants me. It's seeping into my skin. It's not just the way a man wants a woman; it's more than that.

He's inside my head.

"I hate that I let him touch me." I sniff. "The last hands that touched me were lying."

"The last hands that touched you weren't lying." He uses his grip on my hair to tilt my head back to look at him. "I'm touching you right now."

My breath catches in my throat.

"I'm not lying." His fingers tighten in my hair and at my waist. "Do you feel it?"

"Yes." I mouth the word, but no sound comes out.

"In a different world, in a different lifetime, I wouldn't hesitate." His words hold so much promise that I have to believe them. It's not up for debate. "I'm sorry that this is our circumstance and that we have to hold ourselves back from a bond that would be so beautiful; it would be the subject of songs and poetry. Don't ever doubt that I hold back only to spare you from future suffering. For no other reason."

"Well, shit." I whimper. Now I want him even more.

His lips tug up into a smile. "You're so eloquent."

A blush creeps to my already red cheeks. "I should actually shower now."

He holds me, staring at me for another eternal second before setting me on my feet.

"When I get out, I'll order a pizza."

A line pulls downward between his brows. "Order one?"

"I'm about to blow your mind." I can't help but laugh as I close the door between us.

TEN

THE ONLY THING that is worse than being naked in the shower, knowing that he's behind a particleboard door, is knowing that he is naked in the shower behind the same door.

It's like the harder I try not to think about it, the more I can't stop thinking about it.

I'm worried that he knows.

A knock on the door pulls me out of my lust-filled stupor.

Pizza.

Thank god. I'm starving. At least one kind of hunger will be satisfied tonight.

Opening the door, I'm met with the handsome face of a college-age boy.

In any other situation, I would see him and blush, and my heart would be a bit faster, but right now I feel nothing. This is the kind of person I should want. He's attainable, realistic...human.

"Hey," he gives me a nod.

"Hey." I take the pizzas and try to hand him a few folded dollar bills.

"Are you visiting? I've never seen you here before."

"Oh, yeah. I'm just passing through." God, this is uncomfortable. Is this normal? Is he flirting?

Being in the presence of fae royalty has ruined me for regular men. Something is missing. Wings, maybe.

"Are you going to be here a while? I could show you around. There isn't much to do, but if you know what places to go, you can have a good time." He seems so confident when he really shouldn't.

"Um, I don't think—"

"I'm Jason, by the way." He leans against the doorframe.

"I'm Canaan, and this is Kiah." His voice from behind me makes my spine tingle.

Poor Jason looks like he's about to have a heart attack.

"Just leave the pizzas, food bringer. We don't require anything else from you."

"Food bringer?" He whispers, bewildered to himself, as he leaves.

"Canaan!" I try to scold him, but I can't stop laughing long enough to do it.

"What?" He opens the box, and the look on his face makes me burst into another fit of giggles.

Thank god, because he's only wearing a towel wrapped around his hips. He needs to keep making me laugh, or things will turn toward disaster again.

"You were rude to him." I open the other box. "What is that face? It looks amazing."

"This is not the pizza I remember humans eating."

"Well, it's probably changed a lot over the last century." Thick, golden crust and a layer of melty, gooey cheese. For a twenty-four-hour, cheap hole in the wall, this actually looks really good.

"How is this cooked?" He examines it with disgust on his face.

"I don't know? An oven?"

"Not a fire?"

"This isn't a woodfire place, but some places still do that."

He hums and watches me pull out a slice.

"This is very strange."

"I went super basic. Just sauce and cheese."

He hums again, grimacing.

I start to take a bite when his hand comes up and blocks me. "It's too hot. Wait."

"I'm starving."

"Did they not have honey and goat cheese?"

I roll my lips into my mouth, but the laughter escapes anyway. "That's not pizza, not anymore anyway." I blow my slice impatiently.

"Interesting." He's scowling at the food like it has personally wronged him.

"At least taste it." I quickly bite into mine before he can stop me. He was right, it's way too hot. "Oh, my god. So good!"

Forgetting all manners, I scarf down the first piece in three big, unladylike bites.

"Canaan, taste it." I pick up a second slice.

He looks like a toddler being forced to taste a new food.

Almost as soon as the minuscule bite touches his tongue, he wrinkles up his face. "What is this?"

"It's pizza. Tomato sauce, mozzarella cheese…"

"This was not made with a tomato!"

I should have him try ketchup next. His brain may melt.

"I'll make you a real pizza." He promises. "One day, I'll show you how it was originally intended to be eaten."

"I can't believe you don't like this." I dig into my second slice.

"And I can't believe you do. What have you done to the ingredients to make them unrecognizable? A tomato grown from the ground should be the perfect balance of sweet and tangy. Complex but somehow simple, vibrant, rich, and acidic." He sniffs the pizza.

How can someone make a tomato sound so delicious? It's his face. And his bare chest. And his voice.

"Right," I find myself nodding in agreement. I never cared more about marinara in my life.

He takes another bite, shaking his head as he chews. "You really like this?"

"It's actually one of my favorites." I pop the last bite from this slice into my mouth. "Don't yuck my yum."

"What?" His eyes go wide, and he laughs.

"It means don't—"

"I can gather the meaning behind the sentiment. It's just an interesting turn of phrase."

"What is your favorite food?" As soon as the words leave my mouth, a memory floods my brain. Happy and so incredibly sad, it takes my breath away. "Linberry trifle with vanilla cream."

"How did you know that?"

"I had it with Calais." And Mordious, but I still can't say his name without my throat squeezing.

It's almost three o'clock in the morning, but I'm wide awake. I feel jetlagged.

"Can we watch something?" I turn on the television and start flipping through the channels.

"The human realm has changed so much."

By the time I'm able to explain what a television is, I find myself wishing I never suggested it.

But then I flip past something I recognize.

"Oh, my god! I love this movie!" I sit back against the headboard. "She's a tough but dedicated FBI agent who has to go undercover as a beauty pageant contestant to stop an unknown bomb threat!"

He doesn't look impressed, but he sits beside me in the bed.

Every time I look over at him, he's watching. He even smiled at a few parts.

"I don't understand. Why would she go through such an elaborate process to exact her revenge? There must be a simpler way." He turns to me.

"Because it's a movie and it wouldn't be entertaining if everyone were logical and realistic."

"Do you still have theater?"

"Yes, of course."

He hums. "I went to many human shows."

"Really? What was it like?" I roll to face him.

As he speaks, I feel myself drifting away. His voice is so soothing. Even as I fall, I wonder how I'm able to sleep at all. Everything around me is in chaos.

But he is a beacon in the darkness.

"I wish I had known." The words are slurred and muffled. I'm not sure if I actually said them out loud or if they were a piece of a dream.

"I know." His voice is soft. "Me too. I would have done so many things differently."

The softness of lips against my temple almost wakes me up, but it's as if my subconscious knows not to stir or he'll back away.

It might not have been real. But I think it was.

He kissed me.

Tonight felt strangely normal. Almost like we were just two people here together at the same time and place. Lovers maybe.

It was easy. It had that certain intangible something that I'm always looking for but can never seem to find.

It makes my chest ache. I want to do all the things that lovers do.

Not just sexual things. Everything.

Date. And live a life. Eat pizza. Watch movies. The things two beings not separated by realms and tragedy do.

Even in sleep, I'm filled with despair.

He must feel it because he wraps around me, engulfing me in his arms.

We shouldn't.

But we do.

I lean into his chest. He holds me close.

It feels right. Kismet. Fate. Preordained.

As my last conscious thoughts flutter away into darkness, one thing pierces my brain. Is this bond going to last forever?

I need to ask him. But it's already floating away into the land of forgotten things.

ELEVEN

THERE IS an early morning chill in the air when we set out to find a clue. A needle in a haystack.

"And we're off!" I try to be enthusiastic, but my voice comes out croaky.

We barely make it across the street before my anxious rambling starts.

"So, how does this work? You can sense them if they're close by? What if they're already gone? Can you still feel it?" I ask the questions so quickly that he doesn't have time to answer them.

"Yes," He answers calmly, like he's used to my madness. "I'll be able to sense them because my magic is stronger." He takes my elbow gently and moves me toward the inner part of the sidewalk.

"You're a gentleman." I muse out loud. It seems to come so naturally to him. He just does things; it's second nature. It's not performative—just genuine goodness.

"Thank you." He laughs lowly.

We walk the lonely stretch of road, water on one side and Birdsview on the other.

The tiny little town on the bank of a winding river is exactly the kind of place I would go if I were a wicked monster looking to create trouble. No one here would see it coming. They would be powerless to stop it.

"Do you feel anything?" I'm impatient.

I know it's unrealistic to think that we will find them in less than twenty minutes of searching, but I can't help but hope.

"No."

"How about now?" It's only been one minute.

"Still no." His brow furrows just enough to show his growing irritation.

I bite my cheek to keep myself from asking again after sixty seconds.

The river curves slightly, and the bend in the path is shielded by trees.

"The flowers were pulling away from Elion," I whisper, the memory making my stomach twist and churn.

"When?" The concern on his face puts me at ease. He cares.

"After we left the Falls. It felt off. He was being so strange, and alarm bells were going off in my head, but I felt trapped. What was I going to do, run away?" I laugh at the thought of it, like I could possibly outrun him.

"You did the best thing you could've done, which was just to listen to him and keep him calm. If you had tried to run or fight him, who knows what might have happened?"

"I was walking behind him, trying to put space between us, and I noticed it. The flowers were pulling away from him." I shudder at the memory. "I can't stop replaying things. Every time I remember something again, it just reminds me how absolutely useless—"

"Listen to me." He grabs me. His voice is stern but still soft—gentle. "I didn't let you finish that sentence, but I hope you weren't about to call yourself useless."

I look up, craning my neck back to see into his eyes. His eyes are stormy, full of anger and frustration, but not at me. It's never at me.

"I just can't stop thinking about how different things would be if I hadn't trusted him." I can't forgive myself for it. Cheyenne is in the arms of a monster, and people are dead.

"You did know. You felt it."

I don't agree, but I can't speak. My throat feels tight around a ball of emotion threatening to make me cry again.

"He manipulated you." He runs his thumb along my jawline, easing his fingers into my hair at the nape of my neck. "That's not your fault."

Nodding, we walk down the path in silence, his hand still resting on my neck.

To keep myself from asking him about any tingling sensations, I peek up at him every few seconds to see if I can read his expression.

Nothing.

Nothing.

Nothing.

Something.

It's almost imperceptible, but his eyes dart toward the river, narrowing as he studies it. It's just a slight shift in his gaze, but I take it as a sign.

My breath catches, and a prickling feeling rolls down my spine.

This is the human realm. There isn't going to be a bone-eating demon in the water here. My hands tremble anyway.

"No one is here." He squeezes his fingers slightly against my neck, reassuring me. "But I sense something. It's..."

His voice trails off as we round a narrow bend in the path. We freeze.

Police tape.

"Oh, no," I whisper.

A blue tent is set up on the trail, blocking our view beyond it. There are at least twenty uniformed officers and crime scene technicians combing the area.

I can't see anything. There isn't a body or any visible blood, but the eerie silence is frightening. There are so many people here, but it's so somber and quiet that I can hear the water moving down the river.

"Sorry, folks," a woman steps toward us from behind the tape. Her voice is polite but strained. "The trail's closed. I'm going to have to ask you to turn around."

"Can I ask what happened here?" Canaan's voice doesn't wobble at all. I'm amazed at his ability to stay so completely calm.

She hesitates, likely wondering how much she's even allowed to say.

"We found one of the missing men this morning." She looks pale and shaky. Whatever happened behind that tent has her rattled.

Images of wings torn off and blood pooled on the ground flash in my mind. I know what kind of carnage they can cause.

Canaan nods, speaking to her for a moment, but I can't hear it. My blood is thumping in my ears so loudly, I can't hear anything.

After a moment, he gently leads me away.

When we've rounded the corner again and can no longer see the police and detectives swarming the area, he stops.

"We have to come back tonight."

"What? Are you crazy?" I snap out of my trance quickly.

"We have to. I need to be sure."

"And how exactly would creeping around the crime scene help us be sure?" The thought of going there makes me sweat despite the chill.

"I can feel something, but it's just a weak signature. I need to get closer." He looks absolutely resolute.

"Canaan, we can't go back there. It's an active crime scene! They—"

"Those people will not be able to bring justice for the victims. Their very best isn't good enough. They don't even know what they're looking for. And if, by some miracle, they were able to find Elion, what do you think would happen? There is no world where they win that fight."

He's right. I know that. There isn't a single argument I can make.

"I might be able to find them." He sounds like he's still trying to talk me into it. "If I can feel the magic in the blood, maybe I can follow it."

"Really?" My heart leaps into my throat.

"Yes, but don't get your hopes up. It might not work. If it's several days old..."

The air feels heavy, like it's pressing down on my shoulders as we walk back to the hotel. I'm tense. He's tense.

I feel like a foolish child. Why did I allow myself to even hope that this would be simple? Of course, it's not going to be an easy fix.

I'm mad at myself.

This is a disappointment of my own making.

"We weren't going to fix everything in one day, Kiah." His voice is soft and sweet, but I don't really want to hear that right now. It's annoying having someone in your head this way. I can't even feel privately disappointed or upset.

"Right. I shouldn't have expected to. It was stupid." I'm not angry at him. Just angry.

"It wasn't stupid." His tone is clipped now.

"Oh, I'm sorry. Are my private emotions bothering you?" I growl, clenching my fists by my sides.

"No."

It sure looks that way to me.

"You feel things very... loudly." He huffs.

"Again, so sorry. I'm not used to other people being able to feel what I'm feeling."

"Well, I can." He opens the door to our room, holding it so that I can walk in.

Brushing past him, I go straight for the bathroom. It's not even private, not really, but it's my only option. I think too loudly. I feel too loudly. My own brain isn't mine.

I want to wash away everything I feel, letting it flow off my body with the water and then circle the drain.

How many people are going to die because of Elion? I feel a personal responsibility for each one.

I take an extra long time washing my hair. It's all I can do to have a minute to myself. I know as soon as I finish, I'll just have to sit in the hotel room staring at him.

But there is only so much I can do in the shower.

When every inch of me, from head to toe, is spotless and shaved, I finally shut off the water.

Peeking my head out the door, I find an empty room.

I can only guess where he would go.

Once I'm dressed, I clap my hands together and stare at the walls. There is a brown ring of water damage on the ceiling, and the floral wallpaper is peeling on one wall. The bedspread looks like swatches of watercolor paint.

The clock radio on the bedside table looks like the newest item here. The television is a big box from at least twenty years ago.

Clicking the buttons on the radio, I scan the stations for a song that I recognize. When I find one, I sit back against the headboard and close my eyes.

The door clicks open, and he comes in without a word.

Opening one eye, I watch him drop a few slips of paper onto the end of the bed before walking into the bathroom.

I was giving him the silent treatment first.

He showers in the time it takes one song to play.

It's incredibly rude of him to walk around with a towel hanging on his hips like that, knowing how this bond is affecting us. Unless that's the point. He's enjoying the way it tortures me.

Doing my best to ignore him, I hum the song on the radio. It's annoying him. I can tell by the way he's breathing. Good.

Slipping off the bed, I dance just a little bit, but I feel him watching me immediately.

"What are you doing, Kiah?"

Instead of answering, I shuffle toward him, taking his hand and yanking him up.

He stands uncomfortably as I dance around him. I'm still irritated, but I can't help but smile at his expression. He's so confused.

Then, an idea pops into my head.

Once it's there, I can't get it out.

Now might be the best time. The only time. He's too confused, just watching me. He won't be expecting it.

I dance toward him, then shuffle back. Once, then again. Disarming him.

"You don't dance, Canaan?" I come in close again.

"Is that what you call what you're doing?" His eyes rake over my body.

I take both of his hands in mine and move them.

Taking a breath, I plant my feet. Here goes nothing.

I swing my arm, but he catches it so fast I'm pinned to the floor on my back with the full weight of his body on top of mine before I can blink.

"That was a good effort. You almost had me." He smiles, his face close to mine.

"Fuck!" I drop my head onto the carpet. He has me completely pinned.

"You want me on my knees, Kiah?" He says with a laugh, but instantly everything changes. It's like he didn't realize what he was actually saying. "I—"

His eyes darken, and he feels heavier on top of me.

"Canaan..." My heart is hammering against my ribcage.

My legs are wrapped around his waist. I didn't notice until now.

I don't mean to squeeze them, but I do.

His eyes flutter closed, and he drops his face down, closing the already nonexistent distance between us.

The tip of his nose grazes my cheek.

Static electricity sizzles between us. I'm about to burst into flames.

Then he flinches.

A wall goes up, both of us quickly construct it. I have to protect myself. I'm not as strong as he is. I can't keep doing this. It's messing with my head–with my heart.

"Get off." I shove his arm.

He moves back, but not all the way off.

"Get the fuck off of me, Canaan." My voice wobbles.

"Kiah," his eyes flash with something sharp. "Don't do that."

"Do what?" I snap, wiggle out from beneath him. The heat from just a second ago is ice now. "Why did you save me?"

"What?" His body tenses.

"When I gave you my blood, I had no idea that this would happen." I gesture between us. "You knew. Why did you still save me? You could have just let me die, and then you wouldn't have to deal with this!"

"I–"

"You made an informed choice. Don't play games with me now! It's not fair." I fold my arms over my chest, blocking him from my heart.

"I'm not playing games with you!"

"Yes, you are! Every time you look at me like that, or touch me that way..." I bite my tongue to keep from crying. "Then you pull back and leave me here wanting you this way. It's cruel!"

We're both breathing hard now, anger whizzing around the room like a bullet.

"I'll be back." He tugs his pants on and walks out the door.

TWELVE

FOR THE FIRST few hours after he left, I forced myself to sit and watch a movie. I was not about to wait around for him.

But when one movie ended, bleeding into another, I started to worry.

It's been several hours now, with no signs from him.

I brought our dirty clothes to the coin-operated laundry room, mostly to keep busy. But there was a small part of me that was hoping to see him. I didn't. But at least we have clean clothes.

Sliding out of the bed, I creep toward the window and peek out again.

The sun is starting to rise, and the darkness outside is lighter than the last time I checked. But I still don't see him.

Dropping back into the bed, I pull the blankets over my head and force my eyes closed.

He will come back. He wouldn't just leave me here.

Unless he died.

Or was arrested.

Or any number of other threats, both magical and ordinary. He could have been hit by a car!

I shoot upright, a tight ball of panic twisting in my stomach just as the door opens.

He stops, surprised. "You're awake."

"You never came back!" I plop onto the bed angrily, covering myself in the blanket again.

"I'm back right now." He tosses a big, spiral-bound book onto the bed.

"What's this?"

"A man gave it to me. It's an atlas. He had several in his rig and—"

"In his rig?" I scoff.

"That's what he called it. A monstrosity of a vehicle."

"A trucker." I open the book.

"Yes, we spoke at length. He knew every road from here all the way to the northernmost drivable routes. A master of his trade. We will use this book to go up north."

"What's up north?"

"A place I was hoping to avoid." He sighs and rubs his tired eyes. "As suspected, the body they found was killed days ago. At least three, likely more. I searched all night and never sensed anything."

I nod, trying to keep my feelings in check. I'm slightly hurt that he went without me. I would have been his lookout—just to make sure he didn't get caught snooping around where he shouldn't be.

"It was dangerous, Kiah." He turns a few pages, pointing to a large lake in the middle of Canada.

Of course, he acknowledges my feelings. Even after our argument last night, it's like he can't help himself. He has to say something about the way I'm feeling.

I'm not going there right now.

"Lac La Ronge," I whisper, studying the map. "Why are we going there?"

"It is a portal, of sorts. Magic thrives there. I need to speak to someone. She will be there, I'm sure of it." His dread is palpable. It's almost choking me.

"This has to be at least a twenty-hour drive." I trace the pen marks in the book up to the circled lake.

"Twenty-one." He sighs without looking at me.

"Your trucker friend, tell you that?" I huff, crossing my arms without meaning to. I quickly unfold them.

"As a matter of fact, he did." He huffs back, matching my tone.

Clearly, there is some lingering irritation between us. I can't wait to sit in the cramped cab of my little car with him for hours on end.

"When are we leaving?" I throw the blanket back and storm across the room to my backpack.

"As soon as you're ready."

"I'm ready." I grab my clothes.

"Did you wash these?" He lifts up his clean, folded clothes.

"Yes."

There is a pause. Just for a moment, but it's there, a breath.

"Thank you." The hint of attitude that has been present in his voice is gone. His voice is softer now.

"You're welcome." The hint of attitude in my voice is still very much present.

I shove my things in my bag forcefully, leaving out a pair of jeans. I jam everything in the bag like it offended me, taking out my frustration on my clothes.

"Don't wear those." He clears his throat gently.

"What? Why?" I don't even try to hide the bite in my tone. I'm already on edge. He shouldn't push me.

"Just... don't." He carefully packs his clothes, avoiding eye contact.

"No." I shake my head. "I'm not just going to–"

"I can't stop looking at them!" He raises his voice slightly, catching me off guard. "Don't wear them. When you do, I can't stop looking at you. Please."

I freeze. Oh.

"O-Oh." I feel heat creeping to my cheeks. "Ok. I won't wear them."

We stare at each other for just a moment too long. All the things we should say, the apologies for last night, hang in the air above us.

He nods awkwardly. We're both embarrassed now.

"Um, I'll just change, and I'm ready to go." I slip into the bathroom and close the door.

I'm not eager to sit in the car for a full day, but I hurry, anyway. As I wash my face and brush my teeth, I try not to think about what he just said.

But it's all I can think about.

That particular pair of jeans just got bumped up to my new favorites.

Tying my hair into a messy bun, I give myself one last glance in the mirror. I shouldn't be so excited that he's struggling, but knowing that he's looking at that, he likes what he sees has my insides fluttering.

He's sitting at the end of the bed, fastening the ties on his boots.

I would be lying if I said I hadn't taken notice of his clothes. He brought military-looking black uniforms. And he wears them extremely well.

My mouth waters as he slides his rings onto his fingers. That is so...

"Kiah."

My eyes snap up to his, and he's staring at me with a clenched jaw.

"Sorry!" I put my hands up. But I'm not really sorry. He's beautiful, and I look every chance I get.

His eyes trail down, stopping at my pants.

"Are these alright?" I run my suddenly sweaty palms over my thighs.

"No." He looks down at the floor. "Nothing you wear is going to be alright. But those..."

"I didn't bring many options. I could wear your shirt." I look at my slightly cropped t-shirt. It's not sexy by any means, but it is small. "At least it would be big and loose."

He looks up at me through his lashes, darkness flickering in his eyes. "Wearing my shirt–" Whatever he was going to say fades away. He throws his bag over his shoulder. "We need to get out of this room."

The car isn't going to be much better. But sure. "Let's go." I grab my shoes and hurry out the door.

"Show me how to drive. I should be taking some of the burden of this." He folds himself into the passenger's seat.

"Ok." This is a good distraction. I explain everything, and we take off down the road, following the map drawn on the atlas.

"We're only about an hour from the border. How are we going to get you through?"

"Through what?" He looks confused.

"Shit." I groan. "Things have changed since the last time you were here. Canada is a different country. You need a passport to travel between countries." I pull mine out and hand it to him.

"Well, this is a problem." He opens it and looks at my picture. "How old is this?"

"Um, three years, I think."

"Your hair looks different like this."

"Bangs." I cringe. "I was going through a breakup, and I thought it would be a good idea."

"It looks good." His voice is thoughtful.

"Oh, thanks." I'm blushing again.

"Pull over here." He points to an upcoming rest area on the side of the road. "I'll fly over and meet you at a designated point."

"Cool, great." There are so many things that could go wrong here.

"Kiah, we can't be separated." His voice is almost low enough to miss it.

"What do you mean?"

"I'll find you. No matter where you are. I'll be able to find you. We can split up here, and I will find you again." He is so sure.

I pull the car into a parking spot along a lush green, tree-lined walkway, and bathrooms designed to look like log cabins are just outside.

This isn't the most magical place, but it will do.

"Canaan?" My palms are sweaty. "Is this bond going to fade?"

I already know the answer. I can tell just by the look on his face. It's already there, waiting in my blood.

"No."

"Never?"

"No." His raspy voice is low, and he won't look at me.

The cab is quiet. I can hear the thump of his heartbeat. He was right about that. I did get used to it. I hardly notice it anymore. But I hear it now.

Never. That one word feels like it weighs a ton.

He opens the door, letting a burst of cold air in. "Drive through to this road." He points to the map. "I will meet you here."

I nod, swallowing down my nervousness. "Please be careful."

"I will." A soft smile tugs at his lips. "You too."

"I will." I feel breathless.

THIRTEEN

I PULL into the line at the Peace Arch Border Crossing behind a dirty SUV with Alberta plates. The early morning sun beats down on the dashboard, sending a glare across my windshield. Squinting, I tap my fingers on the steering wheel.

I pull the shifter into park. This line isn't moving any time soon. Beside me, a pickup truck pulls into the line with kayaks strapped to the roof. In front of him, there is a big dog hanging out of the passenger's side window.

A minivan stops behind me. I'm boxed in.

I wasn't planning to turn back, but now, I can't even if I wanted to.

Nervous sweat gathers at my neck and hairline. I tug at my collar; it feels tight all of a sudden.

I'm not actually doing anything wrong. I have a passport. I'm not bringing anything illegal in.

But he's up above me somewhere, flying over the border.

A deep, strange panic tugs in my chest. What if they find a gun in my car? I don't own a gun. But what if...

Jerking forward, I open the glove box, just to check. No gun.

The line inches forward. The border agent booth is getting closer. When the dusty SUV pulls under the covered checkpoint, my knee starts to bounce uncontrollably.

I'm next. This is fine.

Turning the dial on my radio, I search for a song, just something quiet to play in the background.

Everything I do feels suspicious. Are they already watching me?

Trying to be inconspicuous, I look around. No one seems to be paying attention to me at all. But maybe that's what they want me to think.

"Oh, god! It's my turn." I gulp as I inch the car toward the guard, who waves me forward.

"Hello!"

"Good morning." I smile, and my lips feel shaky.

"What is the purpose of your visit to Canada?"

"Just visiting."

"Whereabouts?"

"I'm going up to Alberta. Banff." I clarify my lie.

"Alone?"

"Meeting friends." I have to force myself not to look up.

"Can I see your passport, please?" She still looks calm.

"Sure." I clear my throat and hope she doesn't notice the way my hand is trembling.

"Do you have anything with you in the vehicle? Food? Alcohol? Tobacco?"

"No, nothing."

She smiles and hands me my passport. "Enjoy your visit! Welcome to Canada."

"Thanks!" I feel like I can breathe for the first time in almost an hour.

I fall in line with the flow of slow-moving traffic away from the border crossing. I made it through. Now I just have to meet up with him and everything will be fine.

I built up my interaction with the security agent so much that I didn't really have the brain capacity to think about him. Now, it's all I can think about.

What if they shoot him out of the sky?

Pulling over onto a small side street, I crane my neck to look up. Nothing.

I drum against to steering wheel, leaning against the window to see the empty blue sky above me.

With each second that passes, I feel myself getting more nervous. He said he would find me. But Canada is a big place.

I stare at the dust on my windshield. I really need to wash my car.

My knee starts to bounce as I shift uncomfortably in my seat.

I'm starting to regret the coffee I picked up at the gas station this morning. I was so tired; I wasn't thinking about the implications of filling up with liquid.

He will be here any minute. Probably less than five.

Cranking up the volume of the radio, I mumble the lyrics to one song, then another.

Mind over matter. Mind over bladder.

I simply do not have to use the bathroom. That's it. I'll just convince myself that I don't have to go.

I cross my legs and rock back and forth. Then I uncross them. Then cross them again.

Breathe.

I try to distract myself with the radio, changing the station. Squeeze and think dry thoughts.

At this point, even if he shows up right now, at this exact minute, I won't make it to a bathroom.

I sway in the seat, wondering what to do. If I try to stand up, I'm going to pee my pants. I've waited too long. I'm doomed. There is no scenario where this ends well for me.

Swinging the door open, I clench every muscle in my body and climb out of the car.

"Oh god!" Standing is worse! Running into the grass, I duck behind the closest tree.

That looks like poison ivy. Too leafy.

Moving further in, I stop at the next tree. Everything here looks itchy. There is a saying about this.

Leaves of three? Is that three leaves on a single stem or a leaf with three points?

I'm going to have to slather my unmentionables in ointment. "Fuck!" I stomp my feet and pull down my pants. At this point, the choices are piss myself or get a rash.

Holding onto the tree, I lean back so that I'm not going directly into my pants and shoes.

"Holy shit." I sigh, a shudder running up my spine. Nothing has ever felt as good as this.

"Kiah?"

My eyes fly open. Of course, he's standing beside the first tree staring right at me. We make eye contact, and I almost fall backwards into the mud.

"Your timing is fucking impeccable, Canaan! Really!" I don't mean to yell. "Don't look at me!"

He slaps his hand over his eyes and spins around. "I'm sorry I took so long. I had to go to a higher altitude to avoid detection and–"

"Please go wait at the car!" I beg.

"Right. Yes. I'll be right there."

When I'm sure he's gone, I finish and stand, resting my forehead against the rough bark of the tree.

I don't have toilet paper.

Just as I begin to consider using one of my socks, I hear him. The soft sound of his throat clearing.

"I brought you this."

A napkin from my glove box.

"I'll just leave it here."

"Thanks." I can't even look at him. This is a new low.

When he's gone again, I take the napkin. At least we don't have to worry about that pesky attraction anymore. There is no way he still wants me after witnessing that.

"I'll drive." He is waiting beside the open passenger side door.

"Wonderful." I feel hot everywhere. It's not that I was using the bathroom; it's the absolutely ridiculous position. Had he just seen me sitting on the toilet, maybe in good lighting with a calm look on my face, it would be different.

That was... horrible.

My pants around my ankles, clinging to a tree for dear life, squatting in the woods...

Fuck.

Only nineteen hours to go. I cringe.

"Are you hungry?" He finally breaks the silence.

"Are you?"

"I am." He nods.

My embarrassment is suddenly swallowed up by the need to get him something to eat. He always seems to take care of me whenever I need it. He's in my realm now. I need to get him something to eat that won't disgust him.

"We're not far from Vancouver. I'll find you something edible." With a mission on my mind, I'm able to forget everything else. "We need to borrow a cell phone again. Everything would be so much easier if I still had mine."

"Can we get one?"

"I guess we could." I hadn't considered it. "I don't have much money, though."

"Soon, I will have that part covered."

"How?"

"When we reach La Ronge, I will have resources." That's all the explanation I get.

By the time we reach a gas station, I'm starting to feel hungry, too.

With a borrowed phone, I find the healthiest, whole food,

organic, natural place I can. Bright, colorful food cooked in a way that he will recognize.

The closer we get, the more excited I get.

I snuck a quick peek at the menu. I hope he was serious about being able to get some money. This place is going to max out my account.

"Well & Good." We stop the car, and he looks incredulously at the little building.

"You'll like it." I press my hands to his back and push him forward.

Inside the empty restaurant, the smell of garlic and caramelized onions greets us.

Behind the counter, a girl is scrolling on her phone. She doesn't even look up, just waves her hand and gives us a halfhearted, "hey, welcome."

But then she does look up.

Her head snaps up, and her eyes go wide. Her phone slips from her fingers, clattering on the counter.

I know, girl. I'm so used to seeing him, I forget just how magnificent he is. It's not natural.

"Hi." She breathes, her eyes trailing up his chest to his face.

"Hello." He nods, polite but distant. His hand comes to rest on my back, guiding me forward. He leans in, whispering just to me. "I'm following your lead here."

"It's like an assembly line." I come up on my toes. "You pick the base, rice, sweet potatoes, mixed vegetables, whatever you want. Then you pick what things you want to have on top, the meats and sauces and stuff."

"Real food?" He smiles.

"Yeah." My cheeks burn.

When I turn back to the girl behind the counter, she's watching us, slack-jawed.

I order first, and I can't help but notice the half scoops she gives me of everything. Canaan's order is heaping over the bowl so much that bits and pieces are falling out.

We sit in the front of the restaurant, as far away from the counter as we can.

"Did you pick this for me?" He looks at his bowl full of vegetables and steak.

"Yes."

"Thank you. It looks wonderful. I recognize each ingredient."

My tongue feels like it's tied in a knot. I don't know what to say. He always takes care of me. This feels like the least I can do.

"I know you're hungry." I shrug.

"I am." He holds my gaze for just a moment too long. Maybe there was a double meaning behind that.

I won't think about it now.

We eat in silence, the kind that settles between people who are too hungry to talk. I won't admit it to him, but the food is delicious.

By the time we finish, I feel full and satisfied. Fueled.

"We should try to drive until dark." He sighs, looking out the window toward the car. It seems he's dreading it as much as I am.

"Let's get this over with." I stand, stretching slightly. "I'll teach you some car games."

FOURTEEN

"OK, ready? I spy, with my little eye, something black."

"The road." He groans. "Again."

"Yes! How did you know?" I clap my hands. I have to keep this enthusiastic.

"No more. Please." He looks at me warily. "No more."

"I don't know any more games. I think we've played them all." I press my forehead into the cool window. Every single car game. The license plate game was particularly brutal. In seven hours, it seems we've only passed other cars from Canada.

I know he isn't enjoying the games. Hell, about three hours ago, I started to hate the games, too.

But the games are keeping things light, basic, and surface-level. That is the safest place to be.

I can't speak for him, but I know that personally, I can't take another supercharged, emotional, fraught with tension conversation.

We need to keep it light.

"Did you have someone? Before you came into our realm?" He asks suddenly, too casually to actually be casual.

I blink. "What?"

"Were you in a relationship?"

The question drops like a stone in my stomach.

"No." I clear my throat.

He glances at me, a quick look, before setting his sights on the road ahead. "That surprises me."

"Why?" I ask too quickly.

"I just thought someone like you would."

"Someone like me?" This is starting to feel insulting.

"A romantic at heart."

"I wouldn't call myself a romantic." I scoff.

"Your choice in entertainment would suggest otherwise. The music you sing along to is about love, and the movies you watch are all about it." He raises his brow.

That's correct. Shit.

"Well, I did." My shoulders lump as I stare straight ahead. "We broke up."

He doesn't speak, just waits.

"He left me." I shrug, going for nonchalant and unbothered. "For someone else."

I shouldn't have said that.

"Wow." His voice is soft.

"Yeah, it was awful." I laugh. "I was humiliated. Apparently, a lot of people knew before I did. They weren't even discreet about it. But it's fine. I'm over it now."

I glance at him. He's looking at the road, but his grip on the steering wheel is tighter. His jaw is clenched slightly.

"He was a fool."

"What?" I'm sure I misheard him.

"He was a fool." He repeats, louder and more clearly. "For leaving you. For anyone. For any reason."

I spin toward him in the seat. My chest feels tight. "Canaan–"

"If you were mine..."

I'm screaming in my head. Please finish that sentence! But he doesn't.

It doesn't matter. The damage is done. My head is swimming.

If I were his...

My stomach is in a knot. The words are pinging around my skull. I can't stop hearing them.

I want to fling myself at him—right over the center console and into his lap.

This is exactly why I wanted to play the games. The games were mind-numbingly boring, but they were safe. A numb mind is better than a lust-filled one.

He sighs, his head shaking slightly. "I shouldn't have..."

"It's fine." My voice comes out too high, too quickly.

"I—" he suddenly slams on the brakes in the middle of the street. I lurch forward, the seat belt digging into my shoulder. I jerk around to see him, my heart racing.

"What happened?"

"There's something..." he opens the door, and the car starts to roll forward. "How do I stop this thing?" He's frazzled, and it's freaking me out. He is never frazzled.

He moves the car to the side of the road, yanking the gear into park and jumping out, leaving the engine running.

"What is it?" I rush after him.

"There was someone here. Not long ago. The signature is strong." He walks into the darkening treeline, disappearing with just a few steps.

"Wait!" My instincts are to call the police or something. Surely there is someone more trained to handle this.

I hesitate at the tree line for a moment, then run in after him.

The further in we go, the colder the air seems to get.

After several minutes, we come to another road. If we had continued in the car for less than a mile more, we would have come to it.

He steps onto the gravel road and follows it up the slight incline.

"If I tell you to run, promise me you'll go." He walks almost too close to me. "Don't even hesitate. Run. I'll find you."

"Ok." I nod. I don't want to, but I know he won't tell me to run unless it's dire. "I promise."

It's so quiet out here. The gravel road crunching beneath our feet is the only sound, other than the occasional snap of a twig or the sound of the breeze blowing through the leaves.

My insides are jumpy, twitching, and jerking with every sound. But I know I'm going to be alright. It's a strange kind of peace to know that he will do anything to keep me safe.

"It's getting stronger." He whispers. "It's not Elion."

Shit.

"A Shadowrithe?"

"Yes, more than one."

We take a few more steps before he stops, pulling a small black blade from his boot. "Get behind me."

I stumble, my body moving before my feet to stand directly behind him. His wings appear, coming back to a flexed position, almost wrapped around me.

"Your majesty." A wet, snarling voice echoes in the dark night.

"Come out." His voice is cold but poised.

"You brought dinner." It laughs.

Canaan actually laughs too, a dark, menacing sound I didn't know he was capable of. "You won't be able to get close enough to her."

He lunges right so quickly that I almost fall over from the gust of wind the spread of his wings produces. Before I can even look, he's got a Shadowrithe by the throat, and he slices with the blade so deep his head almost detaches completely.

"Did Elion not mention to you that I have had human blood recently?" He turns back to the front, letting the body fall into a puddle of blood and melting ooze.

There is a sound to the right of us again. A shadow moves in the darkness.

"Close your eyes." Canaan's wings come around me again.

He doesn't have to tell me twice. I drop down, crouching in the safety of his wings as he quickly solves this problem. It sounds almost effortless. There is no struggle at all. One squelching sound, then a gurgle, then a thud. Then another. And another.

"They're dead." His hand rubs between my shoulder blades. "There were four of them here."

I keep my eyes pinched tightly closed as I stand.

"There is no one else in the area. Maybe you should go back to the car and wait." He wraps his wings around us, shielding me from the chaos and carnage.

"Please, don't make me go back alone!" I panic, grabbing his shirt with both fists. "Please! I–"

"Stay behind me." He looks past me at the road. "I smell blood."

We walk for several feet in silence. It feels like the forest has swallowed us whole. My car is somewhere out there. It feels miles away.

A light glows in the distance, getting brighter as we approach it.

A porch light illuminates a wrap-around porch on an old farm-style house. It's a beautiful home. A family home.

This long, lonely gravel road is a driveway leading up to their forest oasis. I can't imagine how beautiful it would look in the daylight.

"Are they dead?" I whisper as we reach the cobblestone path leading to the front steps.

Before he has a chance to answer, there is a sound. It's soft, but in the silence, it's crystal clear. A cry.

"Someone is still alive!" I run before my mind can catch up with my body.

"Kiah, wait!" He grabs me as I reach the door. "You can't go inside!"

"But someone is still alive! We can save them!" I yank at his grip on my arm. "Let me go, Canaan! We have to try!"

We freeze when the sound echoes in the darkness again.

"Fuck." He growls, yanking the door open. I run in behind him. The living room is comfortable and clean. There is no evidence that any tragic horror happened here tonight.

He runs into the dining room, then the kitchen.

Everywhere we go, I feel hope blooming in my chest. Maybe they weren't home. Everything is too pristine to be the scene of a Shadowrithe massacre.

He climbs the stairs in front of me.

The creak softly, in that comforting way that old wooden steps do.

"Fuck." He stops. "Turn around, go downstairs."

"Why? What—"

He grabs me with no warning. No warning. No words.

One second, I'm breathing. The next I'm not. Because his mouth is on mine—hard and hungry.

I gasp into his mouth, and he swallows it.

Everything fades to his mouth and hands. They're all that's left in the world.

All is right and good. Every event in my life, every choice, everything that was out of my hands—everything—has led me to this moment. This perfect moment.

He is breathing life into my body. I've been holding my breath, broken and aching, and I didn't even know it.

My thoughts are scattered, and my knees buckle.

His fingers dig in at my arm and my waist, holding me to him too tightly.

It isn't gentle or sweet. It's raw—need and passion. Time fades, collapsing on itself. The world is new. Colors and flowers that didn't exist before suddenly do—they burst into existence.

It aches. It's soft surrender. It's the breeze through the leaves. The depth of the ocean. The vastness of space. I feel how incredibly small we are, just two people in the world, in this realm or any other.

My chest feels lighter as he brings his hand up to my hair and tugs lightly.

We're in time. His heart beating with mine. His breath in my lungs.

I can taste how much he wants me. He doesn't hold it back. It pours out of him, and I drink it all. It's soft and sweet, warm and rich. It bubbles like champagne.

"Canaan." I sigh against his lips.

"Kiah." He is equally breathless.

Our mouths move like they were meant to touch. They speak a silent language that only they know, mouth to mouth.

It's the first kiss, but it's not new. We're coming home to each other after a long time away. It's chaos and calm. Peace and fire.

He lifts me, bringing me up to his height. I melt into him, wrapping around him. His hands are everywhere.

I bring mine to his hair, holding tight, keeping him here.

Consequences be damned. This is the only thing I've ever done that's mattered.

He starts to pull away, and I panic. I'm not ready for reality yet.

His lips are red and swollen, and his chest is heaving. "Kiah." His voice is hoarse now, low and longing.

He doesn't have to long. I'm right here! There doesn't need to be any more heartache or craving so much that we can't sleep.

My feet hit the ground, and I realize that we're in the kitchen again.

"When?" I don't remember feeling us move. My mind feels sluggish, and the kiss temporarily paralyzed my brain.

But everything comes back quickly.

"Canaan?" My heart lurches in my chest when he won't make eye contact with me. The fantasy comes crashing down around me, burying me like an avalanche. "Did you kiss me to distract me?" I don't mean to let my voice crack or my chin wobble, but they do, anyway.

"I didn't want you to see that." He still won't look at me. "No one is alive but a dog."

"So you kissed me?" That kiss was like feeling sunshine for the first time, and it wasn't real?

"Kiah," he reaches for me, but I stumble back.

"I'm going to wait on the porch. If it's that important to you that I don't see it, I won't look." I back away from him, desperate for air that isn't tainted with his presence.

"I'm going to bring the dog outside. Please, just wait."

FIFTEEN

"WE SHOULD REST FOR THE NIGHT."

"Sure." I stare blankly ahead.

"We will just camp tonight. I'll be able to pay for accommodations tomorrow."

"Great."

He mumbles something and pulls off the lonely road into a heavily wooded rest area.

I adjust my seat to lie as flat as possible and close my eyes.

"You're going to sleep here?" He sounds shocked.

"We don't have blankets or anything to sleep outside. This is cramped, but at least it's not the cold, hard dirt."

"I'll make a fire."

"We aren't allowed to light fires at rest areas."

His frustration is growing by the second. "We will go into the trees. You'll freeze in here."

"Go right ahead." I roll over onto my side. "You can do whatever you want, Canaan. With the little bit of free will that I have left, I'm choosing to stay here." To stay here and be ridiculous. I know he's right. It's going to be too cold tonight. But I need some time away from him.

It's cruel and unusual punishment of the worst kind to have to sit beside him and those amazing lips.

I couldn't even let myself think about it or process what happened because he would feel it. It's torture.

The door slams closed behind him, and it echoes in my bones. He quickly disappears into the dark tree line. Good. Go away.

Now that he's gone, I can freak out and overthink about everything. I can fall apart.

He kissed me.

Not just any kiss. The kiss. The only one. Ever.

God, he kissed me.

My chest aches just thinking about it. It was the single most beautiful, painful, wonderful thing that ever happened to me. It's like he branded me with his name. It's hidden somewhere secret, a place that only we know.

I'm rewired on a cellular level. My brain chemistry is different.

He kissed me like he owned me.

I can still feel his mouth on mine. The taste of his tongue and how it felt to breathe his air.

But it wasn't real. At least not to him. He used that kiss, that perfect kiss, to manipulate me.

I search myself. If he had said stop–if he told me he didn't want me to see what was upstairs, would I have listened?

Maybe not.

But that isn't his choice to make. What he did was worse than anything I could have seen. That kiss was cruel. It gave me everything I've always wanted, then snatched it away.

Lying in the car, I can feel the air getting colder. I force my eyes closed and make myself think about how tired I am. The kiss, the cold, and the cramped car seat are all pushed to the back of my mind.

At some point, I drift.

I'm underwater. Not drowning, just there, suspended and

weightless. It's so cold, I feel it in my bones. It's an ancient, frightening cold that feels like it's grabbing hold of me forever.

Everything is blue under the moonlight, my skin, his, the water around us.

He doesn't move, he just sits back, watching me. I reach out to him, but I can't seem to get to him—he's just beyond my grasp, no matter how many steps I take.

My chest tightens. This isn't a dreamweave. This is a nightmare of my own making.

Jolting upright, I grab my chest, sucking in gulps of freezing cold air. White puffs of my breath float in front of me.

"Shit." I roll my aching neck.

It's time to admit defeat.

Opening the door, I step out into the icy air. Wind immediately whips around me, and my teeth chatter.

I stomp into the tree line, squinting in the dark. My boots crunch against the dead leaves.

"Kiah."

The scream that comes out of my mouth echoes through the night. "What the fuck are you doing?" I spin around breathlessly, my chest heaving.

"I knew you would come, eventually. I was waiting for you."

"You—what?" I gape at him.

"Come. There is a fire." His calm voice instantly irks me. Why is he so calm all the time?

"How long have you been waiting there?" In the dark. Like a creep.

Or like a protective, watchful gentleman who waited, giving me the space I needed. Someone who cared more than he wanted me to know.

God damn him.

Fuck. I can't swoon right now. Hardening my expression, I follow him into a little clearing of trees. Low firelight flickers in the dark.

Plopping down, I turn toward the fire, letting the warm flames heat my face.

He sits down on the opposite side, leaning against a log.

Pinching my eyes closed, I ignore the way he's staring. I know he is. I can feel his eyes on my skin.

The fire is helping some, but I'm still freezing.

I'm trying to ignore it, pretending that I'm warm enough, but my teeth are still chattering.

"Come here."

"No."

"Kiah." He growls, his voice and expression tight and fully annoyed. "I'm not asking. Come here before you freeze."

"I don't want to, Canaan." I match his tone.

He exhales hard through his nose before standing with a grunt.

Before I can react, he comes down behind me, wrapping around me without hesitation.

I don't mean to sigh, but it slips out before I can stop it. My treacherous body leans into him.

I'm engulfed in warmth.

Sleep starts to hit me quickly, the comfort of his arms like a weight that drags me down.

It's sturdy and safe. The constant fear that creeps in at the edges seems far away now. He's here. I'm safe.

My body moves, rolling just slightly to shift my hip against the ground, and all the soft, sleepy feelings are violently yanked away.

He's hard.

Not just a little bit.

"Stop!" I snap and roll out of his grasp. "You can't do that!"

His wide eyes meet mine, and for a moment, he's speechless.

"You can't press that into me!"

"I–"

"No!" I stomp my foot on the ground. I don't know what to say. There is so much fury coursing through me that I can only point at him accusingly and storm away.

"Wait!" He jumps up after me.

"No, leave me alone!"

"I–"

"You kissed me!" I spin around, my eyes meeting his in the dark. For some reason, my voice cracks. I didn't think I felt like crying, but now a hot, painful ball of emotions is lodged in my throat.

The golden glow of the fire flickers on his skin. He's just so pretty. It's not fair.

"How could you?" My lip trembles. I don't want to tell him how much that kiss meant to me. Or what it felt like. I'm embarrassed how quickly–how deeply–it pulled me under. "It was a trick. A diversion."

His jaw clenches. The muscles in his wings jerk.

He takes a breath, like he's going to argue, but then he doesn't. His face is full of pain.

"It was cruel," I whisper, wiping my cheek. "You know how affected–"

"I kissed you because I had to!" He explodes, but not in anger–it's something else. "You're an itch inside my brain. I can't think about anything but you." He growls, taking a threatening step toward me. "I couldn't take it for one more second. I can't sleep!"

"You–"

He grabs my arm, jerking me forward so that my chest is pressed to his. My hands instinctively flatten against his chest, steadying myself.

"You don't even realize it. You touch me without thinking. And flip your hair. You laugh, and the sound sticks in my chest for hours." His voice is low and raspy as he hisses through his teeth. "You wear those fucking pants." He's staring me down, hard, direct eye contact as his chest heaves against mine. "And you smell like that. And you bite your lip." His grip tightens. "Every song that plays, you start to sing just one second too early. Every fucking time. It should be annoying, but it's perfect. I find myself waiting to hear it."

My breath is caught in my throat. He swipes his thumb over my cheek, wiping fresh tears away.

"You hum when you read." His lips twitch up into a smile. "It's so quiet, I have to hold my breath just to hear it."

"Canaan," I'm speechless.

"I kissed you because I had to. The timing was wrong, but you had your hand on my neck, so casually–you didn't even realize it was there. But your skin on my skin is painful. It's acid burning flesh from bone. I can't think about anything else. I should have just told you not to go up any further, but my brain was on fire."

"You can't say things like that." I'm unraveling.

"Why not? They're true."

I might regret this. He might reject me. But I grip his shirt in my fists and come up on my toes. Our mouths are so close. Which one of us will be brave enough to close the gap?

SIXTEEN

THE PAUSE ONLY LASTS A SECOND. One eternal second.

When his lips touch mine, I know. It's the match that's going to burn everything down.

There won't be any more denial of this. Here and now, we're surrendering to it.

He lifts me, carrying me back to the fire. I don't care about the cold anymore. I can't even feel it. There is only him.

He sits, my body on top of his.

When my knees hit the dirt on either side of his hips, I feel a rush of adrenaline through my veins. I tremble, not from fear but from the sheer, overwhelming gravity of the situation.

This is it.

We're about to cross the line, and once we do, that's it. Things will never be the same.

His hands come up, hovering over my skin.

"Touch me," I beg against his lips.

His hands are gentle, moving slowly up my thighs. It's tentative at first, but that doesn't last. His grip on me tightens as our mouths move, needier.

I brush my tongue across his lower lip, and he groans low in his throat. Bolder now, I run the tip of my tongue over one of his sharp teeth.

He shudders beneath me. It eases the burning.

The world hums around us, and the forest is alive.

His hands move again, up. He holds my neck gently, then moves into my hair.

I cling to him. My fingers dig into the muscles beneath his shirt, feeling them tense under my touch.

Taking the hem, I tug it upward, throwing it behind me as I quickly shed some of my own layers. My jacket and shirt are discarded in the dirt.

The world tilts, spinning faster than before. The trees sway.

His fingers trace over my bra, leaving a trail of heat behind.

Pulling the straps down my shoulders, I watch his face as I remove it. This isn't the first time I've been naked before him, but he didn't look.

Now he's looking. And touching.

The tips of his fingers graze my skin, leaving yearning behind.

I sit back on my heels, letting myself rest on his body. I can feel all of it.

His jaw clenches.

He leans forward, slow and sure, and one arm slides around me, guiding me down.

The weight of his body above mine, our bodies together this way—it's like they were made to fit just right.

He leans down, kissing me again. Deeper. Hungry.

My teeth chatter, the anticipation overwhelming my body. Reaching down between us, I pop open the button on my jeans and reach for his pants.

He's moving slowly. Reverently. Touching everything. "Slow down, Kiah. We'll never get this moment back. I've ached for so long. What is a few more minutes to commit it to memory?"

"You've ached for so long?" I whisper, more to myself than to him.

"Yes." He leaves a trail of soft kisses across my jaw. When he gets to my neck, his teeth scrape over my skin, and it's like something inside of me snaps.

I gasp and grab hold of his shoulders.

"Slow." He scrapes his teeth again before sucking my skin.

I can't go slow. I can't breathe.

"Canaan, please." I arch toward him, my spine reaching. The throbbing pressure is growing by the second, pressing down on my limbs. I feel it pulsate everywhere. Each nerve is open, raw, and aching—waiting. I'm breaking apart.

He hums, pulling back just enough to tug my jeans down. "I'll take care of you."

For a moment, just a split second, I want to recoil, to pull into myself. I want this. I want him so badly I can hardly breathe. But last time I did this...

A twinge of fear—mistrust in the smallest measure—creeps into my mind.

"Kiah, I won't hurt you." His voice is so soft and genuine.

I believe him. I know he won't. His eyes are too honest. He's too good.

His gaze holds mine, unwavering. It's full of truth, but there is a glint of something else, too. Something dark that wraps around my ribs and squeezes. My heart skips a beat.

"I've tasted your blood. And your mouth..." His voice fades as he lets his eyes drag down my body. "I want you to sit on my face. I want to taste you everywhere." His eyes flick back up to mine. "I want to worship you with my mouth."

He always seemed too regal to have such a filthy mouth. My expression must be a mixture of shock and panic, because he lets out a low chuckle that makes my stomach clench so hard it hurts.

"Come here. Step out of your pants. You said you wanted me on my knees." His lips twitch, one corner of his mouth lifting. He's teasing me.

"I–" My brain is malfunctioning.

He takes my hands and helps me up. Pressing his face between my legs. With my boots still on and my pants around my ankles, I almost fall over.

"Step out." He helps guide my foot from my boot.

I tug at his hair, harder than I mean to, as he slides my pants down and off. The groan that rumbles in his chest makes goosebumps break out over my skin.

"What about yours?" I clear my dry throat.

"My pants?" He tilts his head to one side. "Do you want me to take them off?"

"Yes." I stutter over the single-word answer.

"You want to see it, Kiah?"

My mouth moves, but no sound comes out. Yes. I want to see it.

He comes up, rising from beneath me to tower over me. "Go ahead, pull them down."

I let my finger graze him as I tug them down. His body tenses, and he grits his teeth.

Slowly, I ease his pants down completely.

He's beautiful. It's heavy. I can tell by the way it hangs.

I stare. I can't help it.

"Touch it." His voice is deeper now, rasping.

I curl my fingers around him, and he lets out a low, guttural sound that makes me throb between my legs.

"I've dreamed of this."

"Me too."

"I know about your dreams." He takes my hand, stopping my slow movements. "We shouldn't do this, but since we are, I'm going to make sure you're thoroughly cared for." He drops down to his knees, taking my leg at the knee and lifting it to his shoulder. "If we're going to damn ourselves to pain and suffering, we're going to make it worth it."

The toes in my other foot barely touch the ground. He lifts that leg too, hooking it over his shoulder.

"You're so wet." He presses a kiss against my throbbing clit, then drags his tongue through me in one long, devastating stroke.

My hips squirm, desperately seeking friction.

His hands wrap around me, holding me up.

He buries his face deeper, and the sounds he makes–low groans– they vibrate through my body.

With thorough precision, he wrecks me. His tongue is a torture device that has me unraveling almost immediately.

My fingers dig into his hair, and he growls, moving his mouth faster.

"Look at me." His voice is raw.

I peek down at him. "Fuck!" My eyes pinch closed. He's usually so dignified and composed. Now his face is buried between my legs like it's his life's purpose.

He sucks my clit into his mouth, and I cry into the darkness. My legs tremble, and he tugs me, pulling me harder against his mouth, his shoulders flexing as he holds me steady.

He hums, pleased with himself.

"Give it to me." He kisses me again before diving back in. He said it softly, but it was a command. A demand from a king. And my body obeys.

I'm hit like a wave breaking on the shore. It's relentless and over-whelming. He doesn't stop. He guides me through it, drawing every ripple of pleasure out of me.

By the time he pulls away, my mind is empty. Just a sterile cavern with nothing inside it.

He sets me on my shaky feet and kisses his way up my body. Over my hip and stomach, my chest, my collarbone. When he's on his feet again, he takes my face in his hand and kisses my mouth until I taste myself on his tongue.

Against my stomach, he's swollen and leaking.

When I wrap my hand around it, he jerks, every muscle in his big body tensing at once.

"Kiah." He growls–a warning.

"Canaan." I look up at him and grip him harder.

His jaw clenches, and his eyes flutter closed.

It happens all at once, so quickly, I'm dizzy. He grabs me, lifting one leg around his waist as he moves us to the ground, pressing my back into the dirt with the full weight of his body between my open legs.

He's right there. All he has to do is push forward.

"Do it," I whisper. My voice sounds like someone else.

"You don't understand what you're asking me to do." He rests his damp forehead against mine, breath shaking.

"Yes, I do." I run my fingers through his hair, tugging at the roots.

"Fuck." His hips inch forward, the thick head of his cock sliding into me.

He stops, his eyes focused on the dirt. His composure is slipping; he's losing control. He takes a long, slow breath and presses in again, just another inch.

My leg is hitched up, bent over his arm. He runs his hand over it, stopping at my hip to take a handful of skin.

"I want to take my time." He grits through clenched teeth. "But I can't think. I–"

"Don't hold back," I whisper.

He looks at me. His wild eyes are wide and desperate. "I'm trying not to hurt you." His hips rock forward, sinking deeper. His head falls into my neck as he sobs into my skin. "I don't want to hurt you." He repeats himself. He sounds almost delirious.

"Canaan, you're already shaking." I lift my hips to meet him. "Take what you need."

The sound that comes out of him is more animal than man.

He sinks all the way in, planting himself so deep I gasp and grip his shoulders so that I don't crawl away from it.

"I'm going to devour you." He snaps his hips back, then forward again.

His mouth crashes into mine. It's messy, desperate.

He slams into me so forcefully that it pushes the air from my lungs.

"Tell me it's ok. Tell me you want it."

"I want it!" I gasp. "I–"

Before I can finish the sentence, he's moving. Hard. Each thrust feels deeper than the last.

He hooks my other leg around his arm, holding me open as he drills into me.

I hold his shoulders, his hair, the dirt, searching for anything to anchor myself to the ground.

His self-control is completely gone. He's fucking me like he means it. But there is something else there. Something tender.

He never stops kissing me. Or holding me. He mumbles against my mouth, cursing, praising, choking.

He's falling apart.

The way he says my name makes my body ache. He's ripping me apart and stitching me back together. He's fixing something in me that he didn't break. I can trust him.

My blood burns, recognizing him.

Arching forward, open, I clamp down around him. A kaleidoscope of colors, bright and beautiful, bursts behind my eyes.

I'm somewhere else. Transported to a place so warm and safe, I can't feel anything but him.

It crashes through me, and I cry his name into the trees.

He sobs against my neck, his teeth scraping my skin as he buries himself deep and stills. His body shakes with the force of it. He spills into me but doesn't let go.

Shuddering through the aftershocks, he wraps around me, holding me to his chest.

His cheek rests on my shoulder, his wet hair touching my face. I can feel his heart pounding against mine.

With my eyes closed, I run my fingers over his shoulder. I'm too tired to speak.

As I drift away, I feel an indescribably calm all the way into my bones. His blood and mine are speaking. A language only they know.

SEVENTEEN

SUNLIGHT BREAKS through the canopy of trees as I blink my eyes open.

As soon as I try to move, I feel it everywhere. My entire body protests—pain radiating from so many places I can't tell what doesn't hurt.

"Fuck." I groan, sitting up.

"What's wrong?" If he wasn't already awake, he's instantly up now. Wide awake and already reaching for me.

"I'm just—" I was going to say sore, but then I looked down and the sight of my skin made me forget. "Whoa, holy shit."

My thighs and hips are covered in deep purple bruises. They bloom across my skin like flowers.

His fingers touch them gently. "Come here." He says quietly. "Let me fix it."

"Fix it?"

He nicks the skin on his wrist with his sharp teeth. "Take some. A bruise will heal quickly." Blood drips down into the dirt.

"Canaan!" I grab his arm, looking for something to hold against the wound. "What are you doing? We can't-"

"We can't become more bonded. Just take some. I was too rough with you. The least I can do is fix it." Guilt flashes in his eyes, and I hate it so much that I bring his wrist to my mouth without thinking. Anything to make that look go away.

Shutting down the voice in my head, I force myself to ignore what I'm actually doing.

I'm drinking his blood.

The thought makes me slightly nauseous and very uncomfortable, but I drink a few gulps and pull away.

"I shouldn't have been that rough with you." He pulls me into his lap.

My head feels dizzy. Like taking a shot of something strong. It only takes a second to hit me.

"Shit." I touch my head. "I feel weird."

Pictures flash in my mind. Gauzy white dresses and silver goblets under the moonlight.

"Remember when I watched everyone drinking blood. They seemed so happy. You seemed happy." I run my fingers up his jawline to his cheek.

"I was happy. That is a beautiful ceremony that strengthens our bonds to each other and to our ancestors." He's looking at me with such softness that it makes my insides feel fluttery.

"You're so..." I stop myself.

"You are, too." He smiles.

"I called you a monster that night."

"You did."

"I'm sorry about that."

"That was the night I realized that you would not be a quiet, docile guest." There is a glint of amusement in his eyes.

A thought hits me suddenly, and it takes hold of everything. It's blocking everything out. I can't see past it.

"Do you want to drink from me?"

His eyes snap to mine. "What?" All the lightness of the moment is gone.

"When you gave me your blood, did it make you weaker? You should take some of mine."

His eyes close, and he takes a deep breath. "You're killing me, Kiah. I know you're not trying to, but–"

"Why?"

He leans in, pressing a kiss to my forehead. "You're offering me something that means more than you understand. And because I want it."

"Take it." I take his face in my hands. He offered it to me without hesitation. If it means something, he did it first.

His eyes meet mine, and there is a flicker. Hunger.

"Take it," I whisper again.

"Kiah." He sighs, pinching his eyes closed.

"I want you to have it." In a way I don't really understand, the thought of him taking it excites me. Last time I was half dead. He wasn't conscious. I want to watch him drink it.

Silence stretches between us.

"You're reckless." He whispers.

"Maybe."

With fast hands, he grabs me and pulls me so that we're chest to chest. His mouth is on mine, swallowing down the moan that slips out.

Maybe it's his blood, but I feel bold. Powerful.

It must be from him.

"Canaan, please. I want to watch you take it."

His chest trembles, and he takes a shuddered breath.

One of his hands finds my hair, and he yanks my head back. His lips ghost over my skin, down my cheek and jawline, to my neck. He hovers above my skin, not even touching me, but I feel it in my soul. A tremble.

He pauses long enough for me to feel the tremor in him. Then he takes my hand and brings my wrist up to his mouth.

I watch, captivated, as he bites down. His sharp teeth pierce my skin. I don't feel pain, just heat.

It's like fire—moonlight, sunshine, molten lava— it courses through my veins. He's everywhere. In my bones, wrapped around my heart, inside my lungs.

He pulls back, his lips stained red, and he lets out a ragged breath. "You have no idea what you just did."

"What did I do?"

"Last time, I was so close to death, I didn't really taste it. I didn't feel it in my veins until I woke up, but now—" He leans forward, forcing me back. "We have a job to do here. I can't hide away in bed with you until the world passes into the beyond." He runs his nose over my cheek. "Do you feel it?"

"Yes."

"What does it feel like?" He rubs his cock between my legs.

"Hunger."

"Yes." He growls. "That is what I feel for you."

I wrap my arms around his neck tightly, holding him to me. "I'm hungry too."

"Don't say things like that." He thrusts his hips again.

"But I mean it."

My body barely remembers the soreness. It's almost completely gone now. All that's left is the ache.

"I'll just make you come again." He slides down my body.

"What about you?"

"Oh, I'll come too." He growls, lifting me up again. "Hook your legs around my shoulders."

It all happens so fast. It's a dizzy madness that makes me feel like I'm floating away.

He suctions his mouth over me, sucking and licking so fast and hard I'm immediately delirious.

I can hear his voice in my head. He's not speaking—not out loud— but I hear him. The most filthy, dirty, delicious things are pouring out of him, from his head directly into mine.

He's a wild animal, tearing into me, ripping me open wide.

"Canaan!" I scream, my head falling back.

"Make a mess of my face. Ride it." His voice demands. And so I do. I rock my hips against him, grinding against his tongue.

He doesn't let up until my body seizes.

Tighter and tighter, my muscles cramp. Then another memory hits me.

"Canaan! Can you feed from there?" I jerk my head up.

His body stills completely.

His eyes meet mine. "What did you just say?"

I know he heard me.

"You asked me once, remember? You thought I was working against you and someone had been feeding from me." I shudder at the image in my head. He was so angry. Dangerous and deadly—but just as handsome. "You ran your hand between my legs. You asked if that was where they were feeding."

His pupils are completely blown out.

"Can you feed from there?"

He presses a kiss on my thigh. "Right here."

"Do it."

He growls and buries his face between my legs again. I'm so close, it only takes a few more swipes of his tongue to burst.

As soon as my body starts to tremble, he bites into me at the apex of my thigh.

If I thought the other orgasms were powerful. This one takes hold of me, clawing into my soul. I'm floating above my body.

He comes too, loudly, in thick ropes on the ground.

When his face and his teeth pull away from my skin, I'm drunk.

He unwraps my legs from around his shoulders and brings my limp body down into his arms. "You..."

My head is dizzy, so I let it rest on his chest. I'm not embarrassed. I feel no shame in any of it.

"You have a talented tongue."

He chuckles, tightening his arms around my body. "You're delicious."

We sit, wrapped around each other, the trees swaying around us.

"Let's get dressed. I'll carry you back to the car. We need to get to La Ronge." He lifts me up, grabbing my pants from the ground.

"How did we not freeze to death? I don't even remember falling asleep. It's way too cold to be naked." I feel more sober now.

"I'm not going to let you freeze." He tugs my shirt over my head.

I grab his clothes and start pulling the arms right way-out.

"What are you doing?" He tilts his head, a slight smile on his face.

"You're dressing me like a toddler. I figured I'd return the favor." I hand him his pants.

"I apologize." He takes his pants. "I didn't mean to offend you."

"I know."

He hides his smile as he gets dressed and hides his wings.

"It's still weird to see you without your wings." I watch his back move under his shirt as he stamps out the dwindling embers of fire.

"I imagine it would be." He holds his hand out to me. "How are you feeling?"

"Never better." I ignore the warmth in my cheeks.

"Good."

EIGHTEEN

THE TENSION between us has broken like a fever.

The hours pass in a blur of talking and music. We laugh. He tells me things. I share my secrets. All the irritation is gone.

I've never been more comfortable anywhere, with anyone. An instant best friend. The intimidation that I used to feel around him evaporated. He's not the brooding fae king. He's just Canaan.

Overnight, we are stitched together. It happened so quickly, but it feels so right. It's like I can't even remember a time before him. I'm living in Life AC. After Canaan.

The roads wind through pine valleys. The world is warm and welcoming. Canada is a big, wide wonderland. All the dark, creeping things that have followed us are gone. We're sitting in the sun.

Maybe it's naivete, but it feels like everything is going to be alright.

Our conversation stops when the Cascade Mountain Highway opens up to the mountains in the distance.

"Wow, that's pretty."

"It is." He nods. "Very. I wish we were here to admire this."

"What's so bad about the place we're going?" I feel like he might actually tell me things now.

"When we closed the portals between the realms, there were some that chose to stay behind. Most of them had reasons to do so, like trouble. I would rather have avoided this place. I would also prefer you not to be exposed to it."

I open my mouth to protest.

"But," he cuts me off. "I can't leave you alone, so you'll have to come with me."

"Right. Good." I tuck away the attitude that was swirling around in my head.

He shakes his head, a smile twitching on his lips.

The air shifts, the smile on his face fading to a tight jaw and furrowed brow. "You can't step away from me when we're there. Not even for a second. This place is a black market. I haven't been there in a very long time, but I can only assume it's not a safe place for a human to wander alone. You might see things there, things that will scare you, or upset you." His eyes flick toward me. "We aren't there to right the wrongs or hand out justice. We need information and money. Do you understand?"

"You're scaring me right now. What do you think we're going to see?"

"Humans in various states of indentured servitude."

"Indentured servitude?" A sick heat flushes my skin. "At a black market." My voice is hoarse.

"Remember, these are magic beings that chose not to stay in our realm. Their magic is different here, weaker in some ways, stronger in others. They are lawless outside of my realm. I have no power over them. Stay with me. I will protect you. But we aren't there to step in."

I chew my lip. This is bad.

"So, we're going to see horrible things happening to people, and we have to just ignore it?" I take a deep breath. "That feels awful."

"It does." He nods.

"But I understand." The words taste acidic in my mouth. I do understand. He can't take on an entire group of apparently wild west fairies by himself. We are there for help. Not to help.

I hate it. My chest feels hollow. I'm not sure exactly what I'll see, but I try to prepare for the worst.

The book, Esren, King of the Rimfae, comes to mind.

"I will protect you." He says again, more forcefully this time.

"I know." Fuck, my chest feels fluttery. It's like a tightness that came out of nowhere, and it's crushing me—in a good way.

He is so...

Flashes of last night play out in my mind. His skin. His wings. His hands. The sweat on his forehead.

Fuck.

His body is so big and hard.

It wasn't just sex. I gave him something real—a piece of myself that he still has inside of him now.

He gave me his blood. The look in his eyes when he drank from me. It was reverent.

It was so erotic. I never expected to like it so much. It unlocked something in my brain—cracked it open. A dirty, secret thing I didn't know would cause such a reaction in me.

I could see it changing him. His skin was brighter. He looked more wild and alive. There was a part of me inside of him, something that made him feel good. Something that gives him strength.

In a way that I don't really understand, it makes me feel powerful.

My blood did that to him.

"Kiah." He rolls his neck. He shifts in his seat.

"Sorry." I clench my thighs together.

His hands grip the steering wheel tightly. "You liked it." He's not asking. He doesn't have to.

"I'm surprised, but yes. I did." My voice is quiet. Heat blooms in my chest and travels up to my cheeks.

He rumbles like thunder, a low hum that I feel in my chest.

"We're almost there." He whispers. "The magic is stronger."

"Do you need more blood?" The sexiness of it is gone suddenly, and I feel an urgent need to make him as strong as possible. "You can—"

He smiles, calming me instantly. "I don't need any more."

The look on his face makes me feel soft inside. It's quiet and steady. So very Canaan. "I think I need to stretch before we get there. Just a few minutes to get myself ready."

"I'll stop." He reaches across the center console and sets his hand on my leg. The gesture itself isn't strange. People do it all the time. It's casual, innocent, even. But we both freeze.

I watch his eye go wide, then quickly back to normal. He clears his throat and pulls away slowly, placing it on the steering wheel.

If he isn't going to say anything, neither am I. The air feels heavier now.

When he pulls the car into a rest area, I nearly jump out before he is able to park.

It's almost dark now. We drove all day.

There is only one other car here, and they are pulling away.

The bathroom is dark and cold. A single flickering strip of lights barely illuminates the room, which is probably for the best.

There are cobwebs in the corners and clumps of toilet paper on the muddy, cracked tile floor. One of the two toilet stall doors is hanging on one broken hinge. The other stall isn't much better.

This is not the preferred place to get space from him. But it's the only place I have.

Looking at my reflection in the cracked mirror, I look wild. My hair is a tangled mess, probably from the insane sex and sleeping outside. But I look... beautiful. In a feral sort of way. My skin is clear and bright. I don't look like I've been crammed in a car or sleeping in the dirt.

I wonder if it's his blood. I can see a difference in him. Is this the difference in me? It's jarring. But I like it. The way I feel inside is so visibly reflected in my appearance. I feel different. I am different.

Running my fingers through my hair, I let my mind wander back. Everything is different now. One night together changed the trajectory of my life.

I don't regret it. Not at all.

My lips tug up into a smile.

When we are in the car, I'm going to reach over and touch his leg. I want to. I want him to touch me. And I'm not going to pretend that I don't want it.

Yanking the door open, I almost walk into his body.

He grabs me, pulling me up into his arms, then shooting up into the air.

His mouth finds mine and kisses me so deeply, with so much need, that it makes my head spin.

We're floating on the edge of darkness, the sun setting all around us.

"I'm going to touch you whenever I want." He groans against my mouth. "I won't hold myself back from you."

"Good! Don't." I slip my tongue between his lips.

"And when you want to touch me, reach out and do it."

"I will." I take fistfuls of his shirt.

"Good."

NINETEEN

THE AIR IS CRISP-SHARP. When we finally stop the car on the banks of Lac La Ronge, it's pitch black and cold. The water stretches out in front of us forever, inky under the moonlight. It glimmers slightly, moving and shifting in the dark.

"We have to fly from here." He looks out at the endless dark water.

I wrap my arms around his neck and lean in. He's so warm and solid.

"If I tell you to close your eyes—"

"I'll close them," I whisper. "I promise."

He takes us up and out over the water. His wings are strong and silent. "Do you need to be distracted?" His face is serious, but there is a lightness in his voice.

"I don't need it." I rest my head on his shoulder and run my fingers below his collar to touch his warm skin. "But if you want to talk, I want to."

There is a pause. Just a moment between us.

"I always want to talk to you."

I pull back to look at his face. He's focused on the sky ahead.

"I don't know how." He clears his throat.

"You do just fine." I mean that completely.

We're quiet again for at least a few minutes. They pass by as his wings glide through the sky.

"Were you afraid of me?" His voice is low, hesitating.

I blink, caught off guard by the question. "When we first met?"

"Yes."

"There were moments." I chuckle, half nervous, half amused. "When you thought I was dreamweaving. Or before I understood."

"Understood what?"

"That even in the coldness, you were kind. You've protected me, helped me, and saved me multiple times over. You comforted me when I needed it. It wasn't always warm, sure, but it was constant." I think back to his hand on my shoulder as I cried. "Did you hate me?"

That was a stupid question. I shouldn't have asked it, but my mouth blurted it out without stopping to think. I don't really want to know the answer to that.

"No." His voice leaves no room for argument. "Not for a single moment, even in the smallest measure."

"There were a few times I thought you did." I swallow hard. My throat feels tight.

"I sat in the room with you for hours before you woke, the first time we met." His grip on me tightens.

"You did?" I remember waking up and finding him sitting there, cold and distant, but so beautiful, I was speechless. "Why?"

"I watched you sleep. You seemed plagued by nightmares."

"I was."

"I knew, even then. There was something about you that my subconscious recognized." His lips pull upward. Not a smile, not exactly.

"What do you mean? Like you knew we would end up here?"

"No, not exactly. It wasn't a premonition. I could just feel something in you. If someone had told me, then that we would end up bound together, bonded by blood. I would have believed it. I could see myself in you. It's like I was waiting for you."

My chest feels warm, my heart beating hard against my ribs.

"You saw me coming?"

"I wanted it."

My breath catches in my throat. "Why?" He wanted it? Wanted me?

"You're loyal to a fault— to your own detriment, really. That's rare." He huffs. "It is commendable. Even when I wasn't sure if you could be trusted, I knew you were willing to risk everything for your friend. I just didn't know if that would be harmful to us."

He's quiet for a moment, his piercing eyes still watching the horizon.

"I hated every smile you gave to Elion, how at ease you seemed with him right from the start."

"Me too," I whisper. "I fell for everything."

"Me too." The sadness in his eyes when he smiles makes a sharp pain burn through my heart.

I keep forgetting that my trauma is not the only one. He lost his brother.

"He said you were friends as kids. The three of you."

"We were." He nods. "Calais wanted to marry him." He lets out a dry laugh. His voice holds both amusement and disgust. It's the same way I remember most of my time with him.

"Really?" A shocked gasp heaves from my chest.

"Just a childhood crush. It ended the day she met Mordious. He was the one for her."

"He was so kind."

"He was." The palpable sadness is back. The kind that moves from his chest like a living thing and wraps itself around me.

Lights glow in the distance, rising out of the water.

"That's it." As he slowly descends, I can see that there are islands everywhere. Small strips of land that dot the water.

"I'm nervous." I don't try to hide it. I'm sure he can feel it. He feels everything else; this is no different.

"I'm not going to let anything happen to you."

I watch as the lights get brighter, shapes forming in the dark now, shadows moving.

The strip of land he drops onto is narrow, but from the air it looks long. Trees seem to be surrounding the actual market itself. Where we land is dark and quiet, but I know there is chaos just beyond the darkness.

"Are you ready?" He studies my face.

"As I'll ever be."

Taking his hand, I walk by his side into the tree line. A worn path through the tall grass leads the way.

First, the lights shine through the branches. Then the sound of music and voices carries in the wind. It's quiet and ominous, like a church organ.

The path grows wider as it opens up into an alley-like street. If I didn't know better, I would swear we were back in Noctyra. There's magic about this place.

It's dark, and it's heavy. The air is different here.

It's beautiful and terrifying.

It doesn't belong here in the middle of this tiny stretch of land surrounded by an enormous body of water.

My eyes don't know where to land. There is something to look at everywhere.

A quaint little village, like something out of a fairytale. But if I let myself look for too long, I see the cracks in it. It's not a quaint little village. There's darkness here. Pain.

I feel like I have fallen into Wonderland. I have to actively remind myself that we're not in the fae realm. This is here, in my realm.

It's like an illusion. Parts of it are terrifying right from the onset, but then some things are beautiful. But they're only beautiful if I don't look at them too long. The longer I stare, the more off-putting they become.

"I don't like this place," I whisper to him.

He nods and holds my hand tighter.

"What have we here?" A woman steps in front of Canaan. "Your majesty! To what do we owe this great honor? Are you looking to make a trade?" She sets her eyes on me. She's tall and gaunt. At one time, I know she was beautiful. She has all the right pieces. But it's like she's been here in the dark for too long. Her skin is pale, and her eyes have gone milky

"I'm here to see Zocia." He sidesteps slightly, tucking me just behind his shoulder. "Leave her alone." He grabs her attention, forcing it back to him.

The woman lifts her hands. "I meant no harm. Zocia is all the way at the end. In the cove." Her voice is almost singing.

Of course, she is all the way at the end.

"Stop at my shop before you leave. I'll have something special waiting for you." She bats her lashes.

"Actually." He steps toward her, saying something quiet that I can't make out.

"It will be done." She nods.

"Thank you for your help." He steps around her, tugging me with him. Poised and polite, he walks with his head high.

I can't feel any fear in him. He is power. He doesn't falter, not at all.

As we walk through the busy, compact street, people move, parting around us. They watch Canaan with suspicion and awe. A few of them bow stiffly, but most keep their distance.

We pass by little shops, huts set up to line the single street. Purple and red lights glow from inside, illuminating the slick black cobblestone.

The first storefront we pass is an oddly shaped brick cottage with no door. Strings of beads hang in the doorframe, clinking together in the breeze. A weird smell is coming from inside.

One after the other, we pass little shops of horror.

The deeper we go, the more I feel it. It's oppressive. Fear prickles my skin, and my spine is stiff.

Shadows shift unnaturally, creeping into the corners of my vision.

Maybe it's hallucinations, but then again, maybe it's not.

There are at least a few hundred people here, which feels impossible for how small the space really is. All these fae have chosen to stay here, living among us unnoticed. They're different from Canaan. I can see it plainly.

They are lesser. Worse. He is so superior that they don't deserve to even look at him in all of his wonder and goodness.

I'm used to the fae from Noctrya. These are shells—the skeletal remains of a fairy. They died a long time ago; now they just exist here, ghosts stuck in a body that should have expired.

We approach a shop that isn't like the rest. It's not a tiny cottage or market stall. It's a slick black building, big and modern. It doesn't belong here.

There is a woman standing in the glass doorway. Something about her pulls my gaze. She's haunting, skin and bones with long, silver hair that looks like it has flecks of moonlight in it.

My feet stumble, almost falling.

She doesn't have a face. Nothing. Lips, eyes, nose—it's all missing. A blank canvas of skin with no features.

"Don't look at that shop." He wraps around me. "It's selling darkness."

Shuddering, I lean into him. I feel sick. The air is too warm. It feels thick in my lungs. Sweat drips down my neck.

"Darkness?"

"You can buy a new identity there. Trade your face for a new one."

"What the fuck?" I suck in a sharp breath.

"Just look straight ahead."

"I really fucking hate this place."

"We're almost through." He's still steady. The only thing I can anchor myself to in this awful place.

Each step feels like it's getting harder to take, like walking through sand. It's as if the ground itself is reaching up and holding onto my shoes.

A sign twinkles over the next little shop. It looks like a country cottage where you might see bunnies hopping through the garden. It's precious.

"Memories Bought. Nightmares Sold." I whisper the words as we pass by. Why would anyone want to buy a nightmare?

Canaan places his hand on the back of my neck. His fingers wrapping around, gripping almost too tightly.

The next place is just a shack. The windows are broken out, and it looks almost abandoned. But a light glows inside.

Cages are stacked up outside. Big cages.

"Oh, my god." My voice cracks. I know I need to look at the ground, but I can't help myself.

"Kiah, walk. It's almost over."

"Canaan." I wobble on my feet. Humans. They're selling humans in there. I know we can't help. But, fuck.

"We can't stop here. They might think we're here to shop."

Shop? Everything in me wants to turn around and run. But I know I can't. I wouldn't get far.

He lifts me into his arms, pressing my face into his neck. His wings come up, blocking any attempt to look behind us, if I were brave enough to do it.

"Thank you," I whisper against his warm skin. Clinging to his shirt, I take a shaky breath.

His quick steps take us out of the alley. We're walking down a gravel path now, through the trees.

It's better than the black market, but not by much.

Watching the ground, I notice the way the flowers along the edge of the worn trail reach toward Canaan. They strain against their stems to lean inward, trying to touch him.

As if I needed another reminder of how different he is from Elion —but not just Elion—anyone else. Canaan is something unique. He's set apart.

"We're here." He sets me on my feet, interrupting my thoughts. "Don't speak to her unless she speaks directly to you. Seers are... tricky." He doesn't look afraid, but there is hesitation in his expression. His body is tense.

"I won't."

"Ready?"

TWENTY

BEFORE I CAN ANSWER, a light glows in the distance. It's soft and eerie, a white orb that seems to pulsate with the beat of my heart.

The trees around us seem to block out everything. There is no light, from the alley, from the moon or stars, just the orb.

The cove is a pale blue, just a small circle of water surrounded by brush.

There is a hum in the air, a buzz, like electricity. Everything about this place is magical. But it's dark. I'm not even fae, and I can feel it. It's like a hand on my neck.

"Canaan." A soft, clear voice rings out in the night.

I freeze, my eyes darting around in the dark.

"Come closer." The voice is almost sweet. "Let me see you." It's too peaceful for a place like this.

Canaan holds my hand, stepping toward the water. The ground is soft and mushy beneath our feet. It makes me feel unsteady, like I could lose my footing at any second.

I don't mean to squeeze his hand so tight, but I do.

I'm watching Canaan, barely able to make out the features of his face, when he nods. Following his gaze, I gasp.

There is a woman standing in the cove now, the light is glowing from inside her stomach. I was expecting someone beautiful. Fae.

She looks human. She's small–really small, tiny. Her skin is almost translucent. I can see the silhouette of her organs against the glowing light.

From a purely factual standpoint, she isn't beautiful. She looks like the victim of a violent crime. Or, possibly, the perpetrator. Or both.

Her face is sunken in, skin stretched over bone. Blood-soaked bandages cover her eyes, or the place where her eyes used to be. Her hollowed-out eyesockets seem unnaturally large on her face.

She smiles, holding her hand out. "Closer."

He steps forward, opening his wings fully to block me.

I get the sentiment, but I almost laugh. I'm pretty sure she knows I'm here. I don't think much gets past her.

He's silent and as rigid as stone. Every muscle in his body is tense.

"Ask your question."

Every time she speaks, it makes my heart rate spike. There is something about her voice, so soft and sweet. It's haunting and soothing.

"I am looking for Elion, son of Esren, long-gone king of the Rimfae. And the Shadowrithe army he brought back to life." His voice is low and hoarse. He still sounds like himself, but there is something less noble. It's as if he holds no authority here with her.

She is quiet for a moment. The silence makes my legs wobble. If she can't help us, I'm not sure what we'll do. We never made a contingency plan.

"Has he been to see you?"

She shakes her head and lets out a quiet hum. "They are everywhere. Scattered in the wind. They wear the skins of men now. They leave sorrow in their wake. Death and destruction follow after them."

His wings flex, but he doesn't speak. I peek around him, watching her.

"Would you stop them?" When she speaks, her mouth doesn't move.

"Yes."

"The Vault remembers." Her voice echoes, like it's coming from many people at once. A gust of icy wind blows around us, whipping through my hair. "Beneath the bone, beyond the gate."

He lets out a sharp breath. The kind that means he knows what she's talking about.

She holds out her hand, palm open.

Without hesitation, he slips a ring from his finger. One of his larger, jeweled ones. He steps forward, walking through the water to place it in her waiting hand.

She smiles, closing her fist around it.

Then, she raises it to her mouth and swallows it.

I flinch. Canaan doesn't.

"I need human money." He isn't asking, just telling her.

She smiles, "Go to Zinia. She will give you anything you ask for if you tell her I sent you."

Her face turns to me, like she can see me. "You are important, Kiah."

I freeze. She knows my name, too?

She points her finger at me. "Your blood... your death. When the time comes, keep your eyes on the door."

My heart stops. "What door?" Did she say my death?

Canaan grabs my arm, tugging me away. "She's not going to die."

Zocia only smiles, all of her teeth sharp and gleaming.

"Canaan?" Panic, raw, visceral panic courses through me. I barely register that he's pulling me away, back into the alley.

"Kiah, don't cry. Hold your head up." He growls against my ear.

"W-What?" I can't breathe.

"Kiah, don't show weakness here." He's pleading.

"I'm–"

His lips meet mine with so much force that it would have knocked me off my feet if he didn't have his arms around my waist.

One hand comes up into my hair, tugging hard at the roots. I whimper into his mouth, and he inhales it.

I'm warmer and stronger. It spreads through me. He breathes it into me.

"You can do this. We're almost done. After, I'll explain. But you can't fall apart right now." He holds me too tightly, as if I could disappear.

But I won't. I won't leave him here.

I look into his eyes and take a breath. Everything suddenly feels more manageable. "Ok."

He gives me a tight nod and takes my hand.

"I'm looking for Zinia." He calls out, the alley freezing as his voice booms through it. Everyone stops; the people who weren't already looking look.

A man with patchy, frail wings points his bony hand toward the beginning of the alley. "Between the two fires."

Canaan nods, and we move quickly through the crowd.

I can feel his urgency. It's probably on my behalf.

As we move through the crowds and I try to keep my shoulders up and my gaze down. I don't want to see any more, not another thing, but I don't want to look weak. Don't make him look weak.

A cry, sharp and full of pain, catches my attention, and before I can stop myself, I look up to find it. A man, human, kneeling before a large, muscular fae. From behind, he almost looks like Elion, with long blond hair and white wings. My breath catches. It's not him. But the sight of him sends a chill down my spine.

The man is broken. There are little bleeding punctures all over him. Bite marks.

"Kiah." Canaan's voice is like an anchor dragging me down.

My lips tremble and tears well up in my eyes as I force my gaze away. I feel evil walking past him without offering any help. He needs it.

Canaan lets out a sound somewhere between a growl and a roar.

He stops walking. "Clear the fucking way." His voice booms through the street.

There is a pause, a moment of silence, then everyone scurries away, pulling into the shops and slamming the doors closed behind them.

"That's the best I can do right now," he says, touching my face, wiping my tears away with his thumb.

"Thank you."

We hurry through the empty street, taking advantage of the momentary quiet.

Between the two fires.

There is a tiny hut, hardly tall enough for Canaan to stand upright, between two burned buildings.

"This must be it." He opens the door, and a bell chimes.

A woman is standing behind a glass display counter. She's older, with long white hair that is coiled into tight curls.

She smiles when she sees us. It's sleazy and slimy like the first woman. "Your majesty. To what do I owe this great honor?" Her voice makes my skin crawl.

"Zocia sent me. I need human money." He doesn't return the smile. "I also need to send a message through the Ether."

"Well," she purrs. "I can help you with one of those things. You'll need to see Zephra for the message. She is not here now. But I trade in truths, in memories, in dreams. What do you have for me?" She's looking at me.

"Oh, I–"

She sniffs the air, taking a long draw. "Give me your sorrows." Her eyes roll back.

"No." Canaan snaps. "Don't speak to her."

"I'll give you a fair deal." She's unfazed by his anger. "But I need something in return. And that girl is full of sadness." She's practically licking her lips.

"Don't fucking look at her." He slams his fist down on the glass counter. It shatters immediately, cutting his hand.

I flinch, but Zinia doesn't. She pulls a small copper bowl from nowhere and places it beneath his hand, catching the drops.

"The blood of a king." She smiles, watching the bowl slowly fill. "That, I can work with." There is an envelope on the counter, she slides it toward him, whatever it is, she already had it prepared.

TWENTY-ONE

THE CURRENT MOOD can only be described as tense. Since we got to the car, Canaan hasn't said a word. The silence is loud, humming along with the engine.

I don't know how much money she gave him, or where we're going.

"Um," I clear my throat. "We should stop at an ATM. I'll deposit the money. A hotel won't let us pay cash."

He looks at me, an unreadable expression on his face. His eyes flicker before turning back to the road. "Humans have become complicated."

"Yeah, I guess we have." I lean back in my seat. My stomach is tied in a knot, and I have a million questions for him, but I can't make any of them come out of my mouth.

"Our lodgings have been taken care of."

I know the irritation in his voice isn't aimed at me, but it still makes me shrink back.

He turns off the main road onto a smaller one, driving like he knows exactly where he is going. Tall trees line both sides of the street.

"When?" I sit forward, looking out, trying to figure out where we're headed.

He doesn't answer. And I don't ask again.

The trees break, and a stone and wrought-iron gate opens up before us. The road winds and curves, streetlamps lighting the way.

Then, finally, I see it.

At the end of the driveway, a hotel rises like something out of a dream. A massive, breathtaking mansion of whitewashed stone and ivy.

"This is where we're staying?" I choke.

Four stone pillars rise so high into the air, they seem endless as he stops the car beneath a portico where several attendants are waiting. Their rich, earth-toned uniforms are pressed and creased to perfection.

My car doesn't belong in a place like this. Hell, I don't belong in a place like this.

Canaan climbs out of the car, his tall frame dwarfing the men as he speaks to them quietly. One of them starts to open my door, but Canaan seems to step out of nowhere, opening it before he can.

With his hand on my lower back, he leads me through the door being held open for us.

"What about our bags?" I turn back.

"They bring them."

"Oh, right."

Inside, there is a man waiting in front of the reception desk. "Mr. King. Welcome to The Boneville."

"Thank you." Canaan takes a golden key from his hand.

"Your room is ready. If you will follow Emory, he will bring you up right away."

Canaan nods, and we walk into an elevator that is also being held open for us. Because, God forbid, we have to wait a moment for the elevator to reach the lobby.

"Your last name is King?" I whisper, leaning into him. It's a bit on the nose.

"No." His lips twitch. "We don't have last names. First name and title."

The hallway we step out onto has only two doors. One to the left and one to the right. I stare at the floor as we walk. Glossed marble with a strip of pristine maroon and gold carpet. It looks brand new, like we're the first people to ever walk on it.

"You are in penthouse one, sir." The man opens a white door. He follows us in. "This is the main sitting room. This tablet controls everything in the room, from the window shades to the lights and the Bluetooth speakers. You can also contact the front desk for assistance, room service, or anything you could possibly require. We are here to serve you. Please don't hesitate." He hands the tablet to Canaan, who looks at it with an unimpressed expression.

If the man noticed, he doesn't show it. "The bedrooms are on either side of the sitting room. The master suite has a spa bath."

"Wow." I look around the room. Everything seems so expensive.

This place is a far cry from the motel I paid for.

The tour continues to the fully stocked bar and guest bedroom. Luxury waits around every corner.

I want to move in here.

From the bedroom floor-to-ceiling windows, Lac La Ronge spreads out into the horizon as far as the eye can see. A pitch-black expanse in the dark. It looks a lot different from here than flying over it.

When we're finally alone, an awkward weight settles over both of us. There are so many things to talk about, all of them feel pressing in their own right.

"So," I chuckle nervously, shifting on my toes.

"Maybe we should shower." He picks up the bags.

My heart leaps into my throat. I would love to take a shower with him.

His eyes go wide, and a crease forms between his brows. "I meant separately."

"Oh, right. Sure." My chest deflates like a popped balloon.

"But," he stops, hesitating. "We could."

The bathroom is silent when we enter it. I can hear my heart beating loudly. This is different from a dirty, desperate night in the middle of a dark forest.

This is white marble and soft lighting. The glass shower is huge. A rainwater faucet comes down from the ceiling with four shower-heads surrounding it on all sides.

He doesn't say anything, just starts the water and begins to unbutton his shirt.

My mouth is dry.

This isn't the first time we've even bathed together. But I'm nervous. This is different.

I'm going to look at him. Last time I stared down at the water, holding my arm over my chest to cover up.

I take a breath and undress, painfully aware of every piece of fabric that drops to the floor around me.

I don't know what to do with my hands. My arms don't feel right dangling there uselessly at my sides.

He holds his hand out to me, walking in with me.

As soon as the water rains down on me, I feel more at ease. It's softer in here. The steam and warmth blurring the edges.

He stands with his back to me, water streaming down the long line of his spine. His shoulders rise and fall, steady breaths–calm breaths.

"Turn around." He looks at me, reaching for the pearlescent body wash.

I do it, not hesitating.

His hands are firm and careful as he spreads the lather over my shoulders and back. It's not seductive– it's adoring.

The soap smells like citrus and something floral, blooming in the air around us.

He moves down to my waist, stopping there. I spin around to face him, just waiting.

With slow hands, he moves to my arms, then up to my chest. No one has ever touched me like this. It's reverent–sacred.

Everything about this is different from last night. There is heat but not fire. He's not devouring me, he's just feeling me–memorizing me.

"Can I?" I want to put my hands on his skin.

He nods, swallowing like he can't speak.

Closing my eyes, I let the water run over my face before taking soap and rubbing it into a foamy white lather.

There are tremors in my hands as I place them on his chest.

I let out a nervous laugh, feeling heat creep to my cheeks and chest. I don't know why I'm so jittery.

I run my hands over his arms, wiping away all traces of the forest from his body.

"You okay?" His voice is barely louder than the water.

"Yeah. You?"

His eyes search mine for a moment. "Not really."

I want to ask, but I'm afraid, so I don't.

"You're not going to die." His voice is louder now, firmer. "I will not allow that to happen."

"Are the things she sees set in stone? She said my death—"

"No." He shakes his head. "There are always choices that will change the outcome." He takes my face in his hands. "I will not allow that to happen."

"But what if—"

"Kiah." He grits his teeth. "It will not happen." He punctuates each word angrily. "There is no what if. I will not allow you to die."

"This isn't something you can simply command!"

The muscles in his body roll beneath his skin. A violent rage shaking him from the inside out. They ripple as if he's about to explode.

His wings snap open, hitting the glass wall of the shower. A sickening crack rips through the air, and a spiderweb of fractures breaks across the panel.

I flinch and instinctively step back.

The glass holds but barely.

He doesn't look at me. Water cascades from him, his wings taking up too much space. "You will not die. Do you understand me? I will kill everything that crawls in the darkness before I allow that."

"Wait." I step toward him, reaching, but it's too late. He's backing away, pulling away from me.

I watch helplessly as he storms out of the shower and then out of the bathroom completely.

"Fuck." I breathe, turning off the water and staring at the glass.

Slipping out of the shower, grab a plush robe from a hanger and follow his wet footsteps from the bedroom into the living room. He already has pants on.

"Are you leaving?" I don't mean to sound so panicked.

"I just need a moment."

"Please don't leave. If you want space, I'll leave you alone, but don't go anywhere." I'm not normally a clingy person. But the thought of him leaving me here makes my throat go dry, and my chest tighten.

He groans and lets the shirt in his hands drop to the ground.

"I'll be in the guest room." He looks at me for a moment before brushing past me.

The door slams loudly into the frame, the wall shaking with the force.

Left alone with my thoughts, I stare at the water stretching out under the moonlight. I'm going to give him time and space. I won't bother him.

But when I can, as soon as I get the chance, I'm going to tell him I believe him. I trust him.

He won't let anything happen to me.

TWENTY-TWO

MY EYES BLINK OPEN, and I'm confused. Where am I?

Buried in the luxurious sheets from the hotel bed, I look around for him.

But I'm alone. The sky is dark outside, with just stars hanging over the black water. It must have been at least a few hours because I feel rested as I crawl out of bed.

He's not in the main suite at all. Not in the sitting area or in the bathroom.

I walk through the living room and bar. He's not there.

The door to the guest suite is still closed.

I hesitate for a moment, but test the handle. He didn't lock it. Best-case scenario, he fell asleep. Worst-case scenario, he's still pissed, and I'm barging in on him before he's ready.

Holding my breath, I creep into the room.

It's empty too. He's not in the bed or out on the small balcony.

I stand in front of the windows, staring out at the water from this new angle.

I don't believe he would've left. Maybe he came into the room to tell me he needed to go out, but I was asleep.

As I wonder and worry and make up excuses, I hear a sound.

My knees almost give out.

Tucked on the other side of the room in a small hallway, the bathroom door is closed. And there's light shining from beneath it.

Walking on tiptoes, I creep toward the bathroom.

I know what I heard. That sound is burned into my brain. I'll never mistake it or forget it as long as I live.

I almost say his name, but I don't. I'm not sure why, but I force myself to stay quiet.

I open the door without a sound.

And then I hear it again. A moan.

Sucking in a breath, I break every single rule of basic manners and privacy, but I have to look. My body is moving on autopilot, and I'm compelled forward to see it.

He's sitting on the edge of the bathtub with his back to the wall. His hand is lost beneath the waistband of his pants.

His eyes are pinched closed as beads of sweat or water drip down his chest.

Slowly, his hand moves.

It's like he's torturing himself. His jaw clenches, and he moans again, this time, bracing his free hand against the edge of the bathtub.

His lips part, and the muscles in his chest flex beneath his skin. He's moving his hand faster now, working it up and down in long strokes.

His wings are out; they twitch in time with the movements of his hand. My thighs clench together, desperate to relieve the throbbing that has started to pound.

It looks like pain and pleasure are bound together so tightly that I can't tell one from the other.

I should turn around and walk away. By some miracle, he hasn't seen me yet. I can still leave and pretend I never saw anything.

But I can't move.

Guilt tugs in my chest as I watch him move his hand.

This is private.

He pulls his pants down just enough to pull it out completely. Long and thick and already leaking, he spits on it and grips the base.

Fuck. My body jerks, my muscles twitching.

His cock is beautiful. Soft skin with a thick vein that runs the length of it.

But this is...

His hand moves faster, twisting slightly. His hips buck to meet each thrust.

Frustrated groans spill out of him.

This is how he makes himself feel good, how he looks when he's alone and able to be exactly as he needs. He's not hiding anything. He's unguarded.

He moans and pulls his hand away, denying himself.

My skin hurts, every part of me aches. I want him desperately.

I force myself away, taking a step back.

"Kiah," he groans, low, half choked, and I freeze.

The sound of my name, rough and aching on his lips, is like an electric poker to the knot in my stomach. Fuck.

Caught red-handed, I open my mouth to apologize, but his eyes are still closed.

He didn't see me.

He's just moaning my name. While he's touching himself.

The air in my lungs is punched out in a silent gasp. My legs almost give out. A hot flush spreads across my chest and cheeks. Heat rolls in my stomach, clenching.

He looks close to breaking—unraveling at the seams.

His eyes open and meet mine. I don't leave him enough time to feel embarrassed for being caught like this. I step into the bathroom.

"Don't stop."

"Kiah," he chokes through gritted teeth.

I step inside, my body fluttering with anticipation. The air is thick, heavy, and humming with a palpable tension.

"I know you need sleep." His eyes pinch closed.

I reach him as he starts to hang his head. Taking his face in my hands, I lean into his body. "You could have woken me up."

"I just–"

"I want you to. If this ever happens again–"

He lets out a bitter laugh. "If?"

I lean back to look into his eyes.

"Kiah, you don't understand. I–" He groans. "When we accepted the bond, your body..."

"My body what?"

His hands come up to my hips. "I need it." He whispers. "I can't breathe when you're not near. The former desire to touch you, to smell you, to feel you–it's not just desire now. I have to do it. It's compulsion. It's survival. The ache to touch you is in my blood. I have to. I wake up like this. I fall asleep like this." He shakes his head, letting out an angry breath. "We're here to find them. You're human. I have to resist this urge to plant myself inside of your body and never let go."

His forehead presses against my chest. He feels feverish.

"Everything you do makes it worse." He chuckles.

My heart hammers in my chest. I feel it too. Not to the degree that he does, but I feel it, a pull in my chest.

"I'm starving for you." His low, hoarse voice snaps my self-control. "The taste you left on my teeth is–" his voice fades into a tortured groan.

Reaching up, I yank the tie holding my robe closed. "Then have me. I want you to. Take whatever you need."

He leans back, looking up in confused surprise as I drop the robe to my ankles.

Maybe it's the look in his eyes, the hungry, desperate, primal expression. Or the way he rolls his neck. Or how his tongue slides down one of his elongated teeth. Maybe it's all of it combined. But my heart rate skyrockets, and the temperature in the room goes up by a hundred degrees.

"You asked for this." He smiles, grabbing me. "We're breaking everything in here tonight." He lifts me like I weigh nothing, bringing me into the bedroom.

His mouth comes down to the curve of my shoulder, but he doesn't kiss me; he bites me. Not hard, not painful, just the tips of his teeth pressed to my skin as he takes a deep breath.

My body feels tight, like something is wrapped around me, squeezing.

He drops me to the floor right outside the bathroom door, his arm still around my back. It's a frenzy. He touches me everywhere. We can't make it another step.

"Kiah." He growls when his fingers sweep through the slick skin between my legs. "Did watching me do this to you?"

"Yes." I arch toward him.

"Look at me." His voice is suddenly stern. "If I hurt you, you have to tell me."

"Hurt me?"

"I can't take you like a man tonight."

"What?" I almost choke.

Darkness swirls in his eyes as he smiles. His wings jerk open as he sits back between my legs. I barely register that he's holding my ankles until he places them to rest on his shoulders.

"Ready?" He nudges the head of his cock against me.

"Yes." I don't think I am. He looks like he's about to eat me alive.

He slams forward in one hard thrust. His hand curls into the carpet beside my head, anchoring himself as he pushes forward, inching in as deeply as he can.

I feel it in my molars.

My hands grip his arms, my legs, and the carpet. I don't know what to do. I can't escape it.

He growls and drags it back slowly, never ending. Then, right at the tip, he stops.

"Put your hands up above your head."

His movements are fluid and smooth. As soon as my arms hit the ground, he's bringing his big hand up to pin my wrists down.

I'm open, trapped, vulnerable.

I can't escape from this position. My knees are almost in my ears.

"Take a breath." He smiles.

I nod and try.

He slams forward so hard my mind goes haywire, like a static radio station. All thoughts come screeching to a halt. His cock and the sound of his moans take up all the space in my brain.

It takes only one thrust to know exactly what he meant. He's not taking me like a man. He's fucking me like an animal.

The carpet burns my back, rubbing my skin raw as he pounds into me so hard my brain rattles.

If I needed blood this morning for bruising, I'm going to need a miracle tomorrow.

He's clawing his way deeper, pushing harder, moving faster. There was never any control. He's been manic from the start.

He's wrecking me, brutalizing me. And I love it.

I've never been so fully, completely, desperately wanted before.

"You're so tight around me." He breathes.

I gasp, my muscles spasming, but I can't move. I can't even wiggle. He's got me pinned, fully immobilized.

"Canaan! I can't–" Breathe? Move? Stand it for one more second? Yes.

"Go ahead. Let me feel it. Show me how good it feels." He presses his weight into his hand that has my arms pinned. His other hand comes down to my neck. "Make a mess."

A noise comes out of my chest, a sharp, broken sound that burns my throat.

I'm at his mercy. I can't even speak to tell him what I need. But he doesn't need me to tell him. He knows.

My skin burns, the carpet friction chafing so badly it brings tears to my eyes.

"Come here." He releases my hand. Keeping himself fully planted inside me, he lifts me off the ground.

My back hits the wall, and the cool paint immediately soothes the burn in my skin.

"Wrap your legs around my waist."

As soon as I lock my ankles around him, he starts pounding so forcefully that a painting falls off the wall beside us.

My eyes roll, and my head feels too heavy for my neck.

One.

Then he takes my legs, hooking his arms beneath them to hold me open wide.

In the barely coherent, thoroughly fucked part of my brain, I can feel the sheer strength of his power. It's frightening.

He doesn't ease up.

"All mine." He sucks my skin, blood rushing up to leave deep purple marks. "Do you feel how you're squeezing me? You were made for me. No one who touched you before me matters." He doesn't speak his name, but I don't have to guess who he means. "Say it. Tell me it's mine."

"It's yours!" I cling to him.

That's what he was waiting for. His body jerks, and he stills. It's violent. Waves crashing onto the shore.

He pulls me off the wall and sets me on the bed, right on the edge.

"Again." He smiles.

"Again." I nod, even though I'm not sure if I can actually take it. I'm going to try.

He runs his thumb over my lower lip. "You're so good for me." He starts slowly, rolling his hips forward. "Fucking beautiful."

His teeth scrape against my skin, then he runs his tongue over it. On my neck, my chest, my shoulder. He's marking me. Leaving himself behind.

I'll wear each bruise and scrape like a badge of honor. I earned them.

Arching my back, I open up as much as I can.

He grips the bedspread, grunting as he presses so hard, it feels like I might split open from the force.

"Kiss me, Kiah," he begs.

Sloppy wet lips and tongues collide as he pushes me over the edge.

Two.

I'm falling into endless oceans. I'll never reach the bottom or feel dry land again.

He hikes my leg up, hitting a place that makes my eyes water. A hoarse, brittle scream stretches from deep in my chest.

There is a snap, there is a crack, then a crunch, then the bed dips below us. Broken.

Something like a laugh comes out of me, but I don't have time to think about it. He's not finished.

He pulls out; he comes all over me, spreading it everywhere. Another mark. His territory.

For a moment, I think he might be done. The flames have been extinguished. He drops onto the broken bed beside me, pulling my back to his chest.

I'm barely breathing.

But then I feel it.

He's still hard. With soft hands, he lifts my leg up, sliding in from behind me. My vision blurs, and I panic.

"Just one more. I want to feel the way you milk my cock when you come. One more time. Then I'll lick it all better."

"Oh, my God!" I almost scream.

"I'm not god. I'm the king." He rocks forward.

The rhythm is slow now, but I'm so sensitive; just a little bit is all it takes. My muscles ache as they tense again. They burn like cramps now.

Unable to hold my head up, I drop it back into the crook of his neck. "Just one more." He coaxes, wrapping his arm around me. "Wet my fingers." He holds them in front of my mouth. I know what he's going to do. It's going to wreck me. But I suck them into my mouth anyway.

When he touches my clit, my body jolts.

I moan, and he draws another one out of me. Prying it from the depths of my body.

Three.

This time, he joins me. His body twitching with mine, moaning and groaning incoherently through gasps.

He slips out of me, and I wince. I feel my body moving. He's shifting around me, lifting me, carrying me.

When I manage to open my eyes, we're walking through the living room.

The bed is cool and soft when he sets me down. "Open your mouth." His voice is soft.

"Huh?" My eyes burn as I force them open. His wrist is waiting in front of my mouth, droplets of blood rolling down, dripping onto the sheets. "What?" I'm not conscious enough to understand. I lick it, the metallic taste coating my tongue.

"I'm going to make it all better. You took it so well." He runs his fingers through my hair, moving it out of my face.

My brain is in a fog. I don't really know what he's saying.

Until I feel his tongue sweep between my bruised and sensitive pussy.

"Canaan!" My body folds on itself, my legs clamping closed around his head while I curl into the fetal position.

He isn't deterred. Slow and gentle, he licks me until it starts to feel better.

The rough, feral desperation is gone. He's careful now. And patient.

Four.

My body can't take it, but I can't stop it.

I mumble something as he finally pulls himself away from me. "Come here." He pulls me close, holding me against him. "Sleep."

As I drift away, the soft comfort of his voice lulls me into a deep sleep quickly.

TWENTY-THREE

"YOU CAN'T STAY in there all morning." He slides his pants up his legs. His voice is easy now. You would never know it to look at him that he was in the middle of a bound-fueled frenzy just a few short hours ago.

"Why not?" I pout. "I'm too tired to go out."

"To eat?" He chuckles, raking his hand through his hair. "If you really don't want to come, I'll go get you something and bring it back."

"No. I want to come." I sigh, turning the shower head off. "I'm grumpy."

"I hadn't noticed." He wraps a warm towel around me as I step out. "You look lovely."

His fingers trace over the red marks on my neck and collarbone, his handiwork from last night. I lean into him, letting his chest hold up my weight.

He laughs low in his throat and lifts me, bringing me out to the bedroom. Maybe it's the way last night shifted the energy between us, but I can feel him slowing down, touching me more deliberately. He's not just holding me; his fingers graze my shoulder and move down my back.

There is a language between us now. Our bodies talking.

I want to tell him that I see him clearly. That something changed, and I know him. But I don't. Not yet.

"We need to get out of here. Public spaces." He mutters, pulling away from me.

Smiling to myself, I pull my clothes on and then sit on the edge of the bed to watch him.

Putting a shirt on has never been sexier.

"I want a huge, greasy breakfast." I lick my lips only partially because of the food.

"I'll get you whatever you want. I would like fresh fruit and protein."

I snort. "You should at least taste mine."

"No, thank you." He shakes his head. "You may have made many advancements, but food is not one of them."

"Yeah, yeah," I roll my eyes. "I'm ready." I slip off the end of the bed. "How long are we going to stay here?"

"We'll stay one more night." His voice is clipped. The amusement and lightheartedness from one second ago are gone.

"Where are we going?" I wrap my hand around his bicep, rubbing softly. This might be a bad idea, but I have to know.

"The Vault. We will open a portal in the Ether. I do not want to waste time traveling here in your realm."

I'm flooded with guilt for bringing it up. But he hasn't. I've robbed him of his peace. Even if it's temporary and we have to face everything soon, I want him light and happy as much as possible.

"What is that?" I whisper.

"It is a library of sorts." He places his hand on my neck as we step into the elevator.

"What's there? Why would that help us? Where is it?" Everything spills out in a jumbled-up mess.

"We have to go back to the market. I will send a message to Calais so she can open a portal."

"And what is in the library?" I whisper.

"It holds promises and memories."

I can see by his face that is it. That was the last question on the subject that he will answer. The door is closed on that topic.

And I let it.

We step out into the lobby.

"Are we driving?"

"I've been informed about a restaurant on the lake. We can walk or drive." He watches me, searching for my reaction.

"We can walk."

The hotel has a trail, a cobblestone path cutting through the garden. It winds through the trees, away from the grounds and toward a village.

The small cafe is tucked into a quiet corner, looking out over the water.

I slide into the booth, and he moves in beside me. I like it. I thought he would sit across from me. This is better.

It feels so perfectly normal.

And it wrecks me. Smiling down at the menu, I will the feeling away before he feels it.

This stupid little breakfast is the only thing in the world that I want right now. Just the two of us, sitting together.

I want to watch him cut his food with surgical precision and eat with quiet etiquette.

His hand comes down to rest on my thigh beneath the table. A gentle squeeze. He feels it.

An older woman, who calls us both honey, comes to take our orders.

I wonder what she sees when she looks at us. Just a man and a woman having breakfast, probably.

I watch Canaan. In a place like this, he seems even larger. Like he's too big for this life.

He has no idea how good he is. How utterly devastatingly wonderful.

Kind. And hovering. And frustrating. And perfect.

Sipping my coffee, I force it out of my mind. Focusing instead on this moment, holding onto it for as long as I can.

Taking a piece of my waffle, I drag it through the syrup and hold my fork out to him.

He scrunches up his nose but takes the bite.

"That is very sweet!" He looks shocked. "That's dessert, not breakfast."

"Nope, it's breakfast."

"Agree to disagree." He takes another bite of sausage.

"Want some syrup? Drizzling some on breakfast sausage is so good."

"Absolutely not." He glares at me.

I eat extraordinarily slowly, trying to stay here as long as possible. Eventually, all the food is gone, and my coffee cup is empty. I can't prolong the inevitable anymore.

He pays the bill, and we slowly walk out onto the street, full and tired.

"Can we–"

He grabs me by the shoulders suddenly. "Do you remember how to get back to the hotel?"

"What?"

"Do you remember? I need you to run, Kiah. Now." The urgency in his voice is like a knife in my chest.

"I–ok!" Turning without question, I sprint across the street. I want to turn back, to look at him again, but I don't. I just run.

I reach the trail, and something on the shoreline catches my attention. It's like fate. One second later, and I would have been behind the cover of the trees, and I would have passed right by, missing it.

A woman is standing on a jetty of jagged rocks that cuts out into the lake. Her long hair blows in the breeze.

I can't see her face, but I know.

"Cheyenne?" I scream.

She spins around, nearly slipping. "Kiah?"

"Chey!" Tears pour like a faucet from my eyes. I'm blinded as I stumble down the path and onto the rocky beach.

She's sobbing loudly as she crawls over the rocks toward me.

We slam into each other. Our frantic arms squeezing painfully tight.

"Chey! What are you doing here?"

"I'm looking for you!" She cups her hands on my cheeks. "Are you okay? Let me look at you!"

"Am I okay?" I search her for injuries. "Are you okay? I'm here to find you!"

"Hurry, we have to–"

"Wait." I drag my feet as she tries to pull me. "What are you doing here? Where is–"

"Kiah, he can keep you safe. I promise! Come on. Our hotel is–"

"Cheyenne, stop!" I shout, yanking my wrist out of her grasp. "I am safe. You aren't safe."

"Oh, God!" She sobs. "Do you trust me, Kiah? I promise we will keep you safe. You don't know the truth about him! He's been lying to you."

My heart aches in my chest, and all the food I just ate threatens to come back up. She's brainwashed.

"Listen to me." I take a breath. "I know you think that Elion is a good man. But he's not. He's lying to you, Chey. He's the liar. Canaan is the rightful king. No one stole the crown from Elion; he lost it because he–"

"He told me you would think this." She looks exactly how I feel. Like she's staring into the eyes of her best friend, who has lost touch with reality. I don't know how to pull her back in. What do I do?

"Do you trust me?" I whisper.

"Of course, but you've been tricked!"

"The only person who tricked me was Elion." Hot tears burn in my eyes. "I slept with him."

Her face scrunches up. "What? He–"

"He tricked both of us. I slept with him. Then he left me for dead, and Canaan saved me."

We're going around in circles. Each saying the same thing over and over again.

"No." She shakes her head. "Is that what he told you to say?"

"No." I'm losing her. I can see it. He has his hooks so far in that she won't believe me. "He killed someone. A good man. A man that–"

"Kiah! They aren't good! They kept you locked up there! They–"

"They protected me. They helped me. Canaan has saved my life more times than I can count. Elion tried to kill me." I pinch my eyes closed. "He brought me up and then dropped me." My voice breaks. "If it weren't for Canaan, I would have died."

"Come with me." She grabs me so tightly that her nails break the skin on my wrist. I hardly feel it.

"Chey, wait."

"No. We don't have time to wait."

"Where is Elion?"

"He's meeting with someone."

"Not the seer?"

"Who?" She looks genuinely confused.

"Fuck. I don't know. Please come with me. Just come meet Canaan. You'll see. I promise. He is so good. He'll help you. He's not the bad–"

"Kiah." She stops me with the look on her face. It's heartbreak and pain. "I'm not letting you go back to him. I'll knock you out if I have to."

For the first time, I'm afraid of her.

The sheer determination on her face makes my stomach roll.

"If you bring me back to him, he'll kill me. He'll have to."

"No, he won't. You just have to trust me." She starts dragging me across the rocky beach again.

"Chey," I scream. "Stop!"

"No."

"Canaan and I are bound by blood. Wherever I go, he'll find me. If you bring me to Elion, he'll kill me to keep Canaan from finding him. Let go." I yank my arm back, stumbling out of her grip. The sting of her nail scratching my skin only barely registers.

"He won't hurt you! He loves me! We're going to rule Noctyra together. Whatever Canaan has told you about him isn't true!" She reaches for me, but I crawl back, twisting onto my knees to stumble away.

I'm trapped. If I stay here, Elion might come before Canaan. I can't drag her away, and I won't let her take me.

"Meet me here tonight."

"What?" She stops trying to grab me.

"Come here tonight, alone. I'll come too. We just need time to talk."

She nods slowly. "Ok. I can do that."

"Right after sunset."

"After sunset."

Turning, I run. I never thought I would leave without her. I'm consumed with guilt. I got to her too late. She believes him.

I run up the path into the hotel lobby. Canaan is stepping out of the elevator with wild panic in his eyes.

I rush into his arms, hard, crashing into his chest.

"What happened?"

"They're here."

TWENTY-FOUR

"KIAH, take a breath. I can't understand you."

He pulled me into the elevator so that everyone in the lobby couldn't watch me have a breakdown.

But now we're standing here in this little metal box where his presence is too big, and my heart rate is too fast, and I can't breathe.

"I saw her."

"I felt him."

We both confess.

"You did?"

"That's why I had you run. I felt him close." He holds me so tightly it hurts. But it's what I need right now.

"Do you think he was waiting for us?"

"Unlikely. It doesn't matter that he's drinking human blood. He can drink it every day. I'm stronger than him."

Even though he doesn't say this with even a hint of bragging in his voice, he's just being factual; my insides clench.

"He–" His eyes go wide, and he blinks. "Kiah!"

"What?" I blush. "Sorry. That was just..."

His face hardens, and he pulls me into him, closing the one-inch gap between us.

"Chey is going to meet me on the beach tonight after sunset," I whisper.

He sighs, but doesn't say anything. I expected him to immediately shut it down.

When we reach the penthouse, he has us inside the room so quickly that I'm dizzy.

"It's a trap." He looks at me softly.

"I know."

"So, we have to play it right."

"Wait." I freeze. "You're going to let me go?"

"With me. Obviously."

My heart pounds against my ribs. "I just assumed you would say no."

"Did you want me to say no?"

"No. Maybe?" My thoughts are tangled up. I don't know what I feel or want. "I want to get her away from him, but..."

"We need to talk through this. I really only see two options. She doesn't show up at all. Or she shows up with him. I don't want to give him credit for anything, really, but he is patient. He played a long game, deceiving us over the years. Fighting beside us. Voting against his own interests to appear to be an ally." He sits and pulls me into the chair with him. "I don't see him being foolish enough to walk into this situation. He knows what the bond did to me. He should have made sure I was dead in the Colonnade."

The rage in his voice and the softness of his hands don't match. He's holding me so gently. But his voice shakes.

"We need to be careful today. We'll stay inside and have everything in the car when we go to meet her. I want to be able to leave right away. We can drive, put distance between us and this place. Then, when it's safe, we will send the message to Calais." He starts rushing around the room, gathering my things that are thrown all over. His clothes are neatly folded on the bench at the end of the bed.

"Wait," I stumble after him. "Let me do that."

"No, I–"

We walk into each other, our bodies slamming together.

He huffs and grabs me, holding me into his chest. "Panic is unnecessary. Take a breath." His chest expands slowly. "I'm not going to let anything happen to you. The scenario doesn't matter. If she doesn't come, then she doesn't come. If she comes, and Elion is foolish enough to come with her, I will handle it. We aren't walking into the dark; we know it's a trap."

"Right. We're prepared."

"Kiah," he tilts my chin back. "I need you to understand that this might not end well. I know that you want this to end with Cheyenne here, with us. But it might not. If I have to choose between who I can reach, it's going to be you without question."

I can't put into words why, but that knocks the wind out of me. Hearing him say it, so sure, makes me feel almost frantic.

"Canaan?"

"Yes?" He hesitates.

I can only guess that he thinks I'm going to argue with him.

"You're the best man I've ever met. I had to die to be bonded to you, but I wouldn't change it. I think I'm the luckiest woman alive."

I mean every word of it.

The familiar crease forms between his eyebrows. "I–"

"You expected me to push back." I smile.

"I did."

"Not this time." I wrap my arms around him tightly. "But don't get used to it."

"I wouldn't dream of it."

"I feel strangely calm. Are you doing that somehow?" I lean back to look at him.

"No," his voice cracks with a laugh. "Not in an intentional way."

"Tell me what to do, and I'll do it."

"I'll stay back, out of her line of sight. If Elion is there, he will know that I'm there. I can't conceal it. But neither can he. I'll know if he is there. We will just have to see how it plays out. If we can separate her from him, we will."

"Thank you." I lean into him.

"We have several hours until dusk. I wanted to find Zephra, but we should steer clear of the market right now. You should try to sleep." His fingertips graze the back of my neck.

"I'm too wound up to sleep." I rock on my toes. "I can think of a few things we can do to pass the time."

Without hesitation, he grabs me and throws my body over his shoulder. We're naked and in bed in seconds flat.

The frantic, feverish need of yesterday is gone. This is something else.

I take from him. And he takes from me.

There is no urgency now. His touch is reverent. He is memorizing the parts of me that no one else gets to see. The parts that he feels like his own through the bond.

We give each other comfort, connection, and safety.

His eyes never leave mine.

He uses every minute of the hours we have to wrap around each other.

When the golden rays of the setting sun shine in through the windows, we take our time, showering and packing the final items.

He doesn't rush me. We move around each other, orbiting in perfect synchronization as if we've done this for years. It feels like we have.

"Canaan?" I stop.

He stops too, looking at me like he already knows what I'm going to say. He probably does.

But I don't say it. I swallow it down. I don't want to know.

What is going to happen to us when this ends?

TWENTY-FIVE

MY HANDS TREMBLE as we walk down the path. I know the plan backwards and forwards. Every step plays on a loop in my mind.

I know exactly where he'll be.

When we reach the break in the trees, he stops.

"If you need me, I'll be there."

"I know."

I don't mean to hug him like it's the last time. But my body clings to his. I take a deep breath against his chest. He's so solid and steady. He doesn't shake or tremble. He's Canaan. Like always.

He pulls back and looks at me, all of his thoughts etched into his face. The stoic mask slips, and I see it all. Worry. Doubt. Love. "I don't feel him. Or anyone else for that matter. It's unnaturally quiet."

This does nothing to keep me calm, but I know he's here. That's all I need. If they come or not, he's got me.

I linger a moment longer, wrapping my arms around his waist again to listen to the beat of his heart.

He doesn't rush me away. His arms stay tight around my shoulders until I step back. "I'm ready."

He nods, crouching down in position. "See you on the other side."

The path slops slightly downward, the gravel crunching beneath my feet. The trees fade into the rocky shore of the lake. The water to my right, just a black expanse of ink under the moon.

And then I see her.

My breath hitches, and I take a step forward. I can't stop myself. She's alone.

Or at least, it looks like she's alone.

I force down the brief flicker of guilt. I'm betraying her. It wasn't even hard; I didn't even try or argue. Of course, he was coming with me.

She'll get over it once she's safe. And even if she doesn't, if she hates me for the rest of our lives, I can live with that as long as she is out of his grasp.

Her silhouette moves in the darkness.

My eyes fill with tears. An involuntary release of so much tension and fear, I can't hold it back.

By the time she reaches me, I'm sobbing.

She is, too.

"Chey!"

"Kiah!"

We melt into each other's arms. I'm not sure who is holding who. We're a tangled mess of arms and tears.

"I miss you so much!" Her grip on me is almost painful.

"I miss you too!" I choke. "Are you alright?" I pull back from her, frantically searching her for injuries.

"I'm fine! I'm fine! Are you alright?"

"Yes!" I grab her shoulders, holding onto her dress like she's going to slip through my fingers. "Please, Chey, come with me! We have to get out of here right now. It's not safe."

"You don't understand. I know you think that Elion is the bad guy. He tried so hard to save you. But Canaan confused you. Come with me. He'll explain everything."

I dig my feet into the ground. "No."

"Please—"

"No, listen to me. I'm not brainwashed. Canaan hasn't twisted my mind around. Elion tried to kill me, Chey. There isn't any other way to take that. He grabbed me, flew up into the sky, and fucking dropped me. On purpose. He was taunting me. He was never trying to save me." I would get down on my knees and beg if I thought she would believe me.

She won't, though.

I can see it in her face.

We both seem to come to the realization at the same time. We're at a crossroads, neither of us willing to admit defeat.

Something takes over my body. I don't even realize I'm doing it at first. Without caring if I'm hurting her, I yank her, forcing her body forward. I'll drag her back to Canaan if I have to.

"Stop!" She starts shrieking. "Kiah, stop!"

"No." I shake my head violently, tugging her forward. "You'll understand eventually. I'm getting you the fuck away from him."

"I love him!"

"No, you don't! He's the fucking bad guy, Cheyenne! He's using you for your blood. He lost the throne; it wasn't taken from him. If you help him, you're helping him grow a Shadowrithe army that is going to throw the fucking gates open wide, and no one will be safe! Your mom. Your dad. My mom! Everyone is in danger!"

"No! He—"

"Stop! Jesus Christ! How many people did he pass you around to? How—"

My voice is cut off by Canaan. He flies past in a blur.

The words fade in my throat as I watch him. Two Shadowrithes roll out of the lake like waves.

"You didn't come alone." She whispers as they begin to fight.

"Neither did you."

Something fractures in my heart. We've never lied to each other before. She's an adult. I know that. Her actions are her own. But this makes me hate Elion even more. I blame him.

"We need to get away from here. Please." My voice breaks.

She looks at me, and for a second, I don't recognize her. The look on her face is so entirely not the girl who has grown into my sister.

I see something in her that wasn't there before.

It burns like betrayal before I even realize what is happening.

Her hand comes up. I think she's going to just grab me. But she doesn't.

A sharp pinch. Then a cold jolt in my shoulder, rippling through my arm.

"What the fuck?" I stumble back, immediately feeling dizzy. My legs are rubbery. "What did you—"

Tears drip down her cheeks as she drops the syringe to the ground, catching me before I can fall.

"Wait, no!" My words slur. "Canaan!"

It happens almost slowly. My eyes close, and I'm sinking.

Pressure against my chest makes my ribs feel like they might crack. I can't see or hear. There isn't anything around me. I'm below the surface—so far down there is no light. It feels like he's dragged me into my own personal hell. A place so lonely I feel the light draining from my body.

This is by design. The kind of cold cruelty isn't natural. It comes from hate.

"Hello, darling."

His voice echoes, distant and rippling like water. It's so smooth and mocking.

"No."

"Yes, love." He coos.

A hazy, dreamlike version of him floats before me. A watery hand reaching for me. The tips of his fingers brush up my arm before he swirls around me, disappearing.

"Where am I?"

"Inquisitive as ever." He laughs.

"This isn't real. It's a dreamweave, and Canaan will come get me. You don't have the power to hold me here anymore."

His eyes flicker, annoyed. "You don't know the extent of my power. Canaan is dead. Your body is being brought to me as we speak."

"No." I shake my head. "Canaan isn't dead," I say it with conviction that I don't feel. If he were dead, I would know it. I would feel it.

"You're so stubborn." He drifts into my sight again. "He's gone, Kiah." The wide smile on his face makes my stomach turn. "If you're here with me, it's because she was able to drug you. He's gone."

"But she wouldn't—"

"Wouldn't what? Drug you?" He raises an eyebrow. "You must remember what it's like to be with me. She's wrapped around my finger. She would do anything I asked of her. Including drug her best friend."

I jerk back, but I don't move.

"Now that you've spread those legs for both of us, I would love to know. Who's better, Kiah? I'll never forget the way you clenched around me, coming all over my cock. Did he make you shake that way?" He grins.

"Stop it." I grit my teeth, and my stomach rolls. "I hate you, Elion."

I mean it with every fiber of my being. I fucking hate him.

"Oh, don't cry, love. It—" He stops. His eyes flicker, and he frowns.

Then, just like that, I'm alone.

The silence is deafening. The dark is darker, and it's colder.

"Canaan?" I whisper. "Please, come get me."

Nothing. No warmth. No light.

No response.

I can't feel anything.

"Canaan?" My voice is louder now, more desperate.

He's not dead.

He's not.

But I can't feel him.

Something sharp throbs in my chest. A pain that feels like it's going to kill me. I can't possibly survive it.

If he's gone, death is coming for me too. Elion is going to have to kill me. I'll make him kill me.

But first, I'll make him hurt like this. He will feel this.

Closing my eyes, I cry alone in the dark.

TWENTY-SIX

MY BODY JOLTS. There isn't anything slow or soft about it, no haziness. I'm pulled from sleep like being dropped into ice water.

All of my senses are electrocuted at once.

Gasping, I jerk upright, my arms instinctively reaching out as I scream his name. My vision is blurry, and my chest aches. I'm already crying.

"Kiah!" His hands are on me, pulling me. Then, I'm in his lap.

"Canaan?" I grab his face, and a violent sob rips from my chest.

"Kiah, what happened?" He holds me tight, constricting my ribs.

"I couldn't feel you! I was calling and calling, and you didn't come!" My body trembles against his, my teeth chattering.

"I couldn't get to you, Kiah! I tried, but I couldn't reach you! I didn't leave you. I promise, I was here."

"He told me you were dead!" My voice cracks, and another loud wail heaves from somewhere behind my heart. "I thought–"

"I'm not dead." His fingers thread through my hair. "I'm not dead. I'm right here."

I open my mouth, probably to cry more, when movement in my peripheral vision catches my attention.

We're in the car, on a dark, lonely road somewhere. He has me pulled over the central console into his lap.

And behind us, Cheyenne is bound and gagged in the backseat.

"What the fuck?" I gasp, looking between them.

"I realize this is not great for fostering a trusting relationship between us, but she wouldn't stop screaming." He purses his lips.

"Chey, I'm going to remove the tie from around your mouth. Ok?" I reach back, and she leans forward. Her red-rimmed eyes holding mine.

As soon as her mouth is free, she gasps, sucking in a deep breath so that she can start in on Canaan.

"Let me go, you fucking asshole! I can't–"

I press my hand to her mouth. "Chey, stop. He's trying to save you."

She shakes her head, forcing my hand away. "How can you say that? He tied me up!"

"You drugged me." I don't even try to hide the bite in my voice. I've never been this angry in my life. Ever. There isn't a single instance I can think of where I felt even half the rage that's coursing through me now.

Her eyes go wide, and she stops struggling.

"You can, at the very least, listen to what we have to say. I think you owe me that much." I square my shoulders.

She hangs her head slightly and nods.

"Ok, good." I pull my hand away. "What did you give me? Why couldn't he get to me?"

"It was just a sedative."

"Where did you get it?"

Her spine stiffens. She doesn't have to answer. I already know. But I want her to say the words out loud.

"Where did you get it, Cheyenne?"

"He gave it to me."

Rage boils in my blood, but Canaan touches me, placing his hand on my thigh, and it's like an extinguisher. The fire subsides.

"I know you're mad." She whispers. "But I was trying to get you away from him."

"He would have immediately killed me."

"No! He wouldn't have! He's trying to save you! You don't–"

"You don't understand! I am linked to Canaan. As long as I'm alive, he will be able to find me."

"No–"

My frustration is growing by the second. It's like she has wool over her eyes. I can't make her see the truth.

"They aren't the same. Rimfae don't have the same bond to humans. But we have shared blood. We can't be separated. If you try to bring me to him, you're signing a death warrant! It's the only way he can keep himself hidden from Canaan is to kill me!" I'm shouting by the end.

"And it would weaken me. He wants nothing more than to see me weak and frail. If something were to happen to Kiah, it would be the end of me, too."

"You would die?"

"Yes, eventually." His voice is soft.

"Oh, shit." It feels like I was just punched in the stomach.

"What do you mean you've shared blood?" Chey's disgusted voice cuts into the moment we're sharing.

"Oh, well, I've had his, and he's had mine."

"What the fuck? Why would you have his?" She goes pale.

"Because Elion tried to fucking kill me and his blood saved my life!" I snap.

"Let's all take a breath." Cool-headed Canaan, diplomatic and regal, looks at us both. "Everyone is emotional."

Chey scoffs. "Let me go."

"We can't do that." He's so calm.

"So you're going to hold me against my will? Kiah! He–"

"He what?" I scream. "He what, Chey? He didn't drug you! Are you really so far gone that you can't see how fucking insane this is? You drugged me!" I feel out of body, I can see myself and hear my voice, but I can't control it. I don't know where this rage is coming from, but I don't want to unleash it on her. "You are with the wrong guy. He doesn't fucking love you! He's using you! Canaan just saved your life and–"

Before I can finish the fury-filled tirade, I'm pulled out of the car and placed gently in the grass on the side of the road.

"Hey! You—"

He doesn't have to say anything. With softness that I probably don't deserve, he pulls me into the warmth of his arms.

He's right.

"Fine." I pout. "She's being unreasonable."

"I'm sure she is thinking the exact same thing." He doesn't let himself smile, but his lips twitch.

"Did you see her face when I said I had your blood?" I roll my lips into my mouth.

"She looked nauseous." He chuckles.

Leaning into him, I wrap my arms around his waist. "You're alive."

"I am."

"What happened?"

"There were three Shadowrithes that came up from the depths of the water. I can only assume that he thought I was dead when you went under." He runs his fingers through my hair. "I tried to reach you."

"I believe you." A shiver runs up my spine as the memory creeps into my brain. It was so dark and cold without him. "You can't die, Canaan. Promise me you won't."

He chuckles, but his grip tightens. "I'll do my best."

"No." I pull back, craning my neck to see him in the light of the headlights. "Promise me. Say the words." I feel a desperation to hear him say it out loud. In the logical part of my brain, I know it doesn't work like that, death won't stop for a promise–but I need him to say it. If he says it, he'll be bound by it.

"I will do my best."

My heart sinks, pain radiating through it. He won't promise...

We just stand together, holding each other in the spotlight surrounded by darkness.

"We have to go." He whispers.

"I know." But I don't move.

Neither does he.

"What are we going to do? Is she coming with us?"

"I'll bring her to Calais. We can leave her there if she is too unmanageable."

"Unmanageable?" I scoff.

"Yes. We only stayed here because I needed to send Calais a message. We don't have time to drag her behind us."

I know he's right. But I feel panicked. "I'll talk to her. I'll make her see reason."

He nods, but I know he doesn't believe anything will come from my efforts. A curse of being bound to someone, I guess.

At least he doesn't speak his doubts out loud.

"Ok," I sigh, preparing myself for a fight. "Let's go."

TWENTY-SEVEN

HIS HAND COMES across the center console to rest on my bouncing knee.

I feel ripped in two.

I want to be understanding. I know how easy it is to be manipulated by Elion.

But she's starting to piss me off.

Every chance she gets, she digs at Canaan.

Canaan! The most wonderful, selfless, caring man in the history of men.

At this point, I have the radio turned almost irritatingly loud to drown out her sighs and little comments.

If I thought the drive up to Lac La Ronge was long, this one feels endless. The two-lane road that skirts the lake is oppressive. Pine trees press too close to the road on one side, and vast open water sits on the other.

It's beautiful. But all I can think about is darkness. The shimmering blue water feels like danger and uncertainty.

There has never been tension like this between us, and I hate it. I've chewed the inside of my lips raw.

But she won't hear me. Or maybe she can't.

She doesn't want to be here with us. She keeps referring to herself as our hostage. If she's trying to hurt me, she's succeeding. Each little jab is one more tiny cut.

Canaan is steady as always, his hand on the wheel.

"Hey!" She yells over the music.

Bracing myself, I turn the volume down and turn around.

"Are we just going to drive around all night? What is the plan here?" She lets out a dramatic sigh.

"We're going to the marina." Canaan answers, his voice calm but clipped. "We need a boat."

"Why?" Her tone is dripping with disdain.

I look up at the beige fabric stretched across my car roof. "We need to get a message beyond the ether."

"Why?"

I pause. I wonder how much Elion has told her. Does she know that they can't open a portal from this side?

I chose not to tell her that. Maybe she knows, maybe she doesn't.

"His sister is on the other side. We're just sending her a message." I shrug.

"Why are we going by boat? That will take forever!"

"Well, do you want Canaan to carry you?" I snap.

Her eyes go wide. "No."

"Exactly." I fold my arms across my chest.

She purses her lips and folds her arms over her chest, too. A standoff.

It is right now, in this exact moment, that I realize I'm going to have to shove her through the portal. Alright. Game on. If she wants to be a difficult brat, I'll do it.

"Why can't we just stay in the car?" She raises her eyebrows.

"Right. Because you're going to try to run the second he leaves, and I don't have the energy to deal with that right now." I roll my eyes.

"You act like I'm the crazy one here, Kiah. The natural reaction to being held against your will is to try to run!"

"Chey–" I try, but it's too late. She cuts me off angrily.

"You're in so deep you can't see it. But I see right through you." She glares at Canaan. "I know who you are and what you did."

I see the faint tension pulling at the corners of his mouth, but he doesn't say anything.

He doesn't bite. Doesn't defend himself. He just keeps his eyes on the road ahead.

She smirks like she's won and sits back against her seat.

We pass a shuttered bait shop with a hand-painted sign hanging from the roof. The marina sits behind it. A long, low dock juts out into the water. A few boats, some that look close to sinking, float gently in the water.

Canaan pulls into the gravel lot and turns off the engine. He leans in quietly. "Tell her about the market. We need her to under-stand how serious it is that she stays with us."

"I will."

As soon as he closes the door, I turn around, sitting on my knees in the passenger seat to look at her, head on.

"Chey, did Elion bring you to the market?"

"No." She shakes her head.

"Okay, listen. That place..." A shiver runs up my spine just thinking about it. I never want to go there again. "It's scary there. The fae that live there, they've chosen to stay in our realm because–"

"Because they wanted to live free of Canaan's rule!" She cuts in.

"I mean, technically, you're not wrong."

She looks shocked. She thought I would try to deny it.

"They live there because they want to be lawless and do what-ever they want to humans. So prepare yourself. Those fae are here because they don't give a shit about human life except for what it can provide them. Be careful. If one of them snatches you, you'll be their blood servant, or worse."

She tries to act unaffected, but I see fear flicker in her eyes.

"He's the king, so they aren't going to try anything. But don't put him in a position where he has to act. He's outnumbered." I feel protective of him.

"If it's so bad, why would he bring us to a place like that?"

"Oh my God, Cheyenne!" I yell, finally losing it. "It's not safe for us to stay here! He doesn't leave me alone because–" Because he can't let anything happen to me. "Elion isn't who you think he is."

"Or, Canaan isn't who you think he is."

Before I can answer her, Canaan comes back. "Let's go."

Chey plants herself where she is. "I'm not stepping on any boat until you tell me what's really going on."

Canaan looked at her for a long moment, then says evenly, "We can't open a portal from here. I have to send a message to my sister so she can open one for us. The market's the only place I can do that."

"We're going back to Noctyra?"

"Yep." I open the door and take a deep breath of the fresh air.

"I swear," I turn to him. "She used to be the sweetest person alive."

I follow him down to the dock, my arm linked in hers.

The boat is smaller than I was expecting. The faded blue hull doesn't look seaworthy.

Canaan helps us in, and we sit together on one short bench seat.

The moment we push away from the dock, and the shore falls away, a heaviness settles in my chest. I really don't want to go back here.

I know he can feel it because he reaches over and places his hand on my shoulder.

"We'll find Zephra, send the message, and then leave. In and out."

"In and out." I swallow the fear lingering in my throat.

It was bad enough last time, but now I have to worry about Chey doing something reckless.

The boat weaves through the water, past the scattered islands.

The cold wind stings my face, but that is quickly forgotten when the lights become visible up ahead.

Canaan watches the horizon, searching.

I'm filled with a confusing mixture of relief and fear. I just want to get there and finish this. I wish there were another way.

He slows the boat, bringing it to a little dock, half sunken beneath the water.

"Ready?" He looks at me, clear, strong, steady.

"Yeah." I straighten my shoulders.

His eyes flick toward Cheyenne, but he doesn't say anything.

"It's going to be fine. Everything will be all right. Just keep your head down and don't look at them." I whisper to her as we walk the well-worn trail between the trees.

As soon as we step into the street, Chey gasps and her body jerks.

A fae woman is walking with a naked man, a dog collar secured around his neck. She holds the end of his leash in her delicate hand.

Canaan stiffens, stepping slightly in front of me. "I'm looking for Zephra."

I watch a slow, cruel smile tug at her lips. "Well, you found her." She sways her hips as she walks toward us. "Your Majesty, I'm honored."

"I need to send a message beyond the ether."

"Right this way. Step into my shop." She makes a kissing sound, tugging on the leash. "Come on, love." He follows her without hesitation.

Her shop is nightmare fuel.

Everything here was alive at one point, and now it's not. She has shelves everywhere, with jars set in every available space. Things hang from strings and hooks, like dried flowers, but they aren't flowers.

I pinch my eyes closed. Chey grabs my hand and squeezes. For the first time, she feels like my best friend.

"I need to send a message to Calais."

"Right, well, I take payment upfront." The excitement in her voice makes my knees wobble.

"And what is it that you want?" His voice sounds hard.

"Just a few hairs from the heads of your little humans there."

I jerk my head up to look at her.

"Absolutely not."

"That's what I want."

"Pick something else." He growls. "You can't take from them."

"But–"

"I'll give my hair. Or blood. Or a ring. Or a piece of my skin. Nothing from them." His voice is low and serious.

"I'll take a piece of skin." She smiles.

What? I look between them.

She pulls out a blade and hands it to him. "The length of the handle."

I gasp and cup my hand over my mouth. That's like four inches! "Wait! Canaan!"

"It's alright." He turns, shielding me from what he's going.

He doesn't make a sound. If it hurts, he doesn't let it show.

I feel sick as he steps forward and sets the knife on the counter. I don't see the skin; he doesn't let me.

"Write your message here." She hands him a piece of paper.

He quickly writes his message.

"It was a pleasure doing business with you." She takes the paper and rolls it up.

"Do it now. I want to see it sent."

She chuckles and throws the paper into a flickering white flame. It doesn't burn to ash; it disappears. "There you go."

He grabs me, wrapping his arm around my shoulders. "Let's go."

"You should stick around. We're having an auction tonight! Either of those lovely little women would fetch a pretty penny." She licks her teeth.

"No." He pushes me forward. When we're outside, more people have gathered. "Go, Kiah. Keep your head down, walk."

His arm is bleeding. Blood drips after him onto the ground. He doesn't seem to notice. But it's all I can focus on.

"Hurry." He rushes us onto the path. By the time we reach the trees, we're running. This is different from last time. He's more worried.

We practically jump into the boat. It rocks violently, and no one even cares.

He cranks the engine and tears through the water.

"Canaan, fix your arm." I hold my wrist up.

Cheyenne gasps.

"Don't!" I shout. "You gave blood. You thought he was worth it. Canaan is worth it to me. If you don't like it, fine! But keep your mouth shut!" I turn back to him, climbing across the boat to kneel between his knees. "Please." I'll beg if I have to.

He nods and takes my hand in his. Holding eye contact, he kisses my wrist, then bites into it.

I'm dizzy. Not from blood loss, but from this kind of closeness I never thought was possible.

"Are you okay?" I study his skin. The bleeding has stopped. "Can I bandage it?"

He smiles. "I'll be fine. Calais is opening a portal. We have to get there."

"Where is she opening it?"

"On the shore. We have to get as far away from this place as possible."

TWENTY-EIGHT

THINGS ARE WEIRD.

Ever since I gave him my blood, she's been looking at me with a look that makes me feel so small I want to disappear.

I want to shake her and point out her hypocrisy, but my feelings are so hurt, I can't say anything.

Canaan is tense; every line of his body is rigid, waiting for Calais to open the portal. It's radiating off of him; it ripples in the air around him.

His tension is making me feel nervous. It's coursing through him and spilling over into me. Outwardly, he is calm and cool as stone, but I can feel him. The bond between us won't allow us to hide from each other. It's a blessing and a curse. I know exactly where his head is, but I can't really comfort him.

Just as I start to let the panic and negativity take over—just when I'm sure Calais didn't get the message—a ripple.

Like a mirage in the desert sand, the air wavers.

I suck in a breath, and he lets out a relieved sigh and holds his hand out to me. "Let's go."

"Can he follow us in?" I whisper against his ear.

His jaw flexes before he answers. "It's a risk we have to take. It will be better for us if he does. There will be paladins standing guard until it closes. We don't want any more human casualties."

This isn't just about us. Every decision echoes, affecting every life it touches. I nod, turning to look at Chey. She's already staring at me, with obvious disdain on her face.

"Ready?" I give her a tight-lipped smile, hoping to ease the awful strain between us.

The coldness in her gaze makes something inside of me snap. "Come on. Now." I shout. "We don't have fucking time for this shit. Have a tantrum on the other side. Just go."

Her eyes go wide, but she doesn't say anything. To my surprise, she steps into the portal without a fight. Progress.

Canaan doesn't say anything either, but I notice the way his eyebrows are up in his hairline.

He holds my hand as we step through together.

My lungs heave as I take a breath of the thick, warm air.

"Canaan!" Calais throws her arms around him so fast and hard that he almost stumbles back.

He never lets go of my hand as we walk to the boats, not as we sail the Ebonstream, not when we stop at the docks on the black cathedral.

Chey looks afraid. Out of place. This is the first time she is seeing any of this. I watched her mouth drop open as Noctyra came into view on the horizon.

Canaan fills Calais in on everything.

Well, almost everything. He doesn't tell her about us.

But she knows.

She openly gawks at our interlocked hands. Her looks don't hold the same malice as Cheyenne's.

"Paladins are guarding every gate. I have doubled patrols. There was a small group hiding in the waters in the Hollow Valley. We also found another portal—in the fringes. It was so well hidden I wouldn't have found it if not for the writhes guarding it." There is a glint in her eyes. I recognize it. She slaughtered him.

"I trust you handled it." Canaan doesn't press, but a worried crease forms between his brows.

"More than." She nods, clearly proud of her work.

We walk into the cathedral, and it's as if Calais is noticing Cheyenne for the first time. "The friend?" She points.

"Yes." I feel my shoulders tense. The friend. Is she? I thought we were sisters, but now...

"Does she have information?" She looks through Chey to Canaan.

"If I did, I wouldn't give it to you." Chey growls.

Calais' lips pull into a lopsided smile, her eyes flickering with something dangerous. "I see. So you think you found Prince Charming?"

"I–"

"You are a foolish human." The calm in her voice is almost as scary as the look on her face. "You don't know anything about anything, yet you stand before the king and dare to open your mouth?"

"The king by–"

"Okay!" I yell out, stepping in between them. "This has been lovely, but it looks like rain! We should go inside."

There's not a cloud in the sky, but I need to stop this now. Cheyenne is suddenly much more combative than she's ever been in her life, and Calais is the wrong one to show this newfound attitude to. She doesn't realize the bear she's poking right now.

"Yes, let's." Canaan places his hand on my back, ushering me forward.

I let out a shaky breath and step into the black glass cavern. It's different now. I see more beauty in it than terror. I see Canaan when I look at the details. Like the cathedral is carved from the same stone he is.

I feel like I'm tiptoeing through a minefield.

His hand flexes against me. He feels it too.

"At least we're in it together?" I shake my head.

"It could be worse." The look on his face makes my knees weak.

As we walk through the hallway, a low hum hits me. I recognize it. It seeps into my bones, gathering strength with each step. The corridor opens into the nave.

The cavernous chamber is drowned in shadow. The rows of black pews are filled with solom fae with bowed heads. Their sharp, beautiful faces hold sorrow.

The ornate altar has thousands of candles on it, wax dripping down onto the floor below. The lights flicker like a heartbeat.

The humming is so loud that it makes me dizzy. It's not just a sound anymore, it's pressure. My vision blurs. Chey sways slightly beside me. Her lips part as her eyes dart around the room.

I shudder, and Canaan's arm comes around me, quiet and steady. He presses a kiss into my hair, his lips lingering there, just for a moment. No one is looking, but he doesn't try to hide it– hide me.

I look at them, the mixture of dark and light wings. I wonder how many of them could be standing here right now, looking him in the eyes as they plan to betray him.

But he isn't looking at them with malice.

His eyes are overflowing with love.

"The blood of our ancestors has been stolen. But we carry it within." His voice booms, bouncing off the black glass. "Today, I offer you myself."

My breath catches. Questions overload my brain. If they take his blood, are they taking mine too? Do they know?

The dagger of light slices through his arm with ease. He lets his blood drain into the basin for too long. He's giving too much.

It pours out of him, flowing down his arm into the pool forming below.

"I offer myself." Calais steps forward with her head bowed in reverence.

Canaan almost looks like he's going to protest, but he doesn't. He just takes her arm and cuts it, letting her blood join his.

Now that I know what this means, my eyes fill with tears as I watch them. Their love for each other, the reverence they have for him, it's everywhere. I can smell it in the air.

I don't realize that I'm stepping forward until his eyes jerk to meet mine.

"Can I offer myself?"

The air crackles when I say it. Every eye is on me. I feel them burning into my skin.

"Kiah..." Canaan stares at me, his serious face making my chest ache.

"I know what I'm giving."

He holds his hand out to me, accepting my offer. There are audible gasps around the room as he brings the dagger to my arm.

The tip is cold as he presses it to my skin.

When the cut opens, I don't feel any pain. It's like a surge of something–electric. My blood spills into the basin, mixing with theirs.

It isn't barbaric.

Or frightening.

It is a return.

I feel everyone here, their hearts beating, their quiet breaths.

Warmth spreads through my chest. My blood isn't being taken, it's joining.

Canaan takes my arm, licking the blood trail before kissing the cut.

Calais pours the blood into a silver goblet and hands it to Canaan.

"Drink. Join together. Together we are strong."

The cup is passed through the rows, each person taking a sip. This isn't joyous. They aren't dancing or singing this time.

But it's still magical. With each pass of the cup, I feel closer to them. I'm a part of them now. They will be stronger because of my contribution.

I'll deal with the fallout later. I know Chey will have something to say about this. But for now, I simply can't find it in me to care. One day, she'll understand.

The humming resumes, low and rumbling, shaking the ground beneath my feet.

Their eyes shine. Strength and resolve in their posture and flexed wings.

"Kiah," he whispers, taking my hand in his. "Come with me."

I know where we're going by the look on his face.

My stomach clenches as I hurry beside him. We're not even completely out of the nave when he grabs me. His mouth meets mine with feverish desperation.

"What am I going to do with you?" He growls, lifting me into his arms.

"Are you angry?" I press my palms into his chest, pushing just enough to be able to see his face.

"No." He leans in again. "But I didn't want you to have to do that."

"I didn't have to. I offered it."

"I know, but–" He fumbles with a door, pushing it open so that we can stumble into his dark bedroom.

I pull my shirt over my head and throw it on the ground.

Whatever he was going to say, he groans instead.

"Just kiss me, Canaan."

TWENTY-NINE

OUR MOUTHS MEET VIOLENTLY. I need him. It's like two storms colliding, contents under pressure. The taste of his lips is delicious. The world narrows to this, just the edge of his teeth grazing my lips and the sound of his groans breaking into my mouth.

"Take blood from me." My voice shakes.

He lifts me up, holding my legs tightly around his waist. His body heat and power beneath my fingertips is intoxicating.

"Only if you take from me too." His gravely voice scrapes against my jaw.

I'm dizzy. Not from the blood I've already given, but from him, from the thought of giving and receiving blood again. It's like a drug. It's surrender and possession. My pulse pounds so hard I know he can feel it through my skin.

He groans, his desperate hands squeezing my thighs.

"I want you to." I suck his skin, leaving a deep red mark on his throat. He shudders, and my body churns. There is something about that simple reaction, an involuntary shiver–it makes me needy and insatiable.

The cords of his neck flex against my lips, and I pull back to look at what I've done. His eyes are as drunk and hooded as I can only assume mine are. "Yes." He rasps. "Anything you want."

"Oh, god!" It almost hurts. I want him so badly it feels like I'll die if he doesn't touch me right now. "Take your shirt off." It's not a request. I need to feel his skin on mine.

It's a sharp, beautiful agony. I know he'll fix it. He won't leave me like this for long.

He takes a moment, running the tips of his fingers over my skin before pulling back just enough to rip his shirt over his head.

My eyes move over his body. He is a study in contradictions, strength and grace, power and beauty, darkness and light. The ridges of muscles across his abdomen make my mouth water. He is a masterpiece. Whatever created him, he is their magnum opus. I can't believe I get to touch him.

"You have no idea what you do to me." His voice is jagged and rough.

Me?

"I was just thinking the same thing. How are you real?"

I'm drowning in lust as I reach out, running my fingers down his chest, down his stomach, to the hem of his pants.

For a moment, the air between us vibrates with the weight of this moment. Every sip stitches us together. He said it wouldn't, but I can feel it. The invisible thread holding us together is getting tighter.

He leans down, his breath fanning over my neck. Then he bites.

My knees buckle.

This is a life sentence.

I dig my fingers into his arms, holding myself up as much as I'm holding on to him.

He only takes a little bit, just enough to taste me on his tongue.

His mouth crashes against mine again—not a kiss but a claim. Everything outside of this room is gone. The world spins, but it's empty. We're alone.

He carries me to the wall and presses me against it so hard the stone bites into my back.

His lips leave mine only to leave a scorching path down my throat, teeth grazing, tongue teasing, until I'm arching into him, gasping and begging. Every brush of his mouth is a little fire.

He yanks at my leggings, ripping them, shredding the fabric.

In the midst of the heat, a laugh bursts out of me. "I would have taken those off for you."

"I know." He hums, yanking his own pants down. "But there wasn't enough time for that."

He grinds against me, sliding through the slick mess between my legs.

"You're going to come on my cock and take my blood at the same time." His jaw flexes, giving away his desperation.

Just as I open my mouth to beg, when I can't take another second, he presses into me in one hard thrust.

My eyes roll into the back of my head, and I moan loud enough for anyone and everyone to hear me. And I couldn't possibly care less. Let them hear it all.

He reaches down, sliding his arms into place, one is locked around my waist while the other hooks under my knee. I'm pinned like this, his body and the wall holding me up as he fucks into me so hard I can't remember my own name.

Time fades. Moments of clarity hit me, then disappear as I'm pulled under again. He's everywhere.

"I wish we could stay like this forever."

He kisses me in response, and I fall into him. I sink below the surface, the depths of his power swallowing me whole.

My eyes pinch shut, and my mouth falls open without a sound.

"Come on, Kiah. Let me feel it."

At the top of the wave, just before it all comes crashing down, he shifts, moving his hand from beneath my leg.

When the overwhelming pressure takes over and it's too late to turn back, his blood-soaked wrist meets my mouth.

"Drink." His thick, strained voice makes my eyes fly open. "Fuck! Take it while you come."

He has already ripped his skin open; all I have to do is take it.

So I do.

The metallic taste of him coats my tongue as I feel my body burst at the seams. It's like light rushing through me. Strength and power.

He's the fae king of a realm outside of mine. He is magic. His long life has spanned countless years. But right now we're the same.

Blood for blood. Need for need. Soul for soul.

He roars, and the light flickers. His body melts into mine, his damp face pressed to my shoulder as he groans and grinds into me.

"Oh my god." I can't catch my breath.

He moves first, stumbling away from the support of the wall with my body in his arms. He sinks into his mattress, letting his weight settle on top of me.

We sit in silence, the sound of our hard breathing all we can seem to manage.

"Are you hungry?" He pulls himself up.

"Starved."

He grins, "Come with me. I'm going to teach you about pizza."

His hands are gentle as he strips me out of my tattered clothes. "Wear my shirt."

I slip it over my head, and when the collar rubs against my neck, I gasp.

"Oh!" I slap my hand over it. It hurts more than before. The skin is tender and aching.

"I let my teeth go deeper this time." He looks apologetically at my skin.

"Well, I left marks all over you. We'll call it even." I smile like an idiot. He makes me feel so warm and gooey inside.

He takes my hand, leading me out into the hallway like my partner in a dance. I step quickly, on my toes, and I would let him take me anywhere.

The kitchen is empty. Good. I don't want any witnesses to the things I want to do to him while he's cooking.

Tall, handsome, emotionally intelligent, and he cooks? It

shouldn't be legal. Save some charm and perfection for everyone else.

"Can I help?"

He smirks, probably remembering the last time we did this together. "You can cut the fruit."

Peaches and figs are placed in front of me. As I slowly start to slice the peaches, a dark, little intrusive thought pops into my head.

I halve the figs carefully.

He works the dough against the counter, pressing the heels of his palms into it until it's a smooth ball—the heat from the woodfire oven sizzles in the corner.

He's quiet, and his mouth is tipped down into a slight frown.

"What's wrong?" I take a soft step toward him.

He shakes his head, splitting the dough into two balls. "Nothing."

"Something. That's not just concentration on your face."

I press my back to the counter and slide in beside him, wedging my hip between his and the counter.

Before I give myself away or overthink it, I swing. Not hard enough to actually hurt him–but enough to make his face jerk toward mine as soon as my open hand makes contact.

"You hit me." His eyes are wide and his lips are parted slightly.

"I did."

He drops the dough on the floured counter and stares at me. His chest moves more rapidly, ragged breaths fill the silence.

His lips twitch, and he drops to his knees, no hesitation.

"You were right. I underestimated you." His tongue slides over his sharp teeth. His fingers wrap around my ankle.

Pushing my foot flat against the middle of his chest, I press him back. "And now you're avoiding my question. What is wrong? You can't hide it from me. Just tell me."

He sighs, and his eyes wander up to the ceiling. "I don't want you to come to the vault."

"Why not?"

"I don't want you to see the things that are stored there."

A nauseous feeling rolls in my stomach. "What is stored there?"

"Darkness. Oaths. Broken promises. Lies." He doesn't flinch. "I could slip beyond the ether and be back within an hour."

"Is there a specific thing you don't want me to see?"

He nods slowly. His fingers massage my foot.

The door creaks, and we turn to find Calais in the doorway. She looks between us, at my foot on his chest and his hands.

"What are you cooking?"

"Pizza." We both answer at the same time.

"Sounds good." She looks at us again, her eyes darting around. I watch them narrow, and I feel myself blush. The mark on my neck is clearly visible.

At least his back is mostly to her, so she can't see all the marks I left on him.

When she turns without another word, we don't move or speak for a second.

A giggle bubbles up in my throat. "She didn't even ask questions."

"You thought she would?"

"You're the king. It's not every day you're caught on your knees." I press my toes against his chest, using the leverage to lift myself to sit on the counter.

"That's untrue. I'm on my knees fairly often." He lifts my ankle, pressing a kiss to my calf before moving in.

"We're not finished with that conversation."

"Of course not." He nips at my thigh.

"I want to come with you. I know I slow you down, but..." I gasp as he slides his fingers into my wet, needy skin. "We're better together. We need each other. Don't leave me behind."

"Whatever you want." He growls. "I can't deny you."

THIRTY

"WHERE ARE YOU TAKING ME?" I jog beside him to keep up.

"It's a sacred place. A place so hidden in secret it might have been over a century the last time a human set foot inside."

"And you're bringing me to see it?" I'm not sure I'm worthy of being the only human to see something in over a century.

We walk out into Noctyra.

"It's much less scary now."

"I imagine it was very frightening before." He tilts his head in the soft way that makes me feel gooey inside.

"I've never walked through the streets like this."

His lips tug down, and a deep crease forms between his brows. "I've been a terrible host."

"Look, I wasn't going to say anything..."

He grabs me, yanking me into him as we walk together. It's ridiculous, but I feel myself blushing. This feels so normal. He has wings and we're walking down the cobblestoned streets beneath the slightly orange sky in a realm of fae and magic, but otherwise, normal.

"What is that?" I gasp, stopping in front of a storefront.

"It's a Horticulturist."

"The Pomum." I stare at the fancy filigree.

"Would you like to go inside?"

"Can we?"

"Of course." The moment the door opens, a soft, sweet smell fills the air. Peaches and honey.

"Wow." I step into a fairytale buffet of perfect fruits. Rows and rows of fruit in wicker baskets, slices dipped in honey or chocolate, whole trees growing inside the building. The glass ceiling lets warm light in from above.

"Your majesty!" A silver-haired woman with piercings all over her face dips into a low bow. She jingles, her piercings and jewelry clinking whenever she moves. Even her wings are decorated with delicate silver chains.

She looks at me, a soft smile on her lips as she nods. "I'm Sola."

"Kiah." I feel warm. Not from nervousness or embarrassment but from how friendly and welcoming she it. "Do you grow all of this?" Some of the fruit is recognizable. Some look like a strange mixture of multiple fruits. A pear the color of a plum with the textured skin of a strawberry. A bunch of miniature kiwis in a bunch like grapes.

"I do." She beams with pride. "Pomology is my passion."

With everything that has happened, I somehow forgot that this place is magical, that it has power and beauty beyond what I know or understand.

"Pick something." He whispers.

"Do you have any suggestions?" I'm overwhelmed by the possibilities.

She opens a glass cloche full of small purple fruits. "These melpallows were picked just this morning. They are in season now."

My fingers tremble as I pick one up.

"Do I eat the whole thing?" I look up to find Canaan watching me with a smile on his face.

"There is a seed inside."

I don't know why I'm so nervous. It's just a piece of fruit.

Eating it in front of her is too much pressure.

"I'll take one too, please." He steps in front of me to grab one. I'm not sure it was intentional, it probably was, but I use the opportunity to take a bite while she can't see me.

"Oh, wow!" I gasp. "I've never tasted anything like it!" It has the texture of a grape, but the taste is completely unique. It's not similar to any other fruit.

We sample several other fruits, listening as she explains the growing conditions and how she blends different types of trees to create new mixes.

What was meant to be a quick stop morphed into a full afternoon of eating and chatting.

I make several promises to come back in a few weeks when some other exotic fruit comes into season.

The morning sun is high in the sky now, but the cold wind still whips through the streets.

"That was nice." I tuck into his side, using his arm as a shield from the cold.

"It was. You're very charming." He hums.

"Me?"

"Yes."

"Why do you seem surprised?" I nudge his ribs.

He presses his lips ot my temple and leads me down the street.

It's so painfully ordinary, just a couple out shopping. I'm almost able to forget everything, the pain and fear, the darkness looming around every corner.

It feels wrong. Why should we spend the day leisurely strolling around Noctyra? People died. Mordious. Humans back at home.

My mom is probably sick with worry.

And I'm enjoying myself. Sorrow closes up my throat.

"Kiah." His arms squeeze tighter. "If you don't enjoy the quiet in the midst of the storm, life would be all darkness and shadow. Maybe we can find a way to end this tomorrow. Or maybe it goes on, and on, unending for so long we forget what it feels like to have a normal life. Enjoy these moments when they come up."

"Stop reading my mind."

"I'm not. But I feel it too."

We walk in silence, the city spreading out around us in every direction.

It's almost familiar. But if I look closely, it's not quite right. It's like traveling back. There are no cars on the streets, just pristine cobblestones and raised flowerbeds. Trees grow everywhere, in the middle of the street and on the sides of buildings. It's as if they didn't cut down a single tree when they built the city.

The shops are fascinating. Book stores, flowers, clothes, art. It's like stepping into a different time.

It's a perfect fusion of old and new. Nature and man-made creation.

There is so much beyond the cathedral. People and places. Life.

The longer we walk, the more spread out the buildings become until we're on the edge of the Ebonstream with forest on the other side.

I feel the water immediately.

"Why does the water do that?" My skin itches to touch it. The silvery current looks like it would be so refreshing.

It's cold. I don't need to be refreshed.

It's the water trying to pull me in.

"It is just the magic in the water." He shrugs. "It just is."

"But it doesn't bother you?"

"We're stronger."

"How nice for you." As if I needed another reminder of his strength.

"I won't let it get you."

I know he's teasing, but it makes my skin flush.

"Where are you taking me?" I have to change the subject, or we might get stuck in another detour.

"The Well."

"An actual well, or..."

"It is actually a well, yes, but we don't draw water from it."

"What then?"

"Come see." He looks mischievous.

The path narrows, pulling away from the riverbank and into the forest.

"Remember when Mordious passed, I told you that he was going to the white shores?" His tone is serious now.

"Yes, I remember."

"The magic is alive. It's not something that we own; it is a force by itself, we don't create it." He looks at me, studying my face. "It's a closed loop, a circle. It's ancient, unending. It was always here and it always will be."

"Alright." I nod, trying to keep up.

"It's in us, it knows us. When we're gone, it pulls pieces of us back, reusing. So that we never really die. Parts do, but not everything."

"So, Mordious isn't dead?"

He looks upward, like he isn't sure what to say. "Mordious is dead. But pieces of him are still alive in the magic, and in the blood he left behind."

"Ok. I understand."

"I am Canaan. But I am also everyone who passed on to the white shores before me. The magic gave me things that belonged to them."

In the distance, a well made of shimmering black stones rises from the ground. The air is dense and cold.

It's as terrible as it is beautiful.

My feet drag, my steps take effort to force myself forward.

"The magic holds our true names."

"Your true names?"

"Mine is Adonirum." We stop walking, just far enough away that I can't see into the well.

"Adonirum?" As soon as it leaves my mouth, there is a whisper, an echo. The name pings off the trees.

He shudders, placing his heavy hand on my shoulder. "It's my name in the magic."

I nod, too afraid to speak again.

"Names are powerful here because they carry history in them." He steps forward, looking down into the well. "Come see."

I take his outstretched hand, holding onto it tightly as I lean over the edge to look.

It's a galaxy. A black swirling mass filled with stars. But they aren't stars, not really. Just tiny dots of light.

"What is it?" My body feels drawn to it, like the water.

"It's the magic. The fragments left behind."

It makes me feel small, like standing on the shore looking out at the ocean. It's so far beyond me.

I don't have magic. I'm just a human. But even I can sense the gravity of this. It must be protected. If Elion got control of this...

"Do you understand?" He whispers.

"Yes." I know what I need to do.

THIRTY-ONE

MY HAND TREMBLES as I hold it, hovering in midair, too afraid to knock.

I've prepared a speech. I practiced it with Canaan three times. I'm ready. I can do this.

But I knock wrong. It's too hard and sharp. It sounds angry.

Shit. That isn't the tone I meant to have.

"Cheyenne?" My voice cracks with nerves. "Can I talk to you?"

The door swings open. She's wearing one of the military-type uniforms that everyone here wears. It looks strange on her. Maybe because she always wore loose, lacey skirts and dresses, or maybe it's because she has no allegiance to Noctyra.

"Come in." She sounds as cautious as I feel. Her eyes are narrowed, not angry, but guarded.

I rub my clammy hands together. "Thanks." My throat feels like it's full of gravel. When I step into her room, the door closes with a click that makes my skin prickle.

She's standing there, arms crossed, jaw tight. She looks like she's bracing herself, like she's ready for a fight.

Canaan's voice fills my head. 'Stay calm. Stay steady.'

"Chey, you know me." My pulse hammers in my ears. "Please, I need you to listen to me. I'll hear you out, I'll listen to all of it. But in return, I need you to do the same for me."

She exhales slowly. "Kiah..."

I take a step closer, my hands noticeably shaking. "Please. Trust me. You know me. I would never do anything to hurt you."

Her gaze flickers, something soft passing through her expression, something more like the person that I've known my whole life.

"Please." I take another step toward her.

She exhales sharply and turns her face away, looking out the window. "You don't understand."

"I do!" The words tear through me with more force than I meant to use. "I do understand! I know you don't believe me, but I thought Elion cared about me, too. I thought he..." My voice breaks. "Listen, this isn't even about him, not really. It's about us. You're my best friend. My sister. We can't let something like this come between us. I can't lose you!"

Her lips tremble.

She takes a step toward me.

Suddenly, like a dam breaking, I'm crying—ugly crying. Loud, shaking sobs rip from my chest, all the hurt I've been holding back pours out of me. She grabs me, hugging me so tightly it hurts. I do the same. I wrap my arms around her and squeeze, like she might disappear if I don't hold on tight.

"I'm scared." I choke out.

"Me too." She whimpers, burying her face in my neck. "I don't want to lose you either."

After several minutes of sniffling and crying, we sit down on the floor. It's like an instinct, like we're back home in our bedrooms, sitting cross-legged on the carpet whispering secrets after midnight.

"I need you to understand why." She takes my hands in hers.

"Why what?"

"Why I can't just walk away from him." Her red-rimmed eyes are light and dreamy when she thinks about him. "He's..." She takes in a shuddering breath. "He's everything I always wanted. He listens to me. He makes me feel so special."

I bite the inside of my cheek, forcing myself to stay quiet. Just listen.

She squeezes my hands tighter. "He thinks I'm strong. I know this sounds crazy, but he needs me, Kiah. He wants me to be his queen one day." Her lips tug up into a small smile. "No one has ever seen me the way he does. I'm not a silly girl."

Queen. The words echo in my head like an alarm blaring.

"Cheyenne, I–"

"No." She stops me. "Please, let me finish." Her voice cracks. "He told me his plans for the future. He wants to build a world with me, better than this one. No wars. No blood. It will be peaceful. Humans and Fae will live side by side, like they did before. And he wants me beside him, leading with him. It sounds so beautiful, doesn't it?"

"It does." But not coming from him.

My chest aches. She's so full of hope, so sure. I want to shake her and scream. It's all lies.

He doesn't want peace; he wants power. He wants blood.

"And you believe him?" I whisper instead, pushing my instincts down.

She nods, tears slipping down her cheeks again. "I do. I love him. And he loves me."

Fuck. I can't break her heart.

I don't think I can, even if I try. His claws are in so deep, she can't see past him.

Nausea rolls in my stomach. One of us has to lose. There is no end to this, where we are both happy. Either Canaan wins, and Elion is dead. Or Elion wins, and Canaan is gone.

"*I love you.*" I whip the tears that I can't stop from falling. "I love you, Cheyenne."

"I love you too." Her voice is so soft and genuine, it feels like a knife twisting in my chest.

"What did he tell you about the first war?" I try a different approach.

"Canaan betrayed him. Their fathers had a disagreement and wanted to split the kingdoms. The Rimfae trusted them. Canaan came and spoke to Elion. He made him a promise. Then betrayed him. He killed King Esren and stole his kingdom."

"Did he tell you what they disagreed about?"

"Humans."

I'm surprised she knows that much.

"What about us?"

"Rimfae have always had a more direct relationship with humans. They would even marry them. They–"

"Would bleed them dry and kill them for the high of their last drop of blood." I cut in before I can stop myself.

"No." She shakes her head. "It was jealousy, Kiah! They were jealous of the closeness and afraid that the Rimfae were becoming too powerful."

I swallow down the urge to fight. It's useless. Fighting with her won't bring her back. It's already too late. She's so wrong. Everything is wrong.

What has to be done is the last thing I want to do. She is going to hate me forever. The truth settles over me like ice on my skin. Everything that we've ever been will be shattered.

But it's the only option.

Coming up on my knees, I wrap my arms around her. My voice breaks as I whisper, "I love you, Chey. Forever."

She hugs me just as tightly, "One day, when all this is over, you'll understand."

Her words are like a stone in my stomach. There isn't anything cruel or sinister in her voice, but it's ominous all the same.

I tear myself away from her and leave the room before I completely break down in front of her.

The black glass hallways feel longer and more frightening than before. I know where I'm going this time, but I feel just as lost. The world is tilted, and everything is wrong.

When I throw open the door to his room, I find him pacing. He stops, turning to watch me. The concern etched into his face only adds to the pressure in my chest.

I shrug and shake my head. It's the only thing I can do. My voice is too shaky to speak.

And that's all it takes.

He reaches me in a few long strides, and I'm in his arms. "It's alright, Kiah. You tried."

"But it didn't work." I press my face into his chest. "He's got his claws in so deep..."

"We'll end it." Certain. Steady.

"For everyone's sake."

I melt into his warm, strong body, letting it shield me from the world for a moment.

"Did you make a vow to him?" I whisper.

"Yes. And I broke it." He doesn't hesitate, but he doesn't explain further. His chest tenses, so I close my mouth and don't ask any more questions.

"She's going to hate me."

He doesn't have to respond with words. His arms wrap tighter around me, a silent confirmation.

He doesn't rush me. I know he's ready to leave, and it's urgent, but he never makes me feel like he doesn't have time.

"I'm ready." I steady myself, standing taller than I feel.

THIRTY-TWO

BENEATH THE BONE. Beyond the gate.

The words echo in my head on repeat. I don't even know what it means, but I can't stop thinking about it.

"Kiah, everything is going to be fine. The Vault is a safe place." He wraps his arm around me.

"Can I ask you questions to distract myself?"

"You can ask questions for any reason."

"Why in the vault in the human realm? Wouldn't it be safer in Noctrya? Or at The Falls?"

He smiles, a faraway, knowing look on his face. "There was a human man. Thomas Moore. He was the first keeper. It was his idea to create a place for our truths."

"Your truths."

"The Vault holds everything. Every lie, every promise, every oath. It is a history of every covenant a Fae was ever bound to."

His arms tighten around me as we step toward the ripple in the air. Four paladins stand guard over it, keeping the evil out.

As we step through, they nod to Canaan, to me, a silent vow to keep the gate.

On the other side, there is a surge of light, a soft glow that seems to be coming from nowhere and everywhere.

A path of smooth white stones stretches in front of us, disappearing into the dense trees.

I asked for this. I can't be scared now. There's no going back.

We start up the path in this strange place. It's obviously nighttime, but the glowing light makes it bright enough to see as if it were daytime.

"How many promises have you made?" The question slips out. It's been on my mind, but I didn't really mean to ask it.

His jaw flexes. He doesn't look at me. The shadows cut across his face, and my chest feels tighter.

"A few." He finally answers, his voice like gravel. "Most I have kept. It is the only true test of honor. And I have broken a vow. Maybe if I hadn't, we wouldn't find ourselves walking this path now."

"You didn't–"

"It doesn't matter what I did or didn't know at the time. Elion is responsible for his actions, and I am responsible for mine. For better or worse, I made a vow and broke it. Even if I were to make the same choices now, I have to live with the consequences of that betrayal."

His voice is harsh, but he takes my hand gently, running his thumb over mine.

"What is that?" The silhouette of something dark arches through the trees ahead of us.

"Beneath the bone." His voice is calm and steady.

"That's a bone?" I squint to see it better.

"It's the first guardian."

What does that mean?

My stomach knots together as we approach it. It's high enough that we can walk below it with ease. As it gets closer, I can see that it's not one bone but several built together to form an archway across the path, the ends disappearing into the treeline on both sides.

"What kind of bones are these?" I whisper as we walk beneath them.

"You don't want to know." His tone is laced with amusement.

"You're probably right."

I know each step is bringing us closer, but I feel myself getting calmer. This place is a mystery, but it's not scary. The dark is beautiful here. The air is light. And the sounds all around us are soothing. Bugs are chirping in the trees, and frogs croak all around us.

"Where are we?" I look up at the opening in the trees to see the sky.

"The rainforest."

"Oh, wow." I spin around, looking at our surroundings more closely.

"Look." He points ahead.

"The gates." I'm breathless. The towering gates dwarf Canaan, the metal twisting upward into the sky so high I have to crane my neck back to see the top. It's not natural, but it looks like it belongs here. The vines and leaves covering the gates are shaped from iron. They're so delicate, they look real.

"Beyond the gate." He steps in front of it, his wings open behind him.

"Your majesty." A voice as old as time itself whispers through the air.

My skin prickles, and a chill rolls up my spine.

The gates creek open, slowly. We wait until they are fully open before stepping inside.

It's so strange how quickly the change makes itself known. We're not in the human realm anymore, at least, not in the same one we just stepped out of. The magic is here. I can feel it like a weight in the air.

The path twists, sloping downward toward a sparkling stream.

Little yellow flowers grow on both sides of the white stone path. I recognize them. And in a way I can't explain or even understand, they recognize me too.

"Hello," I whisper, trying to be discreet, but he hears me.

"They like you."

"Do they? How do you know?"

"Can't you feel it?" He places his hand on the back of my neck. "They lean into you. Their roots vibrate in the ground, communicating your arrival to the flowers up ahead."

"Are you sure they aren't doing that for you?"

"It's for you." There is a softness in his voice that settles into my skin; it wraps around me like an embrace.

I feel warm in my chest as he leads me down the path toward the stream. The white stones get narrower until I have to walk in front of him.

When we reach the water, I just know we're going in. The stream runs into a large pool at the bottom of the hill. The lake is small enough to see across to the other side, but big enough to be daunting.

"You won't get wet." He reads my mind. "Hold my hand."

Choosing to trust, I take his hand and step onto the surface of the water. It's like walking on ice.

"Why are all of the magic places in this realm in water?"

"Water is magical. All water. In any realm. It holds onto power. It is alive and receptive to enchantment."

"That makes sense." I hum. It's not a leap to connect the power of water after seeing the ocean. Something that vast and unending must be magical.

We walk out into the middle of the lake, and a rippling current swirls in the water before us.

"We're jumping in there, aren't we?" I cringe.

"We are."

"Let's do it." I sigh.

Stepping into it is a leap of faith, just trusting that he will keep me safe.

And of course, he does.

On the other side, we're in a little bubble. A cottage surrounded by a lush garden that belongs within the pages of a fairytale. I've read enough to know that danger is probably lurking in the shadows; it always is in a picturesque place like this.

The door flies open as we walk up the stone path. A man runs out. He's so small and round, I have to remind myself of my manners. He looks like a cartoon character.

"Your majesty! What an unexpected surprise!"

"Mr. Moore." Canaan shakes his hand with a warm smile on his face. "This is Kiah."

"Oh! I know! I recognize her!" He grins up at me, pushing his round glasses up on his nose.

"You recognize me?"

"From the promises, love!" He steps aside, holding his arms out to let us in.

"The promises?" I whisper to Canaan.

He nods, apparently knowing exactly what Mr. Moore is talking about.

I expected something like a library with rows of shelves filled with leatherbound books. But inside, it's just a room full of candles. Thousands of candles flickering in unison. The lights are small, just tiny flames, but all of them together create a blinding light.

I have to look down at the floor as we walk through the narrow pathway deeper into the cottage.

I'm overwhelmed. There are too many sensory inputs at once. The lights, the flickering, the warmth, the heaviness of the magic.

My skin prickles and I feel wobbly, like my legs might give out.

"It's alright, Kiah." His hand on the back of my neck again, steadying me. Somehow, just knowing that he won't let me fall helps.

The cottage appeared small from the outside, but it goes on forever.

Mr. Moore leads us through the winding pathway cut through the candles. It seems to go on forever. It's as if each candle is lit by the same fire. The flames move in perfect synchronization.

"Here we are." He smiles over his shoulder. "Please, take a seat, make yourselves comfortable. I'll be in the front, out of your way!"

In front of him are two high-backed armchairs next to an empty fireplace. There is so much fire in this building, but the one place meant to hold it is empty.

"Here, sit." Canaan helps me into one of the chairs.

True to his word, Mr. Moore doesn't hover. He disappears quickly, leaving us alone in the room.

"Now what?" I whisper.

"Now, I ask the magic."

I watch him lean back in his chair, asking the magic to help him, to bring forth the promise he needs to see. He's so at ease, like he's speaking to a friend. He's not afraid of it.

A ball of light floats through the air, landing softly in the hearth.

"Oh my god." I gasp, leaning forward. It's a picture, as clear as day. It's Elion and Cheyenne. A crowd of Shadowrithes is gathered around them.

"I vow to you, my love, from this day onward, you will be the queen by my side–"

"Oh my god!" I'm starting to hyperventilate. "This looks like–"

"A wedding."

"Are they married?" I heave for a breath. "She didn't tell me! I can't–" Think? Breathe? Speak? Understand? All of it at once.

"I know where they are." He reaches for me. "We got what we came for. Come here, I'll carry you."

A harsh wind blows through the room, and another ball of light rushes past, lighting up the hearth.

"Kiah, come here." His voice sounds more frantic now. "Let's go."

The picture changes, it's us in the cave by the lagoon. He's holding me in his arms. "Our connection is stronger. He can't keep you there. I can come get you. I'll come in after you. I promise. He can't keep you there." He runs his fingers through my hair.

"Oh," I barely breathe. "You promised me."

"I did." He nods. "Let's go. Now."

"Canaan, why–"

I can't even ask him why he's rushing me before another orb of light comes in. The Vault isn't giving me even a moment to absorb it before it's showing me something else.

"Kiah, don't watch that!" His voice is louder, sharper, panicked.

It's Canaan's face now, soft and broken. Calais is sitting in front of him with tears in her eyes. "If you love her, you can not bind her to you. Promise me, Canaan. Promise me you will let her go when it becomes too much."

He doesn't speak right away. I watch his throat work, his eyes close, his chest rise like he's carrying something too heavy.

Finally, he whispers, "I promise."

My heart stops.

"What?" I whisper as he grabs me, lifting me up in his arms. As he starts to rush out of the room, I see the next image over his shoulder. Canaan and Elion. Younger.

There is an ear-shattering scream that makes us both stop.

Elion is hanging over the edge of a cliff, his body dangling.

"Hold on! I've got you!" Canaan is straining, holding him up.

"I'm slipping!" Elion's voice is sheer panic.

"No! I'm going to cut the rope. I've got you! Just hold my hand!" A bead of sweat drops off his forehead, disappearing into the canyon.

"Canaan!" Elion screams, but he slices through the rope tangled around his hand and wings.

The rope falls, dropping into the abyss, and Elion shoots upward, landing on the ground.

"What was that?"

"A Shadowrithe snare." Elion bends down, picking up a piece of the trap that caught him.

"Here? This is worse than I thought. I have to go tell my father."

"Wait." Elion grabs him, pulling him into a tight hug. "Thank you."

"Nothing to thank me for." Canaan looks genuinely confused. "You would have done the same for me. You're my brother."

"I'm afraid, Canaan." The brutal honesty in his eyes makes my heart hurt. Before he was a monster, he was this young man.

"I swear, I will be your shield. When this is over, you will have your crown. Your throne."

"Brother." Elion throws his arms around Canaan's shoulders. "Thank you."

THIRTY-THREE

"KIAH."

It's not that I don't want to answer him. It's that I physically can't.

I open my mouth, but nothing comes out.

"Kiah, wait, please."

He doesn't touch me. I feel him behind me, but he doesn't grab me.

I march out of the Vault. I need a breath that doesn't smell like ancient secrets and candle wax.

I know he's following me, feeling everything that I'm feeling. But I need a moment. Just one. The air feels thinner, and my body feels heavy.

The white stones crunch under my feet as I pull myself down the path toward the rippling portal door.

He's talking to Mr. Moore. Polite and kind, he thanks him and comes up the path behind me with heavy steps.

He doesn't say anything, but he holds his hand out to me. Even now, I don't hesitate to take it.

We step through the portal together, and just like that, we're back in the middle of the lake. The sun is rising. The picturesque beauty of it only adds to the pain in my chest. The words gnaw at me.

I turn and stare at him. His eyes meet mine, and we're frozen. I'm freaked out. I know Canaan isn't the bad guy here. Seeing a short, out-of-context clip from the past doesn't change what I know to be true. But I feel lied to.

"Canaan," I whisper. "How many promises have you made?"

His jaw flexes, and his gaze moves past me. That's a bad sign.

"Canaan?"

I watch his throat as he swallows.

"The promise to Elion was a mistake. At the time, I did not know how bloody and violent the war would become. I would never have made that vow to him if I had known how hard the Rimfae would fight against our efforts to close the portals. Under orders from King Esren, people were slaughtered to collect their blood to use for strength. When we won, and we only won by a hair, it was decided by our court that it would be better to withhold his crown." His voice is low and full of pain. I can see the weight of that broken promise on his shoulders.

"What about the promise you made to Calais?" My voice wavers and gets weaker with every word. My heart is tearing along the seams. I can't bear it.

His face breaks, a flicker of pain, something raw and aching. I almost wish I hadn't seen it. "Kiah," His muscles jerk, like he's holding himself back from reaching out for me. "You weren't supposed to see those like that. I have never seen the Vault act of its own accord. I–"

"It doesn't really matter how I saw it, does it? I saw it. Now what?" I cut in, my throat drying and burning as I fight to speak.

I want to hate him. To yell and scream and say things that will make him hurt the same way I'm hurting. God, I want to claw at him. But I can't. He warned me. He told me the bond would consume us if we let it. And, like a needy, greedy, love-struck fool, I let it. I let it devour me.

My heart hurts; a sharp, throbbing pain radiates in my chest with every inhale.

All on its own, my body moves. I lunge forward into his arms. I need to feel his touch. It's the only thing that can help me now. Even though it's the same place that's killing me.

He doesn't hesitate to wrap his arms around me. It hurts as much as it helps.

"You're a man of your word. You are good and honorable. You wouldn't make her that promise if you had no intention of keeping it!" I'm growing more frantic by the second. My fingers fist into his shirt, holding on as tightly as I can.

His silence only adds to my unraveling.

"You meant it, didn't you?" I sob. "You're going to let me go. What does that even mean?"

"Kiah, take a breath."

I can't. I can't breathe. I can't think straight.

The silence that hangs over us is deafening. Deep down, I know he's quiet because he doesn't want to lie to me, and the truth won't help.

This feels like the end. We're being cut short right at the beginning.

"You did warn me." I straighten my shoulders. "You told me it would be this way."

"Kiah, please–"

"It's fine, Canaan." I pull out of his arms. "You know where he is, right? We are wasting time."

I take a step and immediately drop into neck-deep water.

I scream, but before the full sound can come out, he's in the water behind me, lifting me up.

"Be careful!" He snaps, wrapping his arms around me.

"I didn't do it on purpose!" I match his tone, jerking myself out of his arms.

"Come here, let me–"

"No! I can swim."

"You're being ridiculous."

"I don't want you to touch me." I don't mean to say it. But the words slip out anyway, and once I say them, I can't take them back.

His mouth snaps closed, and his jaw clenches. He recoils, pulling his arm back.

I watch as he sets his shoulder just as I did a moment ago. I'm not sure what I thought he would do, but I truly didn't expect what he went with.

In a whirlwind of movement, he springs out of the water, his feet landing on the surface beside me. And without a word or a backwards glance, he walks to the shore.

The water is cold, and I'm wearing a long fairy robe that drags as I try to push forward.

My swim back to shore isn't particularly easy or pleasant, but for some reason, I can't stop laughing.

He left me.

"Why are you laughing?" He is sitting on a rock, waiting for me as I stumble in the slick mud at the bottom of the lake.

"You left me!"

"And that's funny to you?"

"Yeah." I shrug, still laughing.

"Stop laughing." He growls.

"Why? Would you rather I were crying?"

He grits his teeth and steps toward me, the golden light of the morning sun singing on his stupid, handsome face. "No."

"Then leave me alone." I turn, attempting to walk away, but he grabs me. It's almost painful. My body spins, crashing into his.

"No. I won't leave you alone. I can't leave you alone. You're going to make a liar out of me once again." His mouth crashes against mine, and I don't try to pull away.

"I wish I hated you." I whimper against his lips.

"I could never hate you." He lifts me, forcing my legs around his waist.

A bird makes a loud, shrill call through the trees as he pulls me away from the lake with his mouth on mine.

I almost forgot where we were until he pins me to a tree.

"Canaan..."

"No. You can't rile me up like this, Kiah." He pumps his hips between my legs. "I need you."

And just like that, I can't think of anything I want more.

"Have me then. Take it."

He groans and drops his face into my neck.

With one hand squeezing my hips and the other shifting his pants down his thighs, I feel my desperation growing.

It's a craving. A hunger.

He rips the fabric of my dress. There was too much material anyway.

"Do it now! Please!" I arch into him, my body writhing in agony.

He smiles, his sharp teeth look longer than usual. It's a wicked smile, a powerful smile. I know he has me trapped here at his mercy.

He slides two of his fingers down and circles my clit.

"Wait! Fuck!" I panic. This is good, but it's not what I need.

I'm a mess. The stimulation is somehow too much and not enough.

"Oh, so you want me to touch you now?" Anger and amusement flare in his voice in equal measure.

"Yes! Please!"

He hums. "Interesting. Because it was just a few minutes ago that you–"

"I want you to touch me! Never stop fucking touching me!" I grind my hips, searching for more friction.

"That's better." He slips his fingers into me and curls them.

"Oh my–" I almost swallow my tongue.

"You're soaked, Kiah." He moves his fingers faster, and my body starts to clench around him. It's all happening so quickly. My mind goes blank, and I pinch my eyes closed.

When he stops abruptly, slipping his fingers out of me, I snap my eyes open in time to see him suck them into his mouth.

"You're coming with me inside you." He whispers. "I want you to scream my name. Do you understand?"

"Yes!" I'll do anything at this point.

He lines himself up, the head of his cock sliding through my wet skin before he presses in and stops. Just the tip, then he pulls out again. He's enjoying torturing me.

"Canaan, please." I groan.

"Tell me how much you want me."

"So much," my voice shakes. "I want you so bad."

"Good." He presses all the way in, finally, stretching me open. "I want it hard." I'm throbbing.

He leans in, smiling against my lips before he kisses me harshly. I can feel his anger.

Each thrust is harder than the last. I can't breathe or speak. I can't do anything but moan. He's still kissing me, but it's not loving. It's dominating. I'm being punished with pleasure.

"Canaan. Oh god!"

His eyes look down at me, merciless. He drags his hand up to my throat. My eyes go wide, startled, but he never squeezes; he just keeps his hand there.

"There is no god here, Kiah. Just me." He growls.

And that's it.

I shake uncontrollably, coming all over his cock.

He starts to thrust faster, but it's sloppy; he's losing the edge. I cling to his shoulders as he drills into me, so deep it's pleasure and pain all rolled together.

When he comes, he grits his teeth and groans my name.

I feel everything. The way he twitches inside me. How his hand tightens around my thigh. His unsteady breaths.

After he comes, he presses his face into my neck again and holds me, still inside me.

He's not angry anymore. But something is off. I can feel it. He's holding me the way he always does, but there is a canyon between us.

"What's wrong?" I run my fingers through his hair.

He shakes his head but doesn't answer.

"Words, Canaan."

He pulls back to look at me. "I don't like seeing you cry, but the hard resolve was even worse. I thought I would be strong enough to resist it. That promise to Calais was before we left together. I'm not a man of honor. Apparently, my words don't mean much. Because I'm about to break another vow."

"Two in two centuries is probably a pretty good record." I run my thumb over his lower lip, but even as I say it, I can feel the tension rolling off him. He's not happy about this, and it hurts like a knife twisting into my chest.

"Once is too many times."

"Well then. Maybe you should keep this promise if it's going to eat you up. I don't want to stand in the way of your honor, your majesty." I push against his chest. "Get out of me."

His face instantly hardens, the same way it used to when I first got here.

He sets me on my feet, the evidence of what we just did leaking down my legs. It's difficult to find dignity in this situation, but I hold my head high and walk away with the tattered skirt of my dress gathered in my hands.

THIRTY-FOUR

"CAN I SLEEP HERE?"

"It's your bed." I roll onto my side, facing away from him. I'll be childish and snappy until the stupid bond draws us back together.

I can't understand his position. I know that. Humans take promises seriously; we have vows, and our word is supposed to mean something.

But we don't have a creepy museum dedicated to preserving every promise every person has ever made. I'm not sure if it makes me feel inspired or appalled.

I pinch my eyes closed and try to force my mind into silence. If I think too much, he'll know. And I wouldn't want to disturb him with my loud emotions.

I'm too worked up to sleep. I don't want to be here with him.

I jump out of the bed so quickly it startles me as much as him.

"Where are you going?" His voice is laced with irritation.

"For a walk. Don't worry, I'm not leaving." I hope that will be enough for him to let me go alone.

"Kiah–"

"I need space, Canaan." I stop at the door. "I'm going to go talk shit about you to my best friend."

"What?" His eyes go wide. I'm sure such a childish, immature activity is beneath him. But it's not beneath me.

"I'm going to vent about you. Leave me alone."

I'm relieved and surprised when he sits back against the headboard with a deep scowl on his face.

A few minutes of letting myself think about everything that I saw today will help me. I just need to flush it out of my system. Trying to keep it locked away only makes me want to think about it more.

And the more I push it down, the more irritated I am.

At him.

And at myself.

He warned me.

That's the worst part. He told me exactly what would happen.

But somehow, I'm still struck stupid by the promise he made her. The only saving grace is that he made it before we gave in to the feelings.

The look on his face is what's plaguing me. It's playing on a loop in my head, and I can't escape it.

The disappointment he seems to feel over breaking a vow.

If it means that we don't have to live the rest of our lives in agony apart from each other, a promise doesn't mean much.

But to him it does.

I've been so wrapped up in this that I haven't even bothered to ask where he's hiding or if Canaan has a plan for how to deal with this.

By the time I reach Cheyenne's room, tears are streaming down my face. I have to compartmentalise all of this. It's too much to deal with at once.

"Chey?" I knock too hard, too desperate.

The door jerks open only a second later.

"What's wrong?" Her eyes bounce over my face.

"I know things have been strained between us. But I just need you tonight, ok?" I whimper.

She tugs me into the room and closes the door behind us. Her arms are around me in an instant. "Come here."

We sit for several minutes, just holding each other. I'm cherishing it this time. I know how quickly it can slip away.

"You're married?" I whisper once I feel steady enough to talk.

"How do you know that?" She gasps, pulling back to look at me.

"We saw it."

Panic flashes in her eyes. "W-What does that mean?"

"I'm not sure." I shrug.

"Is he going to go after him?" She reaches out and grabs my hands, holding them too tightly.

"I don't know. We haven't talked about it." I tell her the truth. I'm not actually going to tell her about Canaan's promises. I don't need to give her anything to use against him.

"Kiah, I need you to promise me that you'll tell me. If he's going to kill him..." She looks pale, like she might be sick at any moment.

"Chey..."

"Please!" She shrieks. "What harm could I possibly do with that information? I have to know if he's going to hurt him! He's my husband!" Her voice wobbles.

"I'll tell you." I hope my expression looks honest.

"Thank you." She holds her head in her hands. "I know it won't change anything, but I can't be left in the dark." She presses again.

"Ok." Unease creeps up my spine.

Something is off. I can't put my finger on it, but it's there, lingering in the back of my mind.

"What had you so upset?" She wipes the tears from her eyes.

"Nothing." I shake my head. "It was stupid. I really just wanted to see you. I miss you."

She frowns, her eyes filling with fresh tears. "I miss you too."

We sit in silence, pretending, even for a moment, that everything isn't monumentally fucked up. I don't know how our relationship works now. How do we move past this? It's even worse than I thought. She married him.

"Thank you for sitting with me. I need to do something." I stand up, ready to run back to Canaan.

"Ok." She holds onto me a second longer. "Please come tell me if he decides to go after him. I have to know. I have to prepare myself."

"I'll tell you." I kiss her cheek and rush out. The momentary peace she made me feel is gone, and now I'm back in the pit of despair I feel when I look at her.

As soon as the door clicks closed, I run, as fast as my legs will carry me.

Down the hall, up the stairs, through an open-air hallway that looks down at a stone-cold courtyard.

I open the door so fast and hard that it slams into the wall.

"Kiah." He spins around, his steps stopping short.

"Something is wrong." I blurt out. "I think."

"Because there is no way he would be stupid enough to hide in a place I would immediately recognize?"

He's clearly been thinking about this too.

"Yes." I step toward him breathlessly.

"He knew I would go to the Vault. He knew I would see it. It's a trap."

"So what do we do?" A panicked, nervous energy creeps up my spine.

"Nothing. We sit on it. If he's expecting us to show up there, that means we're walking into a trap." He reaches out and tucks a strand of hair behind my ear. "I need to inform Calais."

"Ok." A moment of silent tension passes between us.

"I–"

"We–"

"You go." I laugh nervously, rocking from my toes to my heels.

"No, please." He looks as anxious as I feel. "You."

"I just wanted to say sorry." I clear my throat.

"Me too." He looks down at me with a softness that makes my knees weak.

His hands weave through my hair, holding my face. When he leans in to kiss me, my heart stops. It feels nervous and fluttery, like it did before we kissed.

"I made that promise before, Kiah, when I thought I could resist."

"I know." I hold onto his neck, pulling him in closer.

"We will figure it out."

"That sounds reckless." I chuckle against his mouth.

"That's our way."

"I guess it is."

For a moment, just a few seconds, the world feels quiet. The weight is gone, and I'm just a girl in his arms.

"I'll be back." He promises.

"I'll be here."

THIRTY-FIVE

IT STARTS SLOWLY, but with each passing minute, my anxiety grows.

He has been gone for ten minutes. But deep down, something doesn't feel right. It's like a silence that I can't shake. It's hanging in the air.

When the door clicks open, I spin around, letting out a relieved sigh.

"I don't know–" the words fade away. It's not Canaan. It's Cheyenne. "What are you doing here?"

She didn't knock. She walked in.

My skin prickles as I take a step away from her.

"Kiah, there's no time to explain. I need you to come with me." She holds her hand out.

"What? No." I shake my head and take another step back.

"Please. Don't fight me. Just come." The desperation in her voice makes my blood pressure leap.

"Where is Canaan?"

"I don't know." She snaps. "We don't have time to worry about him right now. Come on, Kiah."

The look in her eyes is scaring me. My body reacts to it physically. My muscles tense and my heart beats against my ribs like an alarm bell.

"Chey, listen! Whatever you're doing, it's not too late. Let's talk about this." I'm stalling. Buying time. If I can just keep her here, talking, maybe Canaan will have a chance to come back.

She's looking around the room like she's searching for something.

"Bathroom?"

"What?"

"Where is the bathroom?"

"It's down the hall. There isn't one—" she grabs my wrist and yanks. "Come with me."

I pull and fight against her grip. "Stop. I'm not going anywhere."

She drops my arm and stares at me. The resolve in her eyes hardens.

"I'll be right back." She spins on her heels and runs out of the room.

For a second, just one, I'm frozen, standing numb.

When I step out into the hallway, she's running into the bathroom. I take three steps when she returns. There is blood dripping from her hand.

"What happened? What did you do?" I run toward her. "Whatever you're doing—"

The words die on my tongue. Inside the bathroom, a misty black fog is coming out of the water. It's rising up, solidifying.

"I know you don't understand right now." Her voice is soft as she grabs my hand. "But one day you will. I'm saving your life."

"Oh god. What did you do?" I turn, horrified, looking into her glassy eyes.

Canaan isn't coming. If this Shadowrithe is here, there are others.

I hear myself screaming his name as I'm grabbed by the bony hand.

Please, Canaan. Please come.

I thrash in his grip, but it's no use. I feel the pinch of a needle in my neck.

"Calm down, Kiah. You'll hurt yourself. Please, trust me."

"This is a mistake." I feel myself getting drowsy. "Elion is going to kill me."

Whatever she says, I can't hear it. I slip into darkness, the same lonely darkness from before. But this time, I'm not afraid, and I'm not confused. I know what's happening to me, and I'm fucking furious.

"Elion! You coward!" I scream. "Sending Cheyenne in? You're too afraid to face Canaan, so you send your wife?"

His laughter fills the void, curling around me. "Oh, you're just angry that you followed each step of my plan perfectly."

"This wasn't your plan. Don't try to make it seem like you're some mastermind that was always ten steps ahead. You didn't expect her to be taken. You're scrambling."

He hums. "Maybe."

A sound from behind me makes me spin around, only to find him standing there.

"Maybe this wasn't the plan all along. But it looks like we caught up quickly, doesn't it? As we speak, your body is being delivered to my location. Canaan will follow because he can't help himself. The bond you share will demand it. He's helpless against it. And when he comes, I'll kill him and take back my throne."

"Fuck you."

"I already did, sweetheart. Do you miss it?"

"You are the biggest regret of my life. If I had known what was waiting for me, I never would have allowed myself to have less." I'm disgusted. "And I do mean lesser, in every way."

He smirks, but his eyes flicker. "Oh, come on. Don't be bitter."

"It's not bitter to realize how much better it could be." I shrug.

In a flash of movement, he's behind me. He takes a handful of my hair, right at the root. My head jerks back.

"You screamed for me. Begged. Came all over my cock." He hisses into my ear. "Don't act like you didn't love it."

"So, can you imagine how good it is with Canaan that what you did pales in comparison? He doesn't just fuck me, he dominates me. Somehow, he's rough and gentle at the same time." With each word, his grip gets tighter. "He's a better lover. A better king. Tell me, Elion, what can you possibly offer that measures up? And no, before you ask, betrayal doesn't count."

He growls, a low, animal sound, and shoves me forward, releasing me so I stumble.

I spin around, my mouth full of venom, ready to unleash it on him, but he's gone. I'm alone in the dark.

Good. I would rather be here alone than spend even one more second with him.

With each second that passes, my anger grows until it's a beast completely out of my control. How could she do this? She actually cut her hand and led a Shadowrithe right to me.

Thoughts of Canaan are the only things that are keeping me from falling into a manic rage. I don't even know if he's safe. I can't feel him here. But somehow I just know he's still alive.

Whatever is happening outside of this place I'm locked in, I know he will do the right thing. Calm. Level-headed. Steady. He won't rush in without a plan.

Even now, I feel a sense of peace. He will come for me. He will fix all of this. It's who he is.

I can almost imagine him walking through the chaos. He will come.

But until then, I'll sit here in the black with fury rolling around inside me and curling behind my ribs.

THIRTY-SIX

"HELLO?" I sit up, my body aching with every movement. My head feels like it's filled with water. It's heavy and sluggish. My neck feels too weak to hold it up.

I try to swallow, but my throat is raw. My mouth tastes metallic, the bitter taste of blood on my tongue.

It's so dark in here, I'm not even totally sure my eyes are open.

It's cold, my skin is tight on my bones. The ground beneath me is stone, slick and uneven. The robe I'm wearing is damp and sticking to my body.

"H-Hello?" My voice is a barely audible dry whisper. But it echoes. "Hello?" I call a bit louder. This isn't just a small room. It's big and hollow. A cave? A dungeon?

My pulse pounds in my ears.

I try to stand up, but my legs are too heavy. The stone wall is cold against my back, but I lean on it for support. I stretch my arm out, reaching to feel the floor around me.

A drop of water falls from above me. Then another. Then another. A slow but steady rhythm.

I close my eyes and take a few deep breaths. I won't allow myself to panic.

What would Canaan do?

He would be calm. So will I.

I crawl forward, the rocky ground cutting into my knees as I inch around. I'm searching for something; anything. The ground is wet, with puddles everywhere.

My fingertips brush against something that feels different from the ground. It's wood. Placing my palms flat, I touch it. It's a door.

I stick my fingers under, feeling a cool breeze. But there is no light. I still can't see anything.

Pressing my face flat to the ground. I close my eyes and listen. There is nothing but silence. It feels endless.

Don't panic. Canaan wouldn't.

Using the wall again, I stand on my wobbly legs and inch around the room. It's circular. And there is a draft in two places.

I'm barely able to hook my fingers beneath the second one, but I squeeze them under and tug it, and it slowly moves.

I have to steady myself to keep from slipping. The floor is very wet here and covered in a thick mossy goo.

There is a sound. A powerful booming that comes in rhythmic surges.

"Oh my god! Oh, shit!" I panic slightly as I scrape the door open. The wood drags loudly against the stone before falling with a bang that rings out, echoing in the silence.

I pause, my ears straining to hear. I just rang the alarm bell; someone must be coming for me.

Nothing.

I step toward the opening and peek my head out.

I gasp and stumble back.

"What the fuck?" Tears well up in my eyes.

No.

No!

Canaan wouldn't cry. Stop it now.

Taking a breath, I step forward again.

I'm standing in a small opening in the side of a cliff. Pitch black sky meets pitch black water as far as I can see. The water crashes against the wall, spraying me as each wave hits the rocks.

The water isn't very far below, but the force of the waves would break my body against the cliff.

Damn, it would be really helpful to have wings right now. That's not something I've thought many times in my life.

Do I jump? It seems like the worst possible thing to do, but it's also my only option.

The water isn't far. And I might be able to jump between waves.

"Shit." I sit down, letting my legs dangle out against the cliff

One, two, three...

I count over and over, just to be sure. The waves swell and crash against the rocks every nine seconds.

That's not enough time.

I grab the piece of wood, pulling it with a loud scrape across the ground. I only have one shot at this.

Counting the seconds, I throw the board down into the water and watch it get pulled out.

If I jump, I can swim with the water and hopefully make it far enough away from the wall not to get dragged back.

It's terrible, but it's all I've got.

It's now or never. I step forward, my feet scraping against the ground. I don't jump.

I try again. And again, I stop short of the opening, slinging to the rock on either side.

Again.

A fourth time. Then a fifth.

"Fuck!" I close my eyes and take a breath. "Make him proud. Take charge. You can do this, Kiah."

His face shows in my mind, then I hear his voice. He's like a light in the darkness, a beacon in the storm.

"I'm coming, Kiah. I'm coming. Nothing is going to happen to you."

It's real. I know it, I feel it in my bones.

Tears burn in my eyes, and my breath catches. "But it's a trap! We both know it. Don't come. He won't be expecting that." I panic. "Don't walk willingly into a trap!"

"I can't leave you there. He sent Shadowrithes into the last guarded place in Noctyra to get you." His voice doesn't waver. "He's too bold, and I'm going to take him down."

"Canaan—"

"I'm closer than you think, Kiah. That's why you can see me." His voice is so reassuring that it makes me laugh and sob at the same time. A weight made of fear and panic is pulled off of me.

I open my mouth to tell him exactly where I am, when a rattling sound echoes off the stone.

"Is that you?" I whisper.

"No." His voice is sharp.

"Canaan. I'm jumping." Without giving myself a moment to overthink it, I run.

No counting or waiting. I leap.

I hit the water hard. It's so cold it feels like needles pricking my skin everywhere.

The water pulls me, holding me under as it washes me out in a current too strong to fight against. I kick and use the flow to push myself away from the cliff.

I hear him in my head, but I'm too focused on not dying to really listen.

I'm able to break the surface enough to gasp for air.

"Kiah! Answer me!" He practically screams.

"I'm in the water!"

"Fuck!"

The water is calmer here, just a slow-moving ebb and flow. I spin around and look at the cliff. The hole I fell from is barely visible, just a black spot on the rock face.

He's quiet now. And that terrifies me.

"Canaan?" I whisper. But he doesn't respond.

I search the sky for him, waiting, clinging to hope that his strong silhouette will cut through the dark.

But then I see something.

Light.

And shadow.

Oh god, Canaan! I watch helplessly as the shadows move and flicker. The shadows writhe, twisting in the air. Then something drops from the opening. It's either dead or unconscious because it doesn't tense at all, just falls straight down and disappears into the water.

For a moment, just a second, my heart stops. A scream climbs up my throat, but I swallow it when I see him. He dives out of the opening and swoops over the water.

He's not broken or lifeless. My heart shatters and rebuilds itself all at once. A rush of relief and awe calms my body instantly.

He dips down, picking me up gently.

"You found me."

"I told you I would." The tip of his nose runs over my cheek as his tight grip bites into my skin. "I'll always find you."

THIRTY-SEVEN

"WHAT IS THIS PLACE?" I look over his shoulder at the darkness all around us.

"Hornelen."

"Oh." I don't bother with any more questions. My brain is too scrambled.

The magic is heavy here. I'm dizzy. It's a twisting, changing kaleidoscope of darkness and strange glowing colors. There is no light, no sunlight, no moonlight, just strange orbs of color dotting the sky. But they aren't stars.

It's something else.

I stare up at them, my mouth dropping open. They are sets of two. Two red, yellow, or orange dots.

Are they...eyes.

Quickly, I look away from it. I'm not sure I want to know.

The shoreline is lined with sharp black stones.

He carries me away from the water toward a path cut through the dark, gnarled trees. They look like monsters. Thick, twisting branches with no leaves, just black trunks like skeletal arms reaching out to grab me.

My chest feels tight, and my stomach rolls.

"Wait! Put me down!" I'm sure I'm about to be sick. I push off of him, scrambling over to a tree.

"Kiah!" He follows behind, grabbing my wet strands of hair with his hands.

I cough and gag but breathe through it, the knot in my stomach loosening with each second.

"I'm sorry–"

"Don't apologize." His voice sounds different–not angry but sharper. "It's the magic. This place has always been dark, but it's gotten worse. The evil here is poisoning it, corrupting it..."

"What is this place?"

"It's the cliffs of Hornelen. There are people who live on the other side of the cliffs, but they won't come here. They know better."

"Humans?" I'm shocked. "Are we in the human realm?" It doesn't seem possible.

"We are." He takes my hand, lifting me into his arms.

"I feel awful. Like the air is wet, and it's filling my lungs with water." I wheeze.

My head is pounding, and every heartbeat thuds against my chest like a hammer. A shrill ringing fills my ears.

"Kiah." His voice echoes. "Look at me."

My eyes won't focus.

"Look at me." He sets me on my feet and takes my face in his hands. Look at me." His voice is like solid ground beneath me. "Focus on me. I'm real, and I'm here with you. Don't look out there, stay here with me. Whatever you hear or see, it's probably not real. We are real."

"We are real." My voice doesn't sound like my own.

It dawns on me as he carries me through the densely packed trees on the winding, narrow path that we're sneaking.

The trees on either side of us sway, slowly at first, then faster until they are leaning violently to one side, then whipping to the other.

I gasp, holding onto him too tightly.

There is no wind. They are moving on their own.

The black bark starts to peel, long sheets falling off the trees like flesh being stripped from bone. Thick, red, oozing sap drips to the ground.

"Canaan!" I panic. "What is—"

"It's not real, Kiah."

"Are you sure?" I stare at it, willing it to transform into something else.

"Close your eyes. Don't look at it." His voice is soft and comforting.

I pinch my eyes closed and focus on the movement of his body. With each step, I rock slightly into his chest.

This is fine.

I'm fine.

"Kiah."

I shake my head and keep my eyes shut tight. That wasn't Canaan.

"Kiah."

"No." I whimper, gripping his shirt in my fists. "Leave me alone."

The voice makes my whole body go rigid, and my skin prickles. It's a whisper on the wind, a long, slow voice full of cruelty.

"Kiah." It hisses, growing louder. It's closer now.

"No! Please!" My body trembles. A chill runs through me. Not over my skin but inside of me. It's as if I will never be warm again.

Canaan stops walking. His grip on me is almost painful.

"Stay with me, Kiah. It's not real." His voice is strained, shaking with the effort.

I open my eyes and look up at him. He's pale, staring straight ahead at the path. Whatever he sees, I don't. But it must be terrifying.

"There's nothing there." I press my face to his.

"I know, but it looks so real."

He stands taller and marches forward, not acknowledging whatever he sees there. The world is unraveling, tilting unnaturally.

Everything hums and moves. We're being watched, preyed on. Every leaf and rock is plotting against us.

"Kiah," the voice calls again. It howls. It's a beast with claws and teeth that rip into my chest each time it speaks my name.

I look behind us, over Canaan's shoulder.

A swirling mass of shadow is moving slowly up the path toward us.

"I think that's real," I whisper.

A smile full of razor-sharp teeth splits the darkness in half.

I'm frozen. I can't speak to warn him as it creeps closer. I shake so hard my bones rattle. A scream is lodged in my throat, stuck there. I can't breathe.

Bony hands stretch toward us. Not two. But multiple. Eight? Ten? They are multiplying so quickly, I can't keep track.

Closer and closer. It's right there.

"Shadowrithe..." I choke, the word coming out in a retch.

He spins around, and it disappears.

"We're almost through to the fortress." He kisses my forehead. "There aren't many good things that can be said for this place, but they won't come here. They wouldn't be able to see past the illusions either."

That calms some of the chaos in my mind. At least none of the terrors here are real.

They're waiting for us on the other side.

I force myself to think of Canaan. Pressing my palms flat against his shoulders, I focus on his movements, the tension in his muscles, and the way his chest moves when he breathes. He is here. He is real.

Nothing else. It's all just tricks.

A shadow flies over us, a white winged owl swooping through the air and landing in a tree. It sits, watching us, perched on a branch that hangs over the path.

I watch Canaan's eyes move up to the branch.

"Do you see the owl, or is it a hallucination?" I whisper.

"I see it." His pace picks up.

"It's staring at us."

"I know."

"Shit."

"Yeah."

We pass beneath the branch. As I turn to look over his shoulder at it behind us, its head spins around, continuing to watch us.

"It's not real, Kiah." The owl says. The owl.

"Oh my god." I panic.

"Oh my god." The owl repeats back in my voice.

I slap my hand over my mouth to hold back a scream. Frustration. Fear. Everything is swirling around at the same time.

"There it is." Canaan's voice pulls me out of the spiraling hole of panic and despair that was dragging me down into it. "We're almost out, Kiah." His steps pick up; he's almost running.

The path narrows into such a thin line that the sharp tips of the branches snap against us as he pushes through.

Just ahead, there is a break in the trees. The pitch black void of this awful place opens up in front of us. It looks ominous and unwelcoming, but he's running toward it like it's our salvation.

As we step out, the air changes. It's still heavy and ice cold, but it's different. I can breathe. No shadows are creeping at the edges of my vision—monsters that might jump out at any second.

The path at our feet is wider now. A long road from the treeline, through a field of tall grass, and up to the edge of the cliffs, where a castle sits. A dark, looming castle with a sinister presence.

"Thank you for keeping me grounded." He pulls me out of my fearful thoughts.

"We made it." I wrap my arms around his neck. "Thank you."

"We're going to have to use the grass as cover. If they don't know that you're gone, they might not be at full guard. Or, because this is most definitely a trap, they are already watching us from that tower." He points to one of three tall stone spirals with lights flickering in the windows as he sets me down.

We crouch and hide in the long, swaying waves of golden grass.

"Why don't we just leave?"

I know we can't leave. This has to end eventually.

His expression softens. The crease between his brows eases as he stares at me. "This has gone on too long already. But–" He stops short, and his grip tightens. "But you are going to leave. You can't be here with me for this part, Kiah."

"What?" The panic that washes over me is immediate. "I can't leave! How am I going to leave?"

"Calais is coming for you. She was right behind me when I came through the portal. You jumping into the water wasn't part of the plan. She should be here soon to meet us."

"But who is going to be with you?"

"Kiah–"

"No! You need backup! I know I'm useless, and it can't be me, but someone has to be here to help you! How many of them are there? You can't go in alone, Canaan!"

A woosh in the wind nearly stops my heart until I see Calais. She drops down beside us with wide eyes. "We have to go right now!"

THIRTY-EIGHT

"FUCK!"

It's chaos. Instantly.

The night was eerily quiet, then it exploded.

Calais grabs me, yanking me into her arms and up into the air. My brain doesn't have time to catch up. Everything is moving.

"Wait!" I scream, but it's too late. "Canaan!"

She dives toward the ground, and I see it, a portal. The ripple in the air is barely visible, but it's there. She's taking me away from here.

Clearly, they planned this. I want to stay, but I know I can't. I won't fight. I won't argue. I'm under no illusions about my abilities here. I'll go quietly and worry myself sick on the other side.

I hold on tight, burying my face in her shoulder.

Down, down, down.

But instead of the woosh of air I'm expecting from passing through, she stops, our bodies jerking roughly.

"Oh, no!" She gasps. By the time I turn to see, it's too late. We're falling.

Our screams mix together, piercing the darkness.

We hit the ground hard, her body shielding mine.

"Take this!" She shoves a knife in my hand and pushes me so hard I fly, head over feet.

It's not until I roll through the dirt that I actually see it. A Shadowrithe has her. He plucked her out of the sky.

I sit, my head frantically moving, searching. "Canaan?"

My scream is muffled.

I don't see him anywhere. How did he disappear so quickly? Darkness pours from the treeline, Shadowrithes spilling out like the wave of a tsunami breaking against land.

No Canaan. No Elion.

I stumble to my feet and try to hide, but there isn't anywhere to go.

Nowhere but up. So I run, sprinting as fast as I can toward the cliff. With the knife in my fist, I crouch and move as quickly as I can. My lungs heave, and my feet protest every step over the jagged rocks sticking out of the dirt.

Up.

"Where are you going in such a hurry?" A voice hisses behind me. "The party is down here."

I stop and turn slowly. The knife feels heavy, like I might not be able to use it if I need to.

Two of them. They look bigger than before.

"You smell delicious." One of them almost smiles, its lips curling over sharp teeth.

I take a step back. I would rather Canaan drink every last drop than for them to have a single taste.

They split, side-stepping, circling me like prey. It's like a choreographed dance, they move with precision and ease–they've practiced this.

I've never seen one this close before. Not with a completely unobstructed view.

They are skin and bones, even in full human form. They still aren't exactly human. The shadowy mist moves with them, a part of them.

Inside their chests, something glows. It's a dull, red light that pulsates.

A heartbeat.

For a moment, my mind wanders back to my life before this. Maybe this is my life flashing before my eyes.

I wonder if Chey is watching from one of the towers. If she will finally see the truth.

Maybe this–this moment of terror and sacrifice– is what saves her.

"Kiah! Run!" A voice booms from somewhere behind me.

A gust of wind forces me to the ground.

A fae woman, a sword in her hand and her wings spread wide, swoops down and turns one of the Shadowrithes into a pile of ash and blood on the ground.

Another fae whips through the sky. He grabs the other Shadowrithe and pulls him up into the air. He has him by the throat, dragging him up until they disappear behind the thick gray clouds.

More and more come, circling the sky, diving into the Shadowrithes with no fear or hesitation.

They're coming through the portal.

Tears drop down my cheeks at the sight of them. Fearless.

They fight like they were born for this moment. Strong. Defiant. Radiant. The Shadowrithes don't fall easily, but the fae are stronger. It's almost beautiful. Like a painting or epic story–good versus evil– standing tall against each other.

If I live through it, I'll remember this one day, this otherworldly thing I witnessed, these fae, standing up for humans when they don't have to.

For every one Shadowrithe they cut down, three more appear, like a snake sprouting heads.

I turn and run, continuing to the fortress. I can't help, so I'll stay out of the way.

The ground trembles, and the sky is full of screeching. They cry out as they die, their bodies falling apart.

I can't stop turning to look. I need to find him, need to see him. Just once to prove he's still standing.

The fae are bleeding, bruised, and battered but winning.

And then I see Canaan.

My chest heaves. He's alive!

Immediately, the joy in finding him is slashed. In the sky, two fae clash.

Not a fae and a Shadowrithe.

Two fae.

One with big black wings and dark hair.

And another with smaller wings. A Rimfae.

A hush falls over everything. I hear my blood pounding.

Canaan looks at Calais, nodding. Suspicion's confirmed.

More and more Rimfae come out of the portal, some fight the Shadowrithes, and others fight against Noctyra.

Watching betrayal in real time is unlike anything I've ever seen. It's palpable.

Every clang of their swords aches in my chest.

Someone grabs me from behind. The world tilts, spinning around me.

I swing my arm, planting the knife. It shrieks, and I scream. I roll, just enough to be able to see it.

I hit it, but it's not turning to ash and blood. I didn't do it right.

"Shit!" I panic, pulling the knife out. The blade cuts across my palm, blood filling my hand immediately. "Oh, fuck."

The Shadowrithe almost looks as if it's glitching, his eyes roll back into his skull, and his body twitches as he reaches for me.

I scream and crawl away until I gain enough distance to stand.

I feel eyes on me. They smell it.

My bare feet hit the ground hard as I run as fast as I can, but with the hill growing progressively steeper, they're coming.

My body jerks back, lifted off my feet like a rag doll.

I start to scream, but a hand slaps over my mouth.

"Delicious." A voice snarls before biting into my neck.

The teeth rip into my skin. It's nothing like when Canaan does it. They pull one large mouthful before I'm yanked away so hard I feel my skin tear away.

I brace but never fall. Instead, arms wrap around me gently. I sigh into his chest.

"I'm going to send you through the portal, Kiah. We're retreating."

I wrap my arms around his neck, pressing a kiss to his sweat-slicked skin. "Be safe. Be safe. Be safe."

"You too." He squeezes me tighter. "I'll be in right after you! As soon as everyone is through."

My heart hurts. I don't want to go through without him. I don't want him to be the last one out. But I know he has to. He's the king.

Elion is such a coward; he's not even here. He sent everyone in his place while he's hiding somewhere.

Ahead of us, several fae and shadowrithes are fighting.

On the ground and in the air.

He stops abruptly. My neck jerks with the force.

"No." He gasps. "Kiah, I'm going to have to drop you through. As soon as you're in, you tell them to close it! Do you hear me?"

"What?" I panic, turning to see a ripple of fire in the sky. "What is that?"

"It's Elion."

"I don't—"

We're thrown violently forward, and something explodes beneath us.

"Canaan!" I scream, slipping as his grip loosens. I can't see his face, we're falling so fast, and I am separating from him, his body moving down below mine. His wings aren't moving.

It's been less than a second, but the drop feels eternal, like time has slowed down to let me watch as we both die.

But then I'm grabbed. And he is too.

I whip my head around to see a blond man with smaller white wings. A Rimefae.

"Get him through the portal." He gives me a curt nod, dropping us onto the ground. "Go!"

I don't even have time to thank him; he's gone.

The portal is overrun. There is no way in. Fae and Shadowrithes are fighting all around it, a wall of them trying to block their retreat.

Blood is running down my neck, a hot, sticky blood flowing stream. I'm lightheaded, and my vision is spotty.

I think I see Elion.

With human weapons.

We make eye contact, and he smiles. And so do I.

Leaning over, I press myself into Canaan, forcing his head back so that my blood will run into his mouth.

He swoops down, coming for me, for us, but Calais and the Rimfae that saved us tackle him out of the sky.

Canaan wakes up almost instantly. Brought back— stronger than before.

Around us, portals are opening everywhere. The air is alive, rippling and churning.

"Run, Kiah." He grabs my shoulders, his fingers digging in. "You have to go!"

I turn, ready to step into a portal, when a shot rings out. I freeze; that sound is too familiar.

It was close.

"Canaan?"

He's standing perfectly still, like a statue surrounded by chaos.

His chest.

"Canaan?" I scream as he stumbles forward slightly.

Someone shot him?

Someone shot him.

My mind can't keep up. My brain splinters like cracked glass.

I'm grabbed, pushed forward hard. Someone is holding my arms, claws scraping my skin. My legs give out, and I fall through the portal as Canaan drops forward onto the ground.

The portal closes. And I'm engulfed in screams.

They're mine. I'm screaming.

I land in water. My body is seizing from the icy cold.

I'm too stunned to move. But I don't sink, the water propels me up, forward.

I land hard on the rocky shore of smooth black stones. A waterfall pounds into the water.

Beside me, a Shadowrithe is bleeding. His giant frame shudders, and he shrieks. He's wounded...dying. The red glow of the heart in his chest is getting dimmer.

And I have an idea.

THIRTY-NINE

MY HANDS ARE MOVING, doing things independently from my brain. I grab the Shadowrithe as it lies beside me, dying.

A wet, gurgling sound leaks from its throat.

Reaching in between the bones, I grab its heart and pull it out.

Pluck it right from his chest.

It's not what I expected. It's not warm or soft. It's like a cold stone.

There is a flash, a moment of sanity, that tells me to drop the heart and run. But I shove it down. For whatever reason, I need to do this. My body knows it, even if my brain doesn't understand.

I bite into the heart, hard. I don't have sharp teeth, but I can get the job done.

His blood fills my mouth. It's acrid and makes me gag. It's nothing like Canaan's blood, but I didn't expect it to be. He is all things good and wonderful.

This Shadowrithe is rotting from the inside out. His blood tastes like death and darkness.

I drop the heart into the water just as it, and his body, begin to disintegrate into a bloody blob. Red sludge stains the water for a moment before the current carries it away.

I gag again, crawling out of the shallow water.

What did I just do?

My hands shake as I search myself for him.

Sitting in the mud on the edge of the river, covered in dirt and blood, I stare at the sun rising in the distance.

A rush of anger courses through me, swirling like a riptide. It's just below the surface of my skin.

It's so hot and violent, I know it's from him. It's his darkness.

Somewhere deep in my chest, in a part that is still me, I feel pity for it. What a terrible and cruel existence. To feel like this, to be this full of agony, it must be awful.

As I stand up, harnessing the disgusting hatred, I see Calais.

For a moment, the briefest second, my heart flutters.

Canaan!

But she's alone.

"Where is he?" I race toward her.

"He—" her face twists in horror. "What happened to you?"

"Where is he, Calais? I saw him! He fell! He..."

"They have him."

"But he's alive, right?"

"We need to go—"

"Calais!" My scream echoes off the water and bounces back at us. "Where is Canaan?"

"I don't know if he's alive or not. When a powerful fae dies, there is usually an event." Her voice trembles as it strikes my heart like a physical blow to my chest. My body sways, and my stomach clenches into a painful ball. "There was a clap of thunder. No rain. No storm. Just a clap of thunder." She looks pale, her hands trembling.

"It wasn't because of him." I shake my head. "He's still alive."

She nods, agreeing, but her expression, her eyes, they speak loudly in the silence. She doesn't believe it.

"I would know if he died."

If I say it enough, it will be true.

My body is held hostage by the Shadowrithes blood. My own hurt is right below the surface, but it's only feeding the rage the blood is pumping through me.

I want to cry and rip someone apart.

"What did you do, Kiah?"

"Um," I don't know how to say it. The words are lodged in my throat.

I know Canaan would be angry if he were here.

If he were here.

"Calais," I shudder, my body trembling. "I'm stronger now. We have to go get him."

"Kiah, you don't know what you've done." She takes a step back, looking at me like I'm some kind of monster. "You don't know what that is going to do to you."

"I don't really care what it does to me as long as I can help him. I need to help him. We can't just leave him there. He didn't die. He's hurt, and we have to go get him." I'm screaming by the end.

"Kiah," she sighs and hangs her head. "We can't just rush in. He wouldn't want us to."

"Well then, let's make a fucking plan!" My fists clench at my sides.

She reaches for me, and I recoil. "Don't."

I can't take it, not right now. I imagine anyone's touch would be like sandpaper to my skin. Unless it was Canaan.

"I need a few minutes."

I stumble away from her, swaying and tripping over my own feet like I'm drunk. I feel slightly drunk, like my body isn't quite under my control.

"I need help," I call out loud, just to anyone or anything that is listening. "Please. You know what will happen if Elion wins!" I want to cry, but I can't. The Shadowrithe is taking my sadness and fear and twisting them.

The sound of the falls slowly fades behind me. With each step, I feel more alone.

It's been a long time since I felt the weight of being here. When he's with me, I can let myself forget how far away from home I am.

It's impossible to ignore now.

Too many emotions swirl and spin inside my head. I'm dizzy and feverish, stumbling through the trees.

"Magic? You've helped me before. What should I do?"

Then I hear it.

It's soft at first, but it grows. I duck down, crouching behind a tree to hide.

Someone is speaking.

But the voice isn't coming from here. It's in my head.

It's Elion.

Closing my eyes, I listen.

"They're at the falls. We'll take Noctyra tonight. Then, when they have nowhere else to run, we'll meet them there. And burn it to the ground." He's laughing. I can imagine the look on his face.

They're coming.

Jumping up, I stagger back toward the water.

"Calais!" I scream, running and falling, then running again.

"Miss?" A paladin steps out onto the path, blocking my way.

"I have to find Calais! Now!" I start to brush past him, but he grabs my arm.

"Are you—" he stops, staring at me with confusion swirling in his eyes.

"Please. It's important! I'm not going to hurt her."

His grip tightens, his gaze searching my face. I'm sure he's never met a human with Shadowrithe blood.

"Look, hold your knife to my throat if you want to. This is life or death!"

He pulls a dagger out of a sheath on his belt. "Fine."

I don't struggle or resist; I let him hold the knife point at my throat as we walk.

"Calais!" I scream as soon as I see her.

"Kiah! What are—" she charges toward us.

"It's fine! There's no time! Elion is coming for Noctyra tonight while everyone is here! He's going to take it!"

"How could you possibly know that?" The paladin is still suspicious.

"The blood!" I'm almost bouncing in place. My skin feels like it's bursting, and everything is going to spill out. "Aren't they connected? Elion spoke to a Shadowrithe, and I heard it through the magic!"

"How do you know that?"

"Canaan brought me to the well. He said they were all connected!"

Her eyes flash with surprise, but she quickly changes her expression. "Gather the paladins. Half will stay here, and the other half will go back to Noctyra. Divide anyone willing to fight. We're not losing our home." She barks the order, and he turns, running back to follow it.

She grabs me, her arms wrapping around me too tightly.

"Stay with me so you can tell me right away if you hear anything else."

When she pulls back, I can feel her fear. She looks at me, waiting, her eyes asking the question she's not speaking out loud.

"He didn't mention Canaan." I have to choke the words out. "But he's still alive, Calais. I can feel it."

FORTY

I CAN'T FEEL HIM.

Not at all.

What I feel is the undying hope that he will send me a sign. He can't die.

He's too... alive. Someone so big and strong can't die.

I know from experience that Elion can shield us from the bond. That's what this is. That's all.

He's alive. I just can't feel him.

It probably didn't help our connection that I drank from that Shadowrithe. There are so many things clouding it. That's all.

Standing under the spray of the shower, I realize suddenly that the water is cold and I'm trembling.

It's not just a shower. It's his shower. His bedroom.

I hear him, like he's just outside the door. His voice hangs in the air here.

I keep seeing his face. It's just the little things first, like the gold in his eyes, or the dimple on his cheek when he smiles. His laugh, low and steady with a little rasp in it.

He's not dead.

Outside of this room, they're preparing for war.

Inside, I'm falling apart.

I won't let Calais see it. She doesn't need this right now. There is enough on her plate.

But when I'm alone, I'm drowning.

Each minute that passes feels like a lifetime.

Standing here in his room, I stare at the bed. This is a slow implosion, my body being pulled in on itself. It's not a strike of lightning, it's like poison, slowly seeping.

A dull weight presses in on my chest, building with each painful breath.

Pulling on clothes, I walk out into the hallway. I can't be in here for even one more second. I move through the crowds. The fortress is overrun with people. But I'm alone.

It's like a scene from a movie, the world tilting around me. The frame stretches as I stand perfectly still while chaos bends all around me.

The fact that any of them is doing anything, that anyone can function without knowing... It's cruel. It's disgusting. Everyone should be as affected as I am by the not knowing. Where is he? Is his heart still beating?

I step into the dining room, the makeshift war room. Calais is bent over a map the size of the table, talking strategy.

She looks up when I come in, and our eyes meet.

The depth of sorrow in her tears me apart, but it also fortifies me. She's being strong because there isn't anything else to do. I have to do the same. Push it down and force myself forward. Because that's the only way to bring him home.

"Noctyra is locked down. It looks empty. When they try to breach the court, they will realize their mistake." She stares at the map.

"And as soon as they enter, trapping themselves inside, we will push in from here." The paladine from earlier points.

"Yes. Go."

He nods, and the room clears out. Hundreds suddenly vanished.

"I know I'm useless here. But is there anything I can do?" I'm begging. Please, give me a task. I'll scrub toilets. Anything to keep my mind from folding in on itself.

She gives me a strange look. Almost like she doesn't want to say whatever she's about to. "Blood."

"Take as much as you need."

Take all of it.

"In the kitchen, there is a collector. Her name is Simya. Go see her." She places her hands on my shoulder. "We have to follow the steps, Kiah. One obstacle, then the next. If we rush, we lose. If we go out of order, we lose. This is how it must be done."

"I know." My lips tremble. "But I want to rush in and find him."

"So do I. But without him here, someone has to lead the way he would. This is what he would do. When they took you to the fortress, he rallied and went in with a plan. We have to do the same for him."

I nod, somehow feeling better. We're making him proud.

I run down the hallway, through the crowds of people. I'm in awe of them. Each and every one. There is no fear on their faces, no nervous energy in the room. They are steadfast and ready.

Elion has no idea what's waiting for him.

It gives me a sinister satisfaction. I want him dragged down the hallway by his hair. I want him on his knees, begging, pleading, crying.

I hope I live long enough to see him lose. But not just lose, I want him annihilated. It's the only outcome I'll accept. He deserves as much pain and suffering as he's given out.

I want the world pulled out from under his feet.

I want...holy shit.

I'm standing in the middle of the kitchen, trembling. I have no idea how I got there; I don't remember.

My fists are clenched so tightly that my nails have broken into the skin of my palms.

"Are you alright?" A woman with big dark wings and kind eyes is the only one to approach me. Everyone else is just staring.

"I'm looking for Simya."

"You found her."

"Take as much blood from me as you can." I'm not sure the etiquette around this, and right now, I don't really care. Manners and politeness can resume when Canaan is here.

She looks at me warily. I don't blame her. I probably wouldn't trust me either.

"Calais sent me. I want to help, and it's the only way I can."

She still looks suspicious, but she leads me to the counter, the same counter I sat on while he made me a grilled cheese.

Fuck. If they didn't think I was crazy before, they do now.

My chest heaves, a garbled sob ripping through me. It takes me completely by surprise. A tidal wave that I didn't see coming. It dragged me out to sea, pulling me into a rip current that I can't escape from.

I can't see or hear anything. The pounding of my blood, that's it. I'm thrashed into the depths, slammed into the sand, rolling and tumbling head over feet.

I want to scream, but I can't make a sound. All the pain is locked in my throat.

Warm hands take me, wrapping me tightly in someone's arms. "Breathe, Kiah. We're going to win this."

I know we are. That's not what I'm afraid of. "Why can't I feel him?" I grab her shoulders. "I should be able to. But there's nothing there!"

The tears that roll down my face are like acid; they burn hot until they drip off my trembling chin.

"Live for him now, Kiah." She holds me hard, like I need to be held down. "Honor him or save him, either way, we have to continue, or it was for nothing."

"Ok." I hiccup. "Leave just enough blood for him."

FORTY-ONE

I'M NOT a military strategic genius, but I think I understand the plan.

Half of the paladines are waiting at Noctyra. The other half are here, placed in different locations to attack from all sides if Elion is stupid enough to try to come here. We have the advantage of being prepared.

I repeat it over and over again, whenever the fear starts to creep up my spine.

They are prepared for this.

Sitting here in the corner by myself, I watch them. My useless hands tremble with nothing left to do. They won't let me give any more blood. That was the one thing I could offer.

So, I'm sitting, staring. Just noticing the little details. Not because they are particularly important, but I feel like someone should. Before everything is ripped apart, someone should pay attention. They are so intricate. Each and every one of them has a life, a story.

The woman in front of me has her hair done in at least a hundred tiny braids. They are long, down to her waist, and have silver beads braided into them. Two beads per braid. When she moves, they make a soft, metallic sound. It's beautiful.

The man beside her has a set of rings on his fingers that join together to look like flames. They flicker in the light each time he flexes his fingers.

Another woman has little gold chains dangling from her wings like fringe; they twinkle like crystals.

They are about to go out and fight. Some of them, the people so full of life, standing right in front of me, might not make it back. They are about to bleed for something greater than any one of us. Maybe it's useless, but someone should notice the details. And since I'm completely and utterly worthless here, I take it upon myself. It's the only thing I can offer.

Looking at them helps to keep my mind in a permanent state of panic. If I keep busy, I can almost breathe.

I'm exhausted. The adrenaline I felt before has worn off, leaving me struggling to keep my eyes open.

I don't deserve sleep.

Not knowing where he is, but knowing that he's hurt, is ripping at my sanity. I'm frayed at the edges. He is out there somewhere, in god knows what condition. And I'm here, sleepy and warm.

Maybe if I had been different. If I were stronger and faster, if I could fight back.

Pressing my fingers into my temples, I push hard. The headache that has settled there is pulsating behind my eyes. Too much crying and thinking.

The room hums around me, soft conversations happening all around.

When Calais comes into the room, she's wearing the red wedding dress again. But it's different now, it's ripped at the hem, shortened. She has a breastplate over the lace and beadwork on the bodice.

It's too big for her.

It was his.

I just know it was. It looks like it was made for him.

The room goes silent as she stands in the center.

"He thinks we're weak." Her voice rings like a bell.

No one moves. The silence is palpable now.

"He thinks that we will scatter without Canaan. That we'll crawl into the dark and lick our wounds." Her gaze sweeps across the room.

I can't look away.

"We have his blood in us. Canaan isn't gone. He's right here." Her hand hovers over her heart. "His blood runs through our veins. We aren't going to crawl away and hide. Noctyra won't fall. He can't have it."

"We will avenge him." Someone's voice calls out, quiet and reverent.

"Canaan." Everyone follows a low rumble.

No.

Their voices join together in a chant that shakes the ground.

I feel my feet hitting the floor, my body trembling. No. No. No.

"No," I whisper, my head shaking frantically. "Stop."

They can't hear me. They keep repeating his name like he is already fucking dead.

"Don't give up on him yet." My voice is lost in the sound.

I won't stay and listen to it. This is not his funeral. They aren't going out to avenge his death.

He's alive. This is a rescue mission.

I stumble out into the hallway, leaning on the wall so that I don't fall. My stomach twists. Closing my eyes, I try to picture him, his eyes, his smile, something real and warm to hold onto, but all I see is the way he fell.

Every beat of my heart feels hollow.

I press my back into the wall as they flood the hallway.

Their footsteps hit the ground in perfect harmony, one then the other.

Archers and swordsmen walk past in rows.

How did I end up here? I've fallen through the cracks in the world into another time.

I don't belong here. Yet, I've become so completely intertwined in this fight. It feels like it's mine. I have stakes in this, too.

I hope my blood is enough.

When the endless sea of emotionless fae finally passes through the corridor, Calais stops beside me.

We don't speak, not at first. The silent conversation between us speaks for us.

"I know what you think—" she starts.

"He's alive." The words scrape from my throat. "He's alive, Calais. I know it's not logical, but my heart knows it."

She nods, "More unbelievable things have come to pass."

"Be safe." My eyes meet hers, the gravity of this pressing me into the wall hard.

"You too."

Her shoes click against the ground as she walks, echoing in the vast emptiness.

"Calais! Wait!"

I run after her, my feet moving before my brain can catch up.

I throw my arms around her, squeezing her too tightly.

For a second, she's motionless, but she wraps her arms around me too.

"Open a portal for me." I pull away from the hug, holding her shoulders.

"Kiah," she sighs.

"If they are here, I'll be fine. Please. Let me go." I'll get down on my knees and beg if I have to. "Don't make me sit here uselessly while you're all gone."

Even as she nods her head, I can see that she doesn't want to.

"Come here." She steps into the small library, and my breath catches.

This room. I should have seen it all here. But I didn't want to.

All the answers were in that book, illustrated in graphic detail, but I ignored them— too stupid and naive to see the truth.

Her eyes flutter closed, and she whispers something ancient into the air. It ripples and splits.

"Be safe." She whispers.

I can't speak, so I just nod.

Her chin trembles, and her fingers bite into my arm. "He tried the fight the bond."

"I know."

"No," she shakes her head. "You don't understand. He wanted you before the blood. Drinking from each other only made it stronger." She swallows hard, straightening her shoulders. "He didn't want you to be in the middle of this. He would have denied himself to spare you."

"I know. But I'm glad he didn't."

Her eyes soften, only slightly. "If he's still alive, it's because he's hanging on for you." She walks away, leaving me in the library alone.

I take a breath and step through, channeling his brave spirit. Canaan would do it for me. He did. Now it is my turn, and I'm not going to let him down.

FORTY-TWO

I STEP through the ripple in the air, and the sensation of falling hits me.

I'm not on my feet anymore. There is nothing solid anywhere.

A scream rips from my throat as I plummet through the air. I never hit the ground. There is no end. But suddenly, I stop. My body jerks hard against some invisible restraints.

When the sensation of falling leaves me, I realize that it was hiding the truth. I couldn't feel it within the terror, but now that my heartbeat is returning to normal, it's there below the surface.

I let out a shuddering breath. I know what I have to do, I just hope I'm strong enough to do it.

"Elion." I hold my head up, my voice ringing out in the dark.

"Hello, love." He chuckles, amused by my distress, no doubt.

"What is this? Why am I here?" I squint, searching for something, anything that I can use.

For a moment, there is silence. Just a beat, but the air shifts.

"What is that?" He's suddenly in front of me.

"What?" I tilt my head, pretending that I have no idea what he's talking about.

"What is it, Kiah?"

"Scared?" I can't help the wide smile that splits my face.

He blinks, trying to figure it out before speaking. "What did you do?"

"Where is Canaan?" I'm not going to just roll over and answer his questions.

"Ah, Canaan. He put up a fight, didn't he?" He smirks, but I can still see the shifty movement of his eyes. "A valiant effort to be sure."

"Where is he?"

"He's gone, Kiah."

"Bullshit." I strain against whatever is holding me motionless.

The way he's staring at me, it's clear that he feels the Shadowrithe blood. If I weren't so completely frantic to find him, I would be pleased.

"Take me to him."

"Is that why you're here?" He licks his elongated teeth. "Come to collect his remains."

"Fuck you, Elion. He's not fucking dead." I hope that if I press hard enough and with enough conviction, he'll tell me what I want to hear.

"Tell me, Kiah," he leans in close enough for his breath to fan across my face. "What are you doing here?"

"You brought me here. How should I know?"

"But you're back in the human realm. I've had feelers out, waiting for you. And imagine my surprise when I felt you tugging at the bond again."

"Don't call it a bond." I grit my teeth. If he gets close enough, I'm going to fucking bite him. Any part of him that I can reach is going between my teeth.

"But that's exactly what it is, darling."

"No." I shake my head. "It's not. What Canaan and I have is a bond. What we have is deception. You forced a connection with me. It's not a bond."

He hums, circling me.

"You can't have a bond like we do. Rimfae aren't capable."

I see the words land. They hit him like physical blows, and he can't hold back the violent outburst.

"You don't know anything about Rimfae. Don't speak about things you don't understand, Kiah."

"What's to understand, Elion? You are bloodthirsty and cruel. You used humans. You're selfish."

He lunges forward, grabbing my arms, wrapping his hands around them with ease. "What makes you think bonding with humans is such a gift?"

"Your reaction." I bite back. "You want it so bad, you can't stand it."

Feeling his skin against mine makes my stomach roll. I can't believe there was I time I wanted his touch.

"You think you're so clever, don't you?"

"I do, actually." I grin despite the fear wrapping around my lungs and squeezing.

"I'm glad I found Cheyenne first." He cocks his head in that way that used to make me feel fluttery, but now it only adds to the sickness. "She's so sweet and innocent. Did you know innocent blood not only tastes better, but it's also more powerful."

"Seems almost cruel."

"Magic is cruel, Kiah. Remember that. It's not a beautiful fantasy, not like your little books portray it. Magic is a cunning beast that takes more than it gives."

"Maybe the magic knows when you're using it for the wrong reasons. No one likes to be used, Elion."

"What did you do to yourself, Kiah?" He leans in, running the tip of his nose up my cheek. "You smell different."

"You don't recognize it?" I use every ounce of control I can muster to keep my voice and breathing even.

"No." He breathes again. "It's not even familiar."

"It should be."

He steps back, putting just enough space between us to look into my eyes. "What did you do?" It's a bit more urgent this time. His patience is wearing thin.

"Why are you here with me?"

"What's more important than you, darling?"

"Where is Canaan?"

"Poor Canaan." He pouts, mocking him even now.

"When did you realize that you hate him? Was it after he broke his promise?" I watch his eyes. They flicker with something unreadable; it's dark and murky.

"He–"

"It was before that, wasn't it. You've always been jealous of him. It wasn't even a hard decision, was it? You liked doing it. For once in your life, you felt more powerful than him."

"You don't know what you're talking about."

"Don't I. I know you both... intimately." I push my chest forward. "I think I'm the best person to judge this."

"Fuck you, Kiah." He grits his teeth.

"You should go, Elion."

His eyes narrow. "What do you know?"

I don't want to give away too much. I can't be certain from here that the Shadowrithes have tried to take Noctyra. I don't want to give him as much as a hint.

"I know that on top of being a traitor and a betrayer, you're a coward." I smile, letting all the rage and hatred pour out of me. "You are here, with me, because you're afraid to be out there."

He shouts, pushing me hard as he releases me from his grip. I stumble back, falling onto a hard, rocky surface.

Jerking my head up, I search for him, but I'm alone. Not in the dark abyss, but in a cold, stone hallway.

I jump to my feet and sprint toward a light at the end of the hall.

Steeping into the light, I close my eyes, listening.

"Magic. I'm sure you're sick of me." I whisper. "I don't know if you heard that. I'm not sure how that works. But I don't think you are what he says you are. Please, help me. Lead me. Guide my feet."

The candles hanging in the sconces that light the hallway flicker, all of them at once. Then, the candles on the left flicker.

"Left?" I run down the corridor, listening and watching.

The candles flicker, leading me through this maze. I don't stop sprinting until I reach an open-air hallway that overlooks a courtyard.

My feet stumble against the stones, and I gasp. In a window, across from me, I see her.

"Cheyenne!"

FORTY-THREE

I CAN'T GET THERE FAST ENOUGH. The air presses against me like running through water. I push forward but make no progress.

My feet hit the ground hard, each step sending a burst of pain up through my ankles. I don't care.

"Cheyenne!" I scream again, but the sound is lost in the vastness of this place.

I push open doors as I pass them.

"Which one is it?" I open one door after the next, looking into the darkness.

When I finally see a door with light creeping out from the crack. I push it open and run inside.

"No!" I scream, and she freezes.

Barefooted and bruised, she's standing on the wrought iron window guards outside of her room. The rugged coastline stretches out beneath her. The wind howls outside, whipping the curtains into a frenzy.

It looks like she'll be blown over any second.

"Kiah?" She was already crying, but now she's sobbing.

"What are you doing? Get down!"

"How could I have been so wrong about him, Kiah?" She chokes out between wails.

"Get down, and we'll talk about it."

"No." She shakes her head, snot, drool, and tears mix to drip down her face.

"Listen," I say so much more harshly than I mean to. "This isn't fucking happening, Chey." The anger inside me shakes and rattles. "Like hell. Get your fucking ass down from there right fucking now. We don't have time for this shit!"

It's not tactful or empathetic, but I don't have the capacity for either.

I'm at my wits' end.

She blinks, a few tears dripping from her chin as she stares at me with wide eyes.

"He has Canaan. Help me find him."

She steps down from the ledge.

"I'm sorry for yelling at you." I cross the room and pull her into my arms. She looks small, smaller than I've ever seen her. Her eyes are bloodshot with dark, puffy circles beneath them. Her skin is pale and littered with purple bruises.

The biggest change is in her eyes. She's seen things since the last time we were together. We both have. But hers revealed truths that I already knew.

She hiccups. "I'm sorry for being so unbelievably stupid and blind." She fists my shirt tightly and cries into my shoulder.

"He's tricky. It's not your fault."

"You warned me."

I did...

"He bedazzled you."

"I saw the battle. I was watching from the tower. When I asked him to save you..." her voice fades. "I begged him, Kiah. He said it was time to make a choice. To show where my loyalty lies."

I don't know what to say. None of this surprises me. But I can see how badly she's hurting.

Grabbing her shoulders, I force her up, "Let's go make him pay for it, Chey."

She looks unsure, unsteady.

"Come with me. Help me find Canaan. We aren't magic. We aren't fae. We can't fly. But we're not nothing. Stand up to him. Don't let him crush you."

She nods slowly, like the words are taking their time to sink in.

"Ok."

"He doesn't get to do this. Not to us, not to Canaan. Not to anyone." I feel rage simmering beneath my skin again.

The Shadowrithe blood is like a drug that hits me out of nowhere. Sometimes, I feel mostly like myself. Other times, I don't recognize a single feeling. The rage is the hardest to swallow. It's all-consuming. It starts in my stomach and rises up my throat, burning like bile. Then I feel it burning everywhere. My body trembles under the weight of it.

It takes over. I can't feel anything beyond it.

If Elion were standing in front of me, I would go for his throat.

My fingernails ache with the longing to break into his skin.

I see red. Not just the color itself, but blood, hot, fresh, blood pooling in puddles on the ground.

I've never wanted violence like I want it right now.

I know it's not me, but it's terrifying.

She's looking at me with fear and concern in her red-rimmed eyes. She doesn't know what happened, what I did, but she must sense the difference. There is darkness in me now.

I hold my trembling hand out to her.

She hesitates, looking at the open window with a faraway gaze.

"You didn't deserve it." My voice is hoarse. "Whatever you think, don't let that sink in. You didn't deserve his lies and manipulation."

She slips her hand into mine. "I don't see a way that two humans can possibly help. But if you want to try, so do I."

I tighten my hold on her as we march into the hallway together.

"I asked the magic for help, and it led me to you."

"Really?" A little bit of little shines in her eyes, more like the girl I grew up with.

"Yeah. I guess it wanted me to save you."

She squeezes my fingers, the ghost of a small smile on her lips.

As we creep through the desolate hallways, I tell her about the flickering flames that led me straight to her.

Anything to keep all the other thoughts swarming my brain in the background.

Blood. Revenge. Death.

In no particular order. I want them all.

"What are we looking for?" She whispers.

"I'm not sure. I keep hoping that I'll know it when I see it." It's not inspiring, but it's all I have. The truth.

She stops walking, her gaze fixed on the floor as she chews the inside of her cheek.

"Do you know where he is?"

"No, but I heard something." She looks physically afraid to tell me.

"What?" I take a step toward her, my shoulders hunching menacingly.

"I don't know if it was even him." She cowers slightly. "There was a sound...a scream."

"A scream?"

"It was more than a scream. It was..." her eyes well up again. "It was the worst thing I ever heard."

My blood runs cold. "What do you mean?" I feel a kind of desperation I can't explain. It's fear-laced with despair. "What was it?"

"It was like someone experiencing the worst pain. Then there was a clap of thunder so loud and close it shook this place." She shudders. "I think it was down—" she goes pale.

"Down? Where?"

"In the dungeons."

"Of course, this place has dungeons. Can you get to them?"

She trembles almost violently, her body convulsing under the weight of the memory, "Yes."

"Let's go." I square my shoulders. I'm sure we'll find him there. It's an unshakable certainty.

We move, creeping through the hallways. The fortress goes down, down, down forever. After each staircase, there is another. We'll never reach the bottom.

The floor is wet and uneven, a path etched into stone. It's more like a cave now than a hallway.

"We're close." She whispers, a white puff of breath hanging in the air.

FORTY-FOUR

THE CANDLES, which have been largely behaving as normal candles since they led me to Cheyenne's room, suddenly change.

There is no breeze here. Just freezing cold, stagnant air. But they flicker.

"Did you see that?" She whispers, stopping midstep.

"Yes." My legs wobble.

We stand completely frozen, staring at the candles, our fingers intertwined.

"There." She breathes. "They did it again."

I creep forward, my heart pounding in my chest.

"I can hear your heart beating." A wet, gurgling voice laughs. "You can't hide yourself from me."

Cheyenne's eyes go wide, and she gestures for me to wait as she steps forward.

She comes around the corner, turning to face him.

My mouth hangs open. She doesn't even look afraid.

"I'm lost. Elion told me to meet him at the dock, but I can't find it."

"You're a long way from the docks, love." He chuckles, his laughter echoing off the walls.

"Can you take me there? If I'm not there, he will leave without me!" She sounds absolutely frantic. Her voice trembles with desperation that is so believable I almost question it. "Please!"

"I'm not just standing around." He growls, his tone shifting noticeably from amusement at her expense to irritation. "I'm not your errand boy."

"I know. Please. If you can, please help me. I'll tell Elion that you did."

He groans loudly. "Fuck. Come on. Keep up, or you'll be left behind."

"Thank you so much!" I hear her voice bouncing away.

I wait, listening to the sound of their footsteps disappearing.

Then I move.

I creep around the corner to find a wooden door, just like the one in the room I was kept in. The wood is warped and swollen with water.

Without thinking, I grab the handle and push it open. It gives immediately.

That should have been my first sign to panic, but I rush inside, squinting in the dark. Nothing here is welcoming. This should be locked.

"Canaan?" I whisper into the silence. The sound is swallowed immediately.

High on the wall, a tiny sliver of light peeks through a barred window. It's no bigger than a single brick.

The beam of light that it casts onto the ground is just big enough to make out something on the floor.

"Canaan?" I don't hesitate, running toward him and dropping to my knees.

But it's not Canaan.

Not all of him, anyway.

The scream that rips at my throat is like my vocal cords being scraped against a gravel road. I stumble backward, my hands scratching against the rough stone floor.

It's...

My stomach lurches, and I throw up before I can stop it. The horror of it is too much. Bile burns all the way up.

A pulsating thump settles in right behind my eyes.

It's just his wings.

"Where is the rest of him?"

I would know them anywhere. They're his. Without question.

For a second, I don't understand. The pieces are set in front of me, but I can't connect them. His wings. But not him.

When my brain switches from complete shock to survival instincts, my eyes sweep the room again. He's not here.

The stone beneath them is black and wet, a pool of sticky blood left behind.

My vision blurs at the edges. He's everywhere here. I can feel him in the rough stone, in the blood, in the air, in the tiny strip of light.

"Oh, god, Canaan." I can't pick myself up from the floor. "What did they do to you?" I run my fingers over the wings. "What did they do?" The words barely make it out.

I crawl closer, my knees pressed into the cold stone.

They're beautiful, even now, the light touches them softly, like it knows what they are.

I can almost hear him screaming.

She said it was the worst sound she ever heard. A sound my mind conjures up echoes in my skull, forcing me to hear it.

His face, etched with pain, plays in my mind on an unending loop. I can't stop seeing it.

"Canaan..." I whisper his name in the dark.

I don't know what to do.

He's gone.

Not just missing. Gone.

I can't leave. Walking out of this place is like leaving him here.

As gently as I can, I pull one of the wings up onto my lap. Rocking back and forth, I hold it against me.

If I can hold onto it tight enough, I can trick my mind into believing he's still here.

"Come back to me." I press my face into them, folding my body into his blood. "Don't go."

The air is too heavy to breathe. I gasp and choke, but my lungs never fill.

I can taste it, like ash on my tongue. My chest aches, a slow, deliberate racking, like someone has their hands inside and is prying me open, bones snap, and my heart is shredded. The crack isn't neat, it's a jagged, splintered edge.

He saved me so many times, and I couldn't save him.

I call his name in the dark, over and over again.

He never answers.

I feel the hope die inside of me, the exact moment the flame was extinguished.

"Kiah?" The door creaks behind me.

Her voice is small, like a whisper in the distance.

I don't respond. I can't.

"Oh my god." I hear her retch, the same way I did.

There is no comfort in her presence. There is no comfort left in the world.

She stumbles forward, kneeling down beside me.

"Kiah..." her voice fades.

"I can't leave him, Chey. I can't leave him here." I sob, choking on the words. "I didn't save him."

That man... the strong, gentle king who stood at the gates and held back the hordes can't be left here in pieces.

"Then we'll bring him." She slides forward, taking the other wing. "We'll bring him home."

FORTY-FIVE

SWEAT DRIPS down the side of my face and neck. The back of my shirt is soaked and stuck to my skin.

Every step hurts, my arms burn, and my legs wobble with the effort.

But I won't leave him behind.

Up flights of stairs and through long, dim hallways that stretch on without end, I pull his wing with me. Chey leans on me, our shoulders pressed together as she struggles beside me. I can't tell who is supporting who; we just lean, two shattered things trying to keep from falling apart completely.

It smells like blood, his blood. I'm covered in it. I'm glad for it. In a sick way that burns in the back of my mind, it feels like he's watching out for me. He's protecting me, shielding me.

I earn every inch, moving at a glacial pace.

It doesn't bother me, though. The pain is welcomed.

He deserves this much effort; he's worth it.

I feel outside of my own body. I'm floating above, watching as I cry and stagger. My body aches and protests, but I hardly feel it. The physical pain is so much less acute than the broken pieces of my heart. A hollow, gnawing hole that has been punched in my chest, the place where he used to be.

I'm in a fog. A blinding confusion that muffles the world.

I know where we are. There is still danger here. But I can't find it in me to care.

Chey says something, but I can't make out the words. The thump of my heartbeat drowns her out, slow and aching; it's as if the world is collapsing around me, one pulse at a time.

We reach yet another staircase, and my knees almost buckle.

The wing slips from my grasp, and I panic, dropping to the ground to catch it against my chest. A sound tears from my chest, a sob, an animal howling.

His wing brushes my face, cold and stiff now.

I remember the last time I touched them. His arms were around me. He was whispering softly in my ear.

Where is he? I want to see his face one more time. Even without life and warmth, I need it.

Chey kneels down beside me, her chest heaving. Her hands shake as she touches my shoulder. "We have to keep moving, Kiah." Her voice is barely a hoarse whisper. "We can't get caught here."

I nod, but there is no meaning to it. I'm motionless inside. The world is continuing to move, to spin, to fight. There is a battle going on right now. But I'm stuck here, holding his wing.

She stands first, determination set in her eyes. "Come on."

I follow her, pushing forward. The walls are narrow, closing in on us. The candlesticks flicker as we pass them.

When we finally reach the portal, the ripple in the air before us, I feel trapped.

I know I need to keep moving, but I don't want to leave the rest of him here. This might be my only chance to see him.

"Kiah." She nudges me forward. "Go."

"But..." My throat burns with the urge to sob. "I want all of him."

"I know." She sniffs. "But we have to go."

The magic hums, mocking me. It should have kept him safe. It should have intervened somehow. It's cruel. Elion told me that.

I believe him now.

I step through, the library greeting us in silence.

My cheeks and eyes burn, the constant stream of tears leaving me swollen and sensitive to the bright lights.

The Falls are quiet. There is no battle here.

The hallways are still.

"Where is everyone?" She whispers.

"Noctyra." I grit my teeth and lead her through the hallways toward his bedroom. I can't think of any other place to go.

Up ahead of us, someone steps into the halfway. He's battle-worn and bloody. The sight of us stops him in his tracks.

"Who–" a shudder runs through him as he stares at the wings.

The sight of him draws something from deep inside of me; it rises up from the pit of my stomach, burning like fire, growing until it bursts out of me.

Magic, the very magic I have grown to hate, swells inside of me. I can feel it. Like a parasite. It wiggles and moves, alive and demanding.

"I need to go to the well!" I step toward him.

His eyes snap away from the wings to meet mine. "What?"

"I don't know." I shrug. "I can't explain it. I just have to. I'm compelled. How can I get there from here?"

His brows furrow as he seems to be thinking about it. I'm covered in blood and sweat, carrying the wings of his king; it's probably a lot to digest.

"Come with me." He turns but stops. The look in his eyes when he turns around again makes the ground fall out from beneath my feet. "I'll take that for you."

"No." I grip it tighter, holding it like a precious treasure. "I have to do this."

The golden pattern that once was woven through them like a glinting piece of thread is gone now. They are dull and hard. It's smaller somehow, still larger than me, but the grandeur is gone. They are faded and withered as if it happened long ago.

He nods, his lips tugging into a deep frown.

We move slowly, my body ready to collapse.

At some point, he took the other wing from Cheyenne. She's walking carefully behind me, and her arms reach out to steady me each time I stumble.

"We're going the long way around." It dawns on me suddenly. "Why?"

"There are injured fae in the main hall. I don't want them to see." He swallows hard.

I roll my lips into my mouth, trying to hold the sob in, but it doesn't work. My body sways under the weight of everything, grinding me down until I can't stand anymore.

I slide down onto the ground, holding the wing like a lifeline.

"I need to give these to the well." I sob. "I have to return him to the magic." The words spill out. I don't even know what I'm saying.

His eyes are wide with horror. "Come. I'll bring you to the bridge. Someone will have to fly you there. It's the fastest way."

He grabs the wing, holding it gently.

I don't argue with him. Dragging myself to my feet, the three of us move quietly through the black marble hallways. The beauty of this place feels wrong. Without him here, it should be tainted, it should be crumbling.

A strange hatred tugs in my chest. I hate this place.

I hate everything that has ever happened to me here.

The cruelty of knowing him and losing him is enough to crush me.

We step out into a courtyard, and six fae that I've never met look up. They look at me, covered in blood, and at the wings.

There is a gasp, I can see their hearts breaking in their expression, the realization hitting them, and then their eyes are full of suffering.

"Who will volunteer to take them to The Well?"

"I will." All of them speak at once. They are bloody, one of them has an oozing bandage around his torso, and another is missing an eye. But they all stand, ready to bring us.

"I'll carry you, Kiah." One of the men steps toward me. I nod, swallowing down a sob. "I'm Eamon."

"Thank you for taking me."

"It is my honor."

He is a Rimfae. Light hair and smaller, white wings. For a moment, just a second in time, fear creeps up my spine. Can I trust him?

But the doubts don't last. I don't have the capacity for them.

Maybe he'll betray me. Or he won't. At this point, it doesn't feel like it matters.

Someone takes Cheyenne, and two of them gently take the wings.

We are a caravan of misery.

I can't stop crying. Eamon seems nice enough, but this isn't right.

They lost their king. I lost my Canaan.

FORTY-SIX

TIME ISN'T MOVING; we fly over the bridge and into the clouds. I feel the force of motion, but the minutes are endless. We're in a continuous loop, not making any progress. The wind is restless, blowing hard against us, almost pushing us back.

Eventually, the Ebonstream cuts through the land below us.

Seeing it now does nothing to me. I have no urge to dive in, no draw or pull. It's as if the water isn't there.

Against my better judgment and any self-preservation instincts I have, I peek over his shoulder at the two escorting his wings.

A retaliation hits me and I gasp, slap
ping my hand over my mouth.

"What is it?" He whips around, his eyes jerking quickly over the horizon.

I shake my head; it's all I can do to keep from sobbing. If I moved my hand or tried to speak, I would weep.

This is their last flight. His wings will never fly again.

Will it be like this forever? Will I be bombarded with painful, awful, heartbreaking thoughts for the rest of my life? Moments like this, where there is peace and beauty, will they always be tainted by pain?

It's only the first day, but I'm in a hole that I don't see myself ever coming out of. There is no sunlight down here.

This gaping wound and hollow feeling in my chest is growing by the second.

There is no physical wound, but I'm bleeding out...

I force myself to look again, because someone should pay attention to it. They look different in the fading sunlight. Less dead.

My skin prickles. I can't control my mind. Every terrible thing I can think of keeps popping into my head.

Forcing my eyes closed, I shield myself against his shoulder. I don't want to see anymore. And I don't want anyone to see me.

The wreckage in my mind doesn't rest, but at least with my eyes closed, I can't see the worried look on Cheyenne's face.

I'm tired, but I can't sleep. Every time I start to drift, I'm yanked out of it by the sensation of falling. I'm never falling, but I jerk back, in a full panic, each time.

"We're close." He is gentle with me, speaking softly like I'm a frightened animal.

Whenever I look up at him, the sorrow in his eyes is overwhelming.

My stomach twists. Every inch closer to the well feels like peeling away a layer of myself.

When we break through the clouds, the ground below is strange; it's changed.

The trees lean in a way they didn't when we walked through this forest together. IT's as if they are bowing. As if they can sense what's coming.

The Ebonestream looks different up close; the water seems less like melted silver and more like molten gold.

"What happened to it?"

"Everything feels his wings. The sky, the water, the trees." He swallows hard.

Of course they do.

We land close to the well. On the edge of the little group of trees surrounding it. The air hums, the magic's pulse seems to be faster.

Eamon steps forward first, then they bring the wings forward.

Cheyenne wraps her arm around me, and we walk behind them. I want to call after him to tell him to take the wings back. I changed my mind. But no sound will come out. I can't scream or stop this. But I can't. So I just follow behind his wings in this awful funeral procession.

The well sits, the same as before, but it looks more ominous now.

Eamons turns to me, his eyes reflecting the pain I feel. "It's time."

The words rip through me, and I stumble, my feet simply stopping.

He doesn't try to pull me forward or hurry me along. He just waits.

The escorts place the wings on the edge of the well. They step back and bow, a deep, low, reverent action. Then they retreat.

It's just us now, the wings, the well, and me.

I kneel down in front of them. My hands tremble as I touch them. They're cold and empty, like marble.

I don't know what will happen when the wings hit the magic waiting below, but I hope the world opens up and swallows me whole.

I open my mouth, desperate to send them off with something more than a sob, but I can't manage it.

I want to tell them that they were beautiful and that they deserved so much more than this end.

I shake my head and press my palms flat against them. "They belong to you now," I whisper, and I take a deep breath and push them gently. They teeter on the edge for a moment before slipping over the side. And then they are gone, just like that.

Chey's hands wrap around me, helping me stagger to my feet. The weight of the world, of both realms, presses me down, but I push up.

The air shifts. The trees groan. Somewhere far away, thunder rumbles.

Above us, the sky is pitch black, the light snuffed out like a candle.

The ground shudders, cracks spreading through the dirt like veins.

Tears stream down my face, hot and fast, completely unstoppable.

"Come." Eamon reaches for me. "We have to–" Whatever he was about to say is cut off by a snap. The well collapses inward, the stones falling into a sinkhole.

The ground convulses, deeper this time. Trees buckle and twist, their roots tearing out of the dirt as they fall.

Smoke fills the air.

Eamon is saying something, but I can't make it out. His arms wrap around my waist, and he lifts up into the chaos.

The air burns.

My hair is whipped by the wind as I hold onto him, watching the turmoil with wide eyes.

The Ebonstream overflows, waves bigger than me rolling onto the shore and spreading over the land.

Magic is breaking loose; something ancient is awake. Adonirum.

Thunder and lightning crack the sky open. The magic recognizes him. It's taking him back.

I smile into the storm. Canaan. I feel him everywhere. "Adonirum." I whisper, and the air burns hot.

Eamon races toward Noctyra. The black cathedral rising from the ground on the horizon, like a beacon in the dark. The rest of the city is either on fire or consumed by water.

Rain begins to fall, but it isn't rain, it's something else. It's glowing red. Every drop that falls burns like needles against my skin.

Below us, there is a deafening crack, and the valley splits. The valley collapses in on itself, swallowing the Ebonstream, the trees, the buildings. Everything is there one second, then gone the next.

The cathedral is still standing.

An island in the middle of a vast ocean of blood red water.

He flies faster, holding me so tight it crushes my ribs. He drops down on the black stone steps leading into the cathedral. Calais is beating a Rimfae with her bare hands, hit after hit, until the person is unrecognizable.

The roar is endless. The water crashes like ocean waves. People are screaming.

The air itself is loud, humming a chorus of death and destruction.

I grab Cheyenne and run, pushing myself up the steps, gasping and coughing. My lungs burn, the blood, rain, and ash making a paste on my skin.

Inside, there is death, everywhere. Bodies are piled up on the ground, and pools of the remnants of Shadowrithes are left over.

She takes my trembling hand in hers. "Where do we go?"

"Go?" A voice booms from above us. "Why would you want to go anywhere? The party is only just starting!"

FORTY-SEVEN

I CAN SEE the cruel smile on his face before I even turn around.

Her fingernails bite into my hand as she looks up at him. She's shaking so hard that it moves my arm. Her eyes are wide and wet.

We look like something out of a horror movie. We're covered in blood and ash. When I look at him, I feel nothing. My chest is hollow. The Shadowrithes rage has left me. I can't even muster up hatred for him.

He swoops down and grabs me, ripping me away from Chey and lifting me into the air. I don't fight it. "What did you do, love? How have you managed to cause so much trouble?" There is a hint of amusement in his voice. Predatory curiosity.

"I put his wings into the well." My voice is almost inaudible.

A small smile tugs at his lips as he shakes his head. "I should have known you would find them."

"The magic took him home." There is no pleasure in that; it doesn't bring me any happiness. He's losing. But that doesn't matter anymore. Nothing really matters now, not even victory.

"Ah, come on, darling. Don't look so forlorn." He sighs. Maybe he's disappointed that I'm not putting up more of a fight. It's not fun for him when his toy doesn't play.

I don't dignify him with an answer. I just look past him, over his shoulder, at the carnage below us. The nave has become a war zone.

"I need your help." He says almost gently as he drops down to the altar.

Another Rimfae has Cheyenne, holding her tightly. She's screaming and thrashing, but the sound is lost in the madness. Elion doesn't even look at her.

He places me on the altar.

"You're going to kill me now?" I almost laugh. After everything. I'm almost not surprised.

"We need blood." He looks almost apologetic, but I recognize that lie now. He has a tell. His eyes sparkle, a twinkle that I used to mistake for mischief, but now I know better. He loves it, lying, manipulating, using, and taunting. What I'm seeing is the joy he feels. "The bond is gone, right?"

"No." I shake my head adamantly. It will never be gone.

"Sure it is." He ties a silvery chord of rope around my wrists. "When he died, it was severed."

"But..." I still feel him so acutely. The pain is so visceral. "I don't believe you."

He lets out a laugh, "There she is. Still have a little life in you, yet."

"Not for long, it would seem." I watch as he ties my legs down to the altar.

"It will be easy, love. You'll feel cold, then your consciousness will slip away." He runs his fingers up the length of my leg, then over my arm and up to brush the wet, bloody hair from my face.

"Let her go!" Cheyenne's voice, her hoarse scream, cuts through this strange goodbye.

I lift my head to see her running toward us.

A Shadowrithe materializes around her, misty black shadows taking hold of her arms and dragging her back.

"It's best that you don't see this part, Cheyenne darling." He coos.

Her chin trembles. "Please, Elion. Not her. Canaan is gone. Take your throne. But please, don't hurt her." She's trying to reason with him. To pull on the strings of the bond she thought they shared.

He sighs, turning to face her, really looking at her for the first time. "We need the blood."

"But–" she tries to step forward, but the Shadowrithe stops her. "Take mine instead!"

"That's sweet, but I want hers."

"No!" She thrashes in his grip. "Don't do this!"

He turns back to face me, leaning in close so that only I can hear him. "I've been dying for a taste."

"You're disgusting." I tug at the restraints, but they're too tight.

"I think I'll take mine straight from the vein." He leans in, running the tip of his nose over my cheek.

The crash of breaking glass echoes through the cathedral, and a shadow flashes above me.

Elion growls and bursts into the air. The stained glass windows fall like rain from the apse above the altar, shards of purple and red glass shattering on the ground.

He shoots straight up toward the ceiling, and Calais side tackles him. They roll through the air in a mess of blood and wings.

"Calais." A smile tugs at my lips. She deserves to crush him. And I hope she does.

"Come on." Cheyenne is at my feet, yanking on the chords. "Let's get you untied."

But she can't. No matter how hard she pulls, they won't come loose. With each passing second, her desperation grows. She rips hard, only tightening the thin bands around my ankles. They bite into my skin.

"Chey," I call to her, but she's too busy making my bindings even more secure. "Cheyenne!" I shout.

"Let me look for a knife or something!"

"Stop!" I wish I could reach out and hug her. "You have to get out of here. Run."

"Not without you!"

"You can't stay here! Once he drains me, he might decide that I wasn't enough. One of us has to make it out of here!"

"I'm not leaving you here."

"You have to."

"But you never left me. Even when I wasn't listening. Even when I drugged you." Tears drip down her cheeks, mixing with the blood on her skin. "You never left me."

"Please. After all of this, we can't both die." A bitter laugh bubbles in my throat. "Besides, the seer told me I wasn't going to make it."

"What are you talking about?" Her voice cracks, and she tugs at the restraints again.

"She said I would die."

"Well, she was wrong." She sniffles, focusing on untying the impossible knots.

"Chey, you have to go. Please." I know I'm asking her to make a choice she can't possibly make. I wouldn't be able to leave her either.

"No." She shakes her head. "Stop it. I'm not going anywhere without you."

Above us, Calais and Elion are attacking each other so violently that I can't believe there was ever a moment when they cared about each other. She's snarling, slicing him wherever her dagger will reach. He's bleeding everywhere. So is she. There isn't a place on them that isn't covered in red.

He hits her so hard the crunch of her bones echoes through the nave.

He takes the single second opportunity to dive. He falls toward me with his blade steady in his hand.

I see it in slow motion.

He drops out of the sky, the dagger glinting. The sharp tip slides up my stomach, cutting through my skin up my chest, neck, and into my face.

Cheyenne screams, but it sounds distorted, muffled.

Calais grabs him, dragging him back up, but it's too late.

I choke, warm droplets of blood running out of my mouth.

"Oh god, Kiah." Cheyenne grabs me.

My vision blurs, darkening around the edges.

A sound, far away in the distance, seems to make the room stop. Everyone turns as the heavy door bangs open.

The icy wind blows in, tearing through the cathedral.

I smile, my eyes fluttering closed.

Canaan. Coming to carry me away.

I force my eyes to open. I want to see him. He isn't graceful or light on his feet, but he's beautiful. He moves slowly, like the effort of each step costs more than he has to spare. In my mind, my arms spread open wide, ready to wrap around him.

He's battered and soaked, with his tangled hair covering his face. But his eyes burn beneath it.

In the air behind him, Calais drives her dagger through Elion's chest. His wings falter, and he slips, dropping down several feet.

Then Canaan is above me. And I'm at peace.

He doesn't untie me; he just climbs onto the altar beside me, resting his head on my chest. It almost feels real; the weight is really there.

Calais screams. And something drops out of the air.

A blur of wings landing on the ground. Dead.

Cheyenne sobs beside me. I can hear it, but I can't see her. A gurgling sound comes from my throat, and I choke on blood.

But none of that matters now.

"Canaan." I rest my chin on his head, and my eyes flutter closed.

FORTY-EIGHT

"DO NOT GO. Do you hear me?" His voice is broken, a barely audible whisper. "I won't allow it. Stay with me, Kiah."

The words float in my head like feathers. I'm untied from the altar and lifted into his arms. There is a flicker of hope, a barely there flame that holds onto the idea that I might be alive. But it's buried in the haze in my mind.

My eyes flutter open, then they close again. I slip in and out of time.

I hold onto his voice. Each time the words replay, I feel a tug in my chest. A call that I want to answer. I weave, drifting in and then back out like a dream.

"Canaan, I'll take her." Calais' voice sounds like a bell, clear and steady.

"No."

No one speaks again for a long time. When I manage to force my eyes open again, we're in a boat.

"Where are we?"

Canaan's soft eyes meet mine. "We're going to the falls."

"We're alive?" My voice cracks.

"We're alive."

"But, how?" I remember how soft death felt as it happened. There was a warmth in it. I feel that way now. The moments of my life that made it real are surrounding me. Where the deep, longing ache had hollowed out a place in my chest, I feel full again.

"I told you that I would protect you." His callused hand runs over my cheek carefully.

"Where were you?"

His eyes get darker, the deep honey shifting into something else. Something painful. "I jumped." He tries to smile. "A crazy human woman did it once to escape the fortress."

My hand doesn't feel like my own as I lift it up to touch his wind-rashed cheek. "Glad I could be of service." I think I'm smiling, but my face isn't moving the way it should.

"I'm sorry it took me so long to get back to you. It was a rough road."

I hum, ignoring the burning of tears blurring my vision. "What happens now?"

"Now we have choices to make."

"About what?"

"We don't have to worry about that today." He wraps his arms around me, careful not to put pressure on my chest.

"Are we going to the white shores?" I don't mean to ask it, but once the thought came into my head, I had to.

"No." He looks down at me, steadfast and gentle, as always. "We didn't die, Kiah."

"It felt like we did."

I lean into him, listening to the sound of his heart beating while his chest moves up and down with each breath. I close my eyes and match my breaths to his, in and out.

My lungs hurt, and my skin burns, but I'm alive, somehow.

"Where is Cheyenne?"

"She is with Eamon, in his boat. Safe."

"Oh, good."

I feel myself fading, the water rocking me like a lullaby. I want to stay here, present, with him, but I'm being pulled.

When I open my eyes again, we're not in the boats anymore. I'm Canaan's arms.

The falls are in front of us on the horizon, like an island in the sky, surrounded by thick fog.

"We made it, Kiah." He whispers. The strain in his voice makes me panic. He's in so much pain.

There is a note I've never heard before. A quiet breaking that reaches into my chest and squeezes my heart.

"Canaan, you have to put me down!" A burst of energy courses through me. "I can walk."

"You cannot." His grip tightens. "And even if you could, I can't let you, Kiah. I need to have you close for a while. Please." There is something raw in the way he says it. His chest trembles against my cheek.

"I'm afraid." My voice cracks.

"Don't be."

"You should be resting. You're injured."

"When we get to the falls, we will lie in bed together until we are fully recuperated." He clears the tension—the strain—from his throat, as if he can force it away with sheer willpower.

I know how badly he's injured. Even with my head in this state of underwater confusion, I know that much.

I can feel it, it's seeping from his skin. Pain and suffering.

I rest my uninjured cheek in his chest, but something catches my eye.

Calais is holding something in her clenched fist that makes my body go rigid.

My eyes fix on it, and I can't pull them away.

It's Elion.

His severed head dangles from her hand, her grip tight on his blood-matted hair. His mouth is still twisted into a sick little smirk.

"Oh, my god."

Sometimes, even now, after everything, there are moments that I forget. Being with them blurs the reality of it.

But we are not the same.

The differences between us sneak up on me.

"That's his..." I can't even say the words.

"Yes." Canaan doesn't have the same tremble in his voice that I do. He's not disturbed by the bodiless head; he looks at it with disinterested disdain.

The bridge has glowing blue lights, floating like balloons above it. They shimmer and ripple like portals. For a moment, they draw my gaze away from the trail of blood dripping out of Elion's gaping neck.

They're mesmerizing. Magic.

"What are they?" My mouth drops open as he steps onto the bridge. Warmth radiates from them like sitting beside a fire.

"I've never seen them before." He watches them too.

"Maybe the magic is apologizing for kicking our asses."

He lets out a pained chuckle, but it stops short, turning into a groan.

"We're almost there." I know I can't convince him to put me down, so encouraging him is the next best thing.

The bridge is cruel. It's only now that I realize the mercilessness of it.

We're at the end, the fortress is in sight. We're almost to the safety and security of a place to rest. But we have to make it across this fucking bridge first. It's taunting, growing longer somehow as we cross it.

It's never going to end.

His feet might give out at any moment, but this god forsaken bridge doesn't care.

The only comfort is the beating of his heart and the warmth from the glowing orbs—whatever they are.

Ahead of us, Calais marches triumphant and proud. When she crosses over onto solid ground, she pulls her sword, caked with dirt and blood, she shoves Elion's head onto the end of it, and raises it into the air above her head.

"Mordious!" Her voice cracks as she screams, carrying her trophy into the waiting open doors.

The ground shakes as everyone stomps in unison, cheering his name, then hers, then Canaan's...then mine.

They chant my name. Loud, full of pride and honor. I roll my lips into my mouth, but I can't hold back the sob that hurts my chest so badly, it makes me cry harder.

Canaan tips his head but doesn't speak. I'm not sure he can.

His jaw is clenched tight from pain, and the cords in his neck are taut beneath his skin.

Inside, Calais is hammering the sword down into the stones, forcing the grout apart so the sword can stand upright. A pike for his head to sit on, right about the blood-stained ground where Mordious died.

It feels barbaric and necessary at the same time.

Canaan doesn't stop; he walks through the hallways packed with fae. They go quiet when they see him, averting their eyes and bowing their heads. Many of them are injured, bruised, and bleeding.

A relieved sigh pushes from my chest as we finally reach his door.

We're covered in every nasty thing imaginable, but he walks straight to the bed. He sits in the center, holding me to his chest.

Finally alone, I let out the whimper that's been lodged in my throat.

"I'm so sorry, Canaan."

"Don't apologize for things that were not your fault." His voice is stern but still soft.

"Your wings..." tears blur my vision.

"I am less concerned about them than..." he stops, his voice breaking on the last word.

"Than what?" I pull back, just enough to see his face, forcing myself to move through the searing pain in my chest.

"Our bond was severed."

I didn't believe Elion when he told me. "Why?"

"When they cut the wings, I was almost completely exsanguinated. When you gave my wings to the magic, it gave me renewed magic from the well, but it was the blood of our ancestors then, not you."

"Oh." I don't like this. My stomach twists.

He looks almost nervous, swallowing hard as he looks at our fingers laced together. "Last time, when you gave me blood, you didn't know what you were doing."

My heart swells. "Right..."

"I knew, but you weren't given a choice." He touches my hand so gently. "You could go home now, Kiah. We will seal the portals and deal with the Rimfae and Shadowrithes. You aren't trapped here anymore. It's over."

"Or we could bond again."

His eyes jerk up to meet mine. "Kiah—"

"I know exactly what I'm signing up for this time. I can't go home. Not after everything. That's not my home anymore. I've seen too much. I've lived too many lives." Tears burn my skin as they fall. "We might not be bound by blood, but the way I feel about you, I can't just leave you here."

"So you would choose to bind yourself to me again?"

"Let's heal each other." I hold my wrist out to him.

His eyes search mine.

"I'm sure. I know what I'm saying. Please."

He takes my hand softly and brings it up to his mouth, kissing the pulsating vein in my wrist. When he bites down, my eyes flutter closed.

I feel him drawing from my soul, pulling at the strings, and stretching it into him. I feel where he starts, and I end, the tattered, broken pieces of us stitching together to create a whole.

When he removes his teeth, I'm lightheaded.

"Take mine." He bites his own wrist and holds it up to my mouth.

I do. Without hesitation.

The moment his blood touches my tongue, the fire in my skin goes out. My wounds are stitched closed, and the ache that wrapped around my heart loosens its grip.

His heartbeat pounds in my ears, keeping time with mine.

A choice.

When I pull back to look at his face, the color has already started to come back to him.

"We lived." He whispers.

"We did."

"And you're mine again."

"I never wasn't."

FORTY-NINE

HIS FINGERS RUN over the scarred skin on my chest, softly tracing the raised lines. It's become almost a habit now; whenever he can reach them, he touches them.

I can't even feel self-conscious about it.

"Are you nervous about today?" I crane my neck to look back at him.

His eyes blink open, "No. There isn't anything I can do about it. Whichever way the vote goes, that is the voice of the people. I'm the king, but this is beyond me."

"But what if they vote to allow the Rimfae to return to the kingdom with no consequences?"

"I'll be disappointed. But we have to move forward. The portals are closed. The remaining Shadowrithes have been stripped of their human forms and banished to the other side. The Rimfae that remain are divided. The ones that didn't turn will watch the ones that did. They won't allow this to happen again." He sighs. "To heal, we have to walk away. If we hold onto it, we won't ever be strong again."

"And that's why you're the king." I hum.

The laughter that rumbles in his chest shakes my body. "It's not that I'm above it. There are times that I want to hold onto the anger."

"Are there?" The laughter dies, a hollow throbbing replacing it in my chest. I know what he's talking about. I've seen it.

When we shower, he keeps his back turned away. He sleeps with his shirt on. It's been weeks since I've seen it.

"Yes. But I won't let it fester. Things could have been so much worse. We didn't get out unscathed, but we're sitting under a tree, in the warm sun beside the Ebonstream. And Elion isn't ruling over Noctyra."

"Elion doesn't have a head." I cringe. "But you're right." I've been waiting to bring it up, looking for an in. This seems like as good a time as any. "So, I was wondering."

He hums, waiting.

"I know this is a touchy subject." I take a nervous breath. "But I just want to say this, and then I'll leave it alone. I want it spoken out loud clearly, then I won't bring it up again." I chew the inside of my cheek.

"Kiah, what is it?"

"I just want you to know that you're the most beautiful man alive. Still. Whatever scars you have, you don't have to hide them from me. If you don't want to show me, I understand, but don't hide them because you think I don't want to see them. I do. I want to see all of you." I blurt out without taking a breath.

"You want to see them?"

"They're a part of you now." I meet his gaze. "You've seen mine." On instinct, my fingers come up to touch the thick scar on my cheek. "Not that I can really hide them."

He sits for a moment, still and silent. Then he sits forward, yanking his shirt over his head. "Go ahead. Look."

Crawling off his lap, I sit on my knees beside him. There are two thick patches of gnarled, melted flesh.

They are pink and raised like mine.

My hand trembles as I reach out, running my fingers over one, then the other.

He lets out a shaky breath and hangs his head.

I scoot behind him, face to face with the wreckage, and press my lips to it.

A shiver runs up the length of his spine.

I press another kiss, then another. "You're beautiful, Canaan. The wings weren't even a factor. I can't imagine the loss, but you don't have to hide from me."

I've tried to chalk it up to healing, but this feels worse than when we denied ourselves before. Now I know what I'm missing.

He never stops touching me, but it's not the kind of touching that I need.

I'm being devoured by it.

I run my fingers over the jagged circle, the entrance wound in his back that cuts through his chest and exits from it. A gunshot wound.

"I can't believe he brought human weapons."

"I can." He huffs.

I guess I can too,

Leaning in, I kiss it. "I miss you."

A low, relieved groan rumbles in his chest. I feel it vibrate against my lips. "I miss you. All the time. So much." He spins, grabbing me quickly and tucking my body beneath his in the soft grass and dirt.

"Won't someone see us?" I look over his shoulder toward what is left of Noctyra standing in the distance.

"No." He hums without checking.

"Canaan." I try to sound assertive, but my back arches up, pushing my chest into his.

"I need it, Kiah. I need you. It's been so long since I touched you."

"Why didn't you say something? You—" I stopped my voice, fading away when I realize I've been feeling the same way, and I've also stayed silent about it.

"I didn't want to rush you. I didn't want to push you too soon."
He sucks my neck, leaving little red spots all over my skin.

"I should have told you." I tilt my head, giving him better access
to my throat. "You've been distant."

"Not on purpose. I thought—" his breath trembles. "I thought
maybe you wouldn't want a mutilated king."

"Do you want a scarred, mutilated woman?"

"More than anything." He groans, running the tip of his nose up
the scarring on my cheek.

He hasn't even touched me yet, not really, and everything feels
too sensitive. Just having his hands on me again is healing the leftover,
shattered pieces.

His chest is heaving above mine as the heaviness of his body
settles over me. I'm desperate for it. Wild. For him.

With rough hands, he yanks my skirt up.

"Don't be gentle, Canaan. Touch me like you did before, when
we weren't fragile. When we weren't broken."

The muscles in his chest shake violently as he pulls his own pants
down. Big and hard, ready. I can feel the frenzy beneath his skin.
Whatever strength he had to hold himself back has snapped like a
rubber band.

He drags his shaft through my wet, swollen skin.

"Put it in." He pants hoarsely.

When I wrap my fingers around it, I watch his face. His jaw
clicks, his teeth clenching.

He presses inward, an invasion. Slow, inch by inch, he sinks in
until our hips are flush. I gasp, and he groans. Finally.

When I look up at him now, I can't see past his face; there isn't
anything else. Scars or wounds, wings or wars. It's just Canaan.

His weight pins me down, pressing my hips into the dirt.

The throbbing ache and discomfort are gone, but this alone isn't
enough. "Please, move." My fingers dig into his shoulders.

"I've got you." He reaches below me, scooping me into his hands to hold me at an angle. He shifts, pressing deeper until I clamp down around him.

He drops his head down, resting his forehead on mine as he rides me through it. A perfect rhythm. Exactly what I need.

It's a frenzy.

I snake my hand down between us, pressing my fingers into my clit.

His eyes open, looking down to watch me.

"Oh, fuck." He moves faster. "I want to bite you, Kiah. Can I? Can I have just a little bit?"

"Yes!" I throw my head back.

I know he's going to use it as a tool right as he feels me about to come.

"You feel so good. So wet and warm and perfect for me." His fingers bite into my skin, pulling me up so that he can go so deep it sends a deep, rippling ache through my stomach.

"Oh, god! I–" I gasp, reaching down to take handfuls of dirt–anything to ground me. It's been so long, somehow I forgot how full he makes me, how much he stretches me open.

"Kiss me," he begs, pressing his mouth to mine.

The kiss is much too slow for how aggressively his hips are moving, snapping into me. It's soft but insistent. His tongue presses against mine, sweeping into my mouth. I suck his tongue, and my body bucks forward into his.

God, his tongue tastes good. His lips.

The kiss barely muffles our moans as I feel myself starting to clench and shake.

He chokes, sliding his lips down the side of my face to my neck, preparing for what's coming.

"Fuck," he sobs. "I need to come."

That admission sends me over the edge.

Pleasure bursts through me, bringing me up so high, then dropping me. But I don't fall, I float. Tears well up in my eyes and pour over, unstoppable. This is what it felt like to fly.

He bites into my neck, his teeth piercing the skin.

I scream, and he grunts, his body jerking above me, inside of me, surrounding me.

He draws my blood out as he pulls my orgasms out of me with so much force that my muscles start to cramp.

Again and again, I writhe beneath him, pinned down.

He pulls his teeth from my neck and collapses, letting the full weight of his body land on me, except for the little bit he holds on his forearms.

"Oh my god, Canaan." I gasp for air.

"Never again." He presses his lips to mine. "I need you every day."

"Every day." I agree, nodding.

FIFTY

SLABS of black marble are stacked on either side of the street with pallets of slick cobblestones lined up in neat rows.

Everyone is here, rebuilding this place side by side.

The votes are being tallied right now. It's hard to concentrate on stones and grout when the fate of the remaining Rimfae is hanging in the balance.

But everyone here seems completely content to lay stones. The street is coming together quickly, hundreds of fae working in unison.

When I take a moment to stop, to look up, it's gut-wrenching in a way, but somehow beautiful.

The magic is dimmed. It must feel like gravity is pressing down on them if even I can feel the changes. The air is lighter. The hum that was always there, pulsing, is almost completely silent.

They're using their hands to rebuild what was lost. Not magic. Just hard work. Grueling work, as if each one of us is trying to earn peace and healing with every stone we place.

And maybe we are.

Sweat drips down the side of my face, and my mind is running in a million different directions, but my body feels better—it feels good.

I'm leaving a mark on this place. In one hundred years, the work I did here will still stand. I'm a part of Noctrya now.

For the fifteenth time in ten minutes, my head jerks toward the Cathedral, looking across the shimmering water to the little island. How long does it take to count a few thousand votes?

"The more you look, the longer it will take," Canaan whispers from behind me, amusement laced through his voice.

"Yeah, I know, but I can't stop myself. Even this isn't enough of a distraction." I pick up another stone and place it in the row.

"No matter what happens, it's the will of the people. The votes have already been cast, and it's been decided. There isn't anything we can do now."

"I know." I let go of some of the tension in my shoulders. "I'm nervous." I let out an embarrassed laugh. "It's stupid—"

"It's not. I'm nervous too. I voted, and I stand by it, but there is still a part of me that wonders." He runs his fingers through my wind-blown hair.

I nod, closing my mouth and rolling my lips inside. I can't talk about this here. It's too much to unpack it all again. We've talked about it for hours. For days. We've gone over every scenario.

All the talking doesn't mean much. The votes are in. He's right, there isn't anything we can do.

We move like a well-oiled machine. The road winds up the hillside, brand new and gleaming under the sun.

Cheyenne weaves through my thoughts. I wonder what she's doing. If she's happy. It's strange to think of her back at home—so far away but not really. Saying goodbye to her plays on repeat in my mind. I don't regret the decision, but I miss her already.

Canaan is going to bring me home in a few weeks to visit my mother. He promised me a few times a year. It's everything he can offer.

I push the thoughts down, forcing them away until they pop back up again later.

"Is this where the Ponum was?" I look around, gauging the distance from the dock.

"Yes." His lips tug up into a smile that is equal parts happy and sad. "It was just there." He points to a cleared-out space that used to have buildings standing on it.

"That was a good day."

"It was."

"Is she going to rebuild? Have you heard?" I look around for her.

His face falls, a deep frown pulling his smile downward. "She didn't make it through the fight."

"Oh." Sola. I didn't know her, not really, but she was so kind to me. The world feels lesser without her in it.

For several minutes, we work in silence. I don't want to talk anymore. The air feels thicker around us, almost tangible. Words feel small and useless, so I just shut my mouth. We set a whole row of stones, and when there is a sound, a bell.

The ring is crisp and clear in the bright blue sky.

My eyes immediately jerk toward the cathedral.

Calais, Eamon, and the other members of the court walk out onto the steps. There isn't a single sound anywhere. The birds are silent. No one breathes.

"It has been decided," Calais' voice echoes. "Unanimously, that the Rimfae that betrayed the crown who have not denounced their actions, will be held at the fortress in Hornelenm, without their wings, until such a time as we can dispatch them. The Rimfae that betrayed the crown but have already renounced their betrayal are forgiven."

My throat feels tight.

The words hand there, heavy, immovable.

The vote was unanimous. I look around at all the faces staring in the same direction. Everyone voted the same way. Their faces are all the same now, too. There is no victory here; no one is winning. Each face is carved with the sharp lines of sorrow and pain.

The Rimfae here in the crowd, the ones whose loyalty was never in question, look shattered. Their wings hang heavy, and the brightness has gone out of their eyes.

Over six hundred Rimfae betrayed the crown. And over two hundred of them will have their wings removed and be... dispatched. The thought makes me sick to my stomach, even though I cast a vote for it.

"They can't be trusted, Kiah. If they cannot take accountability for their actions, they can't rejoin our society." His voice is steady, but there is a crack in it, buried deep down beneath the words.

"I know." I nod, slipping my hand into his. "I get it, but..."

"It seems almost impossible." He sighs. "Ending so many lives."

"It is done." Her voice moves over us like a breeze.

Done.

I take a breath, letting myself lean into Canaan's chest as he stands behind me. "The magic is rewriting itself. It's healing. We're going to be different now." He whispers. "We'll be better."

Everyone agrees to stop for the day. I think we all need it.

"Come with me. I want to show you something." He tugs me gently, leading me up, away from the street we spent the day lying down.

It only takes a moment, a few steps, to realize where he is taking me.

"Canaan, wait..." My knees wobble. "I don't know if I can."

"Do you trust me?" He smiles, so soft and sweet that I can't deny him even though I don't want to go.

Everything in me physically protests; my feet scrape against the ground, dragging like lead.

But I trust him. So I keep my head high and follow him through the strange new terrain.

The path up to the well is gone. The water ran down the side of the mountain, washing everything away.

We move slowly, walking up through the trees that are mostly intact. It feels like we're the first people to ever walk here.

"You're trembling."

"I'm nervous."

"There's nothing to be afraid of. I promise. I wouldn't bring you here if it was going to be awful." He wraps his arm around my shoulders, holding me against his side.

"I know that." I pull in a shuddering breath.

We reach the spot, the edge of the tiny clearing of trees where the well used to stand. I hold his arm tightly, taking a breath as we step inside. The air is warmer here, thick and humid.

Flowers have sprouted all around the open hole in the ground. Every color is here. A kaleidoscope of oranges, yellows, and pinks, blues, and purples in every shade. I stand completely frozen. I'm afraid that if I take another step, I'll trample one of them by accident.

"Can you feel it?" His voice is as full of wonder as the awe swirling in my chest.

"Yes."

"Everything will be alright. We will be strong again."

There are no doubts. We will. It's as if I can see it in the gentle breeze that blows through the petals.

THE END

DID YOU ENJOY THIS?

Visit myrandaraebooks.com for 40+ more spicy romances

ALSO BY MYRANDA RAE

SERIALS

🐺 👑 **fantasy/shifter**

Beyond the Ether

1 Blood of the Innocent

2 Blood of a King

The Fairytales series

1 Captivated, Cursed

2 Love You Anyway

3 Finding Iris

4 Sucker for You

5 The Lost Girl

The Playlist series

1 Fix You

2 Beloved

3 Cherry

4 A Warrior's Heart

Sons of Sorsha (The Playlist) mini-series

1 Jack

2 Lucas

3 Samuel

4 Asher

👽🛸 scifi / aliens

Coiled Throne Series

1 The Coiled Throne pt. 1

2 The Queen Trials pt. 2

The Astrynian Warriors Series

1 The Destroyer's Little Pet

2 Havoc

An'eo Chronicles

1 Callisto

2 Proximus

3 Nyon

4 Kieran

5 Loide

Tribute to the Alphagods

1 Wrath

2 Pride

3 Envy

4 Lust

🍃🔥 contemporary

The Underworld duology

1 What's Done in the Dark

2 Will Come to Light

3 Zion (bonus mini-short)

STANDALONES

🐺👑 fantasy/shifter

- Alpha's, Kings & Play-things
- BEAST: Destined to the Hellhound
- Mark of the Damned
- Bound: Mates at War
- The Queen in Shadows
- Suck Me Slowly

💋🔥 contemporary

- Enemies Closer
- Unplanned: A One Night Stand
- PINK
- Lewd & Lascivious
- In His Bones
- When I Whisper His Name
- Just the Two of Us
- Going for Gold
- The Void He Fills
- Bound to Break

* Indicates Work in Progress